Love

&

OTHER
PERENNIAL HABITS

EMMALINE WARDEN

EMMALINE WARDEN LLC

Digital Edition ISBN: 979-8-9874003-0-2
Print Edition ISBN: 979-8-9874003-1-9

Cover design by Lily Bear Design Co.

FIRST EDITION
Print Edition

To my kids – for being your silly, supportive, loving selves. You're by far my favorite creations
Love always,
Mom

To Bethany Bennett, Marielle Browne,
Daphne Chase, Alissa Davis, and Catherine Stein –
For all the writing sprints, verbal processing,
and simply being the best group of friends a girl could
ask for.
Your love and support have been invaluable and I
can never repay it, but will spend my life trying.

To Nicole McCurdy – Your insight when editing this book
was invaluable. Thank you for answering a multitude of
emails, and for helping to make this book shine.

CHAPTER ONE

THE EARL OF Everly was dead, thank God.

The bastard had met the grim reaper in his sleep at the ripe age of sixty-six, an easy way to go for someone so terrible as him, but nevertheless, he was dead. Margaret Reedy, Countess of Everly, watched the carriage pull away, the black plumes on top of the horses' heads dancing in the wind as they merged into the traffic of Mayfair. Everly would be buried at the family estate in Salisbury, and Margaret, being a lowly woman, was not allowed to attend the proceedings. Not that she would have. Her husband was a miserable man who had made it his purpose in life to ensure her days were a living hell. No, she would bid goodbye to the arse from the front steps of their Grosvenor Square home, then head inside for a nice cup of tea and some biscuits.

"How are you, dear?" her mother, Lady Veerson, asked from the couch of the sitting room. Her blue day dress showed nary a wrinkle as she sipped from her teacup, her perfectly coiffed grey hair immaculate, not a single strand out of place. The woman had not moved from the spot since she arrived that morning, and Margaret envied her carefree existence, but that was it. Her mother, after all, was married to her father and that was a sentence she would not wish upon anyone. It had been her sire who had determined the trajectory of her fate, forcing her to marry the aged earl, a man nearly forty years her senior, and sentencing her to an existence of wretchedness that only death could save her from. Unfortunately for them all, her father was very much alive.

"I'm well. Ready for this all to be completed." She brushed at her black crepe dress before sitting and taking the proffered cup of tea from her mother.

"The hard part is over, dear. The earl will be buried and once his will is read and Lord Harrison officially takes over the title, you'll be the dowager countess. Do you have any notion of what your settlement will be?" Lady Veerson sipped her tea so delicately at the question it set Margaret's teeth on edge.

She shook her head. "Walter wasn't too forthcoming about what his plans for me were once he perished. I'm sure he intended to outlive me."

Her mother frowned at her words. The acknowledgment of oppression she had been dealt at the hands of her husband was a topic her parents wanted little to do with. Just the mere mention of Walter's domineering personality sent them both into lamentations of her being overly dramatic. It had not mattered when Everly demeaned her in public, calling her all sorts of horrible names, and it certainly did not matter now. No, her parents cared very little for the well-being of their eldest child, only that she married well, and gained a title in the process. After all, what were a few harsh words when you could be a countess?

Margaret pasted a smile on her lips. "I can only hope

Daphne's marriage is nothing like mine. It's a shame she could not come today."

"What nonsense, Margaret. She's at finishing school, readying herself to become a nobleman's wife. That is much more important than sitting idly by as her sister tends to her husband's funeral." Lady Veerson glanced at the clock but shook her head as she realized the timepiece remained unmoving because of mourning constraints. "I should be off. I have my monthly orphan society meeting. You should be grateful I was available to support you in your time of need."

"Of course, Mother. You are very thoughtful." The words left her lips with force, their necessity grating, given the circumstances.

Lady Veerson nodded. "I am." She set down her tea-cup and stood. "Let me know once the will is read and you learn your fate. Your father and I will be happy to have you return home for the duration of your mourning. I know he is eager to begin the search for your next husband."

Margaret bit the inside of her cheek to hold in her re-tort. Her mother did not need to know that she would never remarry, nor that she would rather live in a shack than return to her parent's household. No matter the outcome of the will, Margaret knew this was her chance for a new beginning, and she was not intending to let it pass without a fight.

After her mother took her leave, Margaret walked the home, her fingers dancing over the furniture that Everly had picked. Walter designed each room to his taste after he stated without affliction that she had little knowledge of what was up to fashion for the home. He had picked each piece meticulously. And he had lorded each room over her, another dagger in his reasonings for why she would never be a good wife and countess. The temptation to break each piece had her removing her hand and holding them tightly behind her back. Lord Harrison would not appreciate learning the items had become damaged in a manic rage, no matter how terrible her husband had been.

Yet the idea held merit. She imagined lining each precious possession on top of the dining room table, then maliciously hitting each of them with a Pall Mall mallet. Margaret smiled at the joy the image brought, allowing her mind to run through each cherished item Everly had boisterously taunted her with. She catalogued them from most hated to least, then imagined each swing and the resounding crash of the beloved item as it met its end. In terms of comfort, it was minimal, but she would take what she could get. After all, anything was better than Everly being alive.

The clearing of a throat behind her brought her out of her musings and she smiled at their butler, Sterns. "Sorry to interrupt, my lady, but the solicitor is here. I've already informed Lord Har-er, I mean the earl, that I have set him up in the study."

Margaret chuckled at his stumble of the title of the new Earl of Everly. It seemed it was not just her that was adjusting to the new life that did not include a temperamental old man with a penchant for malevolence. "Thank you, Sterns. If you could have some refreshments sent in, it would be greatly appreciated."

The butler nodded. "Of course, my lady."

Heading to the study, Margaret could not contain the nerves that danced around in her stomach threatening to bring up her breakfast. Her impending fate would decide the entire trajectory of her escape, and if Everly had ensured she be in hell even after he was gone, she was uncertain what her next steps would be. But she would escape, of that she was certain.

Inside the study, Lord Harrison Metcalf sat across from the solicitor, who presided over the previous earl's massive desk, the ankle of one leg resting on his knee as his brown eyes met hers, his usually meticulous blond hair falling over his face. A single sheet of paper sat before the solicitor, a stoic-looking man, and Margaret swallowed the bile that attempted to rise from her throat.

"My lady," the solicitor said, bowing to her. Lord Harrison nodded his head at Margaret as if to reassure her that all would be well. He had been her biggest champion and closest confidant during her marriage to the earl, and his friendship now was invaluable. And if the will read as she suspected it would, Lord Harrison would no doubt do everything in his power to ensure that she was taken care of. While she was grateful for his thoughtfulness, it did not escape her notice that she would be indebted to another man for the rest of her life.

Lord Harrison had been Walter's nephew and only heir, his presence truly underscoring the age difference in their marriage, but Harrison's always ready smile and quick wit had soothed the sting of her husband's vicious treatment. Within very little time, his weekly dinners with the earl had become the highlight of her week, the only bright spot in an otherwise dreary landscape of her marriage.

Taking the seat beside Lord Harrison, Margaret folded her hands primly in her lap and took a deep breath.

"First, I want to extend my condolences to you, Lady Everly, on the passing of the earl. I wish you comfort and support in this terrible time," the solicitor said, his voice a croak.

Margaret nodded even as his words made her hands tighten. "Your words are more comfort than you know," she said, forcing a smile to her lips. "I've rung for some refreshments before you read the will."

The solicitor nodded his head. "Thank you, my lady, but that will not be necessary. It seems the previous earl kept his legal matters rather simple, so I do not believe it will take much time at all to go over it."

Margaret's stomach dropped at the words. "What do you mean?"

The solicitor rubbed at the back of his neck before adjusting a pair of spectacles and picking up the solitary piece of paper that sat before him. "Perhaps I should just get to it." He cleared his throat, not that doing so would make the croaking of his voice any less pronounced, and said, "I, Walter Reedy, twelfth Earl of Everly, being of sound mind and body declare this to be my last will in testament. To my wife Margaret Reedy, Lady Everly, I leave the jewelry I gifted to her, which includes a pearl necklace, a sapphire ring, and a pair of emerald earrings. I also leave to her the unentailed property known as Baron Manor with the hopes she puts the same amount of love and care into it as she has shown to our other homes."

The solicitor adjusted his spectacles once more. "He mentions your marriage settlement, where it seems a provision of ten pounds a year is allotted if you should become a widow."

Lord Harrison growled beside her. "You cannot be serious. How is she expected to live off ten pounds a year?"

"I believe the intent was for the countess to return to her family with the hope that she remarries," the solicitor said, swallowing audibly at Lord Harrison's rough tone.

"She is the Countess of Everly. The only one to decide she should remarry should be herself. This is unacceptable." Lord Harrison stood as if to lunge at the man, but Margaret placed a hand on his arm. His knight in shining armor act, though thoughtful, was entirely unnecessary. Walter's will, evil as it was, was set in stone and there was nothing either of them could do to change it.

"It's all right, Harry," she said, even as her mind replayed the solicitor's words on repeat, a soft chant that slowly grew louder as the moment went on.

"It's not all right, Meg. The bastard gave you a rundown property to call your home as a dowager and almost no money to get by. I won't stand for it."

Margaret squeezed his arm before turning back to the solicitor, who seemed paler than he had before. Poor dear. "Please continue."

The man nodded and glared at the paper before him. "I'm afraid the rest is regarding the new earl and the entailed properties that come with the title. I'm sorry, my lady, but that was the only mention the previous earl made regarding your settlement."

"That's quite all right. If you'll both excuse me, I'll leave and allow you to get on with the rest of the will." Margaret stood and smiled at the solicitor before nodding her head to Lord Harrison and taking her leave. Her hands shook as she headed to her apartments and quickly shut the door behind her, turning the lock. Leaning against the portal, Margaret took a deep breath.

She was free.

Most widows would respond to her settlement with shouts of outrage followed swiftly by someone fetching the smelling salts, and yet Margaret could not contain the smile that overtook her face. The jewelry meant nothing and could easily be sold for a respectable profit, but the house, oh heavens, the house.

Everly had referred to Baron Manor as Bitch Manor, the estate he had relegated his late mother to. Their relationship had been tenuous at best, and he had found much delight in telling all and sundry the story of his mother's involuntary isolation in Woodingdean. After she passed, the home sat in disarray and disrepair and was no doubt in a rather shabby state, but it was hers. Never mind that Everly had gifted her with the manor he most hated, never mind that he had written a final barb to strike her heart in his assumption that she would never care for it. The blighter could kiss her arse, thank you very much, because what he failed to realize in his idiotic attempt at revenge was that she could purchase an unentailed property. And now, not only did Margaret have the funds, but she had very little fears when it came to getting her hands dirty.

The smile that took over her lips was painful it was so

large, and even as tears filled her eyes, she could not help the laughter that bubbled from her lips. It began quietly, then turned into a raucous noise. Combined with the tears, the pair of emotions were so contradictory yet meshed with one another in a display so awful, so joyful, that, for a moment, fear nearly overcame her. It was like a dream and Margaret was scared she would awake at any moment to find Everly still alive and the gilded bars to her prison firmly in place.

A knock at the door had her jumping, and she shook her head, wiping away the tears. Unlocking it, she found Lord Harrison on the other side. "May I come in?" he asked.

"Of course. It is, after all, your house now."

"Meg..." he said, his tone exasperated.

"Harry."

"Meg, let me help. You can stay here, or if you insist on going to Baron Manor, I'll pay for the renovations. I'll hire a full staff and make sure the place is at least habitable before you journey there."

She shook her head at him. "No. I'm going to do this on my own."

"Why must you be so stubborn? That bastard left you a dilapidated building that he called Bitch Manor and barely enough funds to pay for food and clothing, let alone renovate an entire home. Half the rooms aren't even safe enough to venture into."

Margaret laughed at his outrage. "Well, then I shall just avoid those until they are repaired."

"Repaired by whom? And with what money?" Lord Harrison stalked the floor of her sitting room, his brow in a deep furrow. "You're talking nonsense. Why won't you let me help?"

"I know you won't understand, but I need to do this on my own."

"That's utter bullshit and you know it." Lord Harrison rubbed at his face. "I'm sorry, Meg. I just hate knowing that he's done this to you." He sat in the chair near the fireplace, his hands clenched together as he stared at the floor. "I wish you'd let me fix this."

"There's nothing to fix. Whether or not you see it, Walter gave me the key to my cage and I'm going to take it." She smiled at him. "If I promise to ask you for help should I need it, will that pacify you?"

"I think the only thing that will pacify me at this point is bringing the blighter back from the dead so I can kill him." With a sigh, Lord Harrison stood and walked over to her, placing a comforting hand on her shoulder. "Shall I send up some maids to help you pack?"

Margaret smiled at him. "Not for packing, but I would appreciate the help."

He raised a brow at her. "Do I want to know what you have planned?"

She went to her closet and examined the mass of gowns inside. "I plan to take my life back."

CHAPTER TWO

October 1819

THE SALTY SIREN Inn was a bloody nightmare, each bit of its wooden floor taken up by bodies that reeked of sweat and liquor. Oliver Ludlow, Marquess Greenwood, heir to the Duke of Hedley, took one last fortifying breath on the inn's cobblestone steps before pushing his way inside. His desperation for food outweighed the stench that emanated before him, plus the idea of a pint, no matter how watered down the ale might be, was enough to pull him in further. All the tables sat occupied, so making his way to the bar, Oliver signaled the barmaid and put in his order before standing against the wall to watch the ongoings before him.

It seemed to be a celebration of some sort, given the numbers of cheers that were being exchanged by men and women alike. One slight female with brown locks that were in a braid down the back of her head held the attention of the crowd, but what caught his gaze, even more, was the fact that she wore a soft linen shirt and trousers, just like the men surrounding her. On her feet, brown boots covered from toe to calf, hugging the skin in a gentle embrace, and outlining muscles he was certain no noblewoman would ever have. And judging by her boisterous laughter, and ample glass of ale, she certainly acted like no noblewoman ever would.

She was intriguing. A bright light that kept pulling him in even through all the noise and clutter that surrounded him. As if she could sense his gaze on her, she glanced at him. Her eyes were an indiscernible color, but the raised brow she sent his way, along with a small smile, propelled his pulse to race. Oliver turned away; certain the smile was not meant for him. The barmaid approached with his food and he found a rough tabletop to stand at, switching back and forth between eating the stew and drinking the ale, all the while the boisterous crowd and the sultry laughter of the woman in trousers played behind him like a melody.

"There you are!" a feminine voice said behind him as thin arms slid around his stomach. "I was wondering what was taking you so long to get here."

Oliver turned around to find the woman in trousers locked around his waist, her wide brown eyes motioning to the overbearing brute that stood behind her. Oliver sized up the large bloke, uncertain what part he was meant to play, but her arms tightened around him as the man moved closer to them and Oliver slid his arm around her shoulders, pulling her in close instinctively. Her sweet vanilla scent surrounded him, pushing out the stench of the inn as she pushed herself deeper into his arms. "Sorry I'm so late. There ended up being more work at the cottage than I had originally thought."

The man glared at Oliver, his gaze unsteady as it volleyed between him and the woman wrapped around him like a snake. "You know this chap, Meg?"

Meg, for certainly that had to be her name, smiled at the man before planting a big kiss on Oliver's cheek, the action leaving him stunned as her plump lips caressed his cheek before answering. "Sure do. This handsome man is my husband." She pinched Oliver's side. "Dear, introduce yourself to Charlie here." Her upper crust accent made him pause, his brow raising at the enigma currently wrapped around his waist.

Oliver held out the hand that was not wrapped around Meg's shoulder. "Oliver Ludlow. Nice to meet you."

Charlie stared at the extended hand before frowning and turning back to Meg. "Your husband? This scrawny thing?"

With a frown, Oliver looked down at himself. Sure, he was lean, but scrawny? Rather rude of Charlie if he did say so himself.

Meg shrugged her shoulder and snuggled deeper into Oliver's side. "You can't help what the heart wants, Charlie." She stood on her tiptoes and eyed the group that was shuffling out of the inn. "It seems the party is turning in for the night. Better head to your carriage and make sure your wheels aren't stolen come time for the next leg of the race."

Oliver's hand still hung in the air, and when Meg grabbed it and wrapped it around her waist, he nearly stumbled at the effects of her lithe body against his. "Good luck with the rest of the race, Charlie," she said.

Charlie scowled at her, and Oliver prepared himself for a fight, but the man turned and left the inn, the slam of the door behind him a massive relief. Not that he could not fight the man if required. Well, no he could not, truth be told, but also, he did not want to. The exit of Charlie had Meg unwrapping herself from around his waist and huffing a strand of unruly hair out of her face. "Well, that was unnecessary." She smiled at Oliver. "Thanks for that. He wouldn't take no for an answer and it was either start a brawl in my friend's establishment or find another means of removal."

"And I seemed to be the sort that looked interested in helping?" he asked, perplexed by her calculations.

She smiled, her eyes crinkling at the corners. "You have a friendly smile. I'm not the best judge of character, but a pleasant smile is always a fabulous place to start." She clapped her hands together and eyed his table. "Can I get you another ale? It's on the house. Consider it payment for services rendered."

"Ale is compensation for your friend Charlie nearly desecrating me?" Oliver laughed. "I'm intrigued by what you consider even." She raised a brow at him. "How about an ale and the tale of how you became acquainted with said Charlie? It sounds like an interesting story."

She nodded her head. "Deal."

After acquiring another ale for him, and one for herself, Meg stood across from him at the worn table, one booted leg crossed over the other and a smile on her face. Mahogany tendrils of curls shot out around her head like a halo, and a smattering of freckles covered her plump face. Blonde, barely indiscernible lashes framed chocolate brown eyes, and plump pink lips curved when she smiled, which seemed to happen often given the lines that bracketed her mouth. She was just an ordinary girl. So why did it feel like he had been blessed by her presence?

Meg took a sip of her drink, the foam on top leaving a small line of residue on her upper lip that she brushed away with the back of her hand. "There was a carriage race from Brighton to Woodingdean and the party stopped here for the night. Charlie is one of the racers and it seems he has a penchant for collecting bed partners at every inn he stops at. I was his latest conquest and he would not take no for an answer." She sipped her ale and chuckled. "Some men, Charlie being the example, take rejection better when they think the woman they're after is already claimed, and thanks to you, he took it at a loss."

"I'll be honest, most men are idiots."

She laughed at his pronouncement. "Would you include yourself in that tally?"

Oliver pondered her question before shrugging his shoulders. "Probably. Not as terrible as Charlie, but I've been known a time or two to act more like a beast than a human being."

Meg rested her chin on her hand as she eyed him. "Why do men do that?"

He took a sip and frowned. "We're stupid?" She snorted, and the sound was so unexpected that Oliver laughed in response. "I wish I were lying, but truly, we have no other excuse except sheer stupidity. The only reason the world is still turning and humans still exist is because of the female species."

"That's true. Every war fought has to have been started by a man."

"Exactly." Oliver looked around the now quiet inn. "How did you come to be anywhere near Charlie and his unfortunate proposition?"

Meg smiled at him. "I was in the race with him."

"Pardon?" Oliver asked, certain he had heard incorrectly.

"I was one member taking part in the race. Left him in the dust on his arse and it seems he found himself quite intrigued by a female who could hand him his man bits in a sack while looking like a queen." She shrugged, sending a wink and smile his way before picking up her cup. "But I appreciate your help in averting him." She glanced around the inn and sighed. "I should help Marty with the dishes and cleaning before I head home. Thank you again for your assistance, Sir Oliver. I am grateful for your help." She sketched an animated bow before leaving him alone, her departure so sudden, Oliver wondered if he imagined her.

This slip of a girl befuddled him. Her demeanor was friendly, open, and yet she somehow seemed reserved. After all, what sort of woman took part in a carriage race, spoke like the queen, and then tended to menial tasks such as cleaning and dishes? No, she made very little sense, and if there was anything Oliver liked most in life, it was things that made sense. Reasoning and purpose kept everything simple, and Meg, no matter how oddly beautiful she was, did not fit those requirements.

He kept his eyes on her the rest of his time at the inn, just in case Charlie came back and pushed his proposition once more, but Meg did not seem interested in his presence. She flitted from table to table, clearing dishes and wiping them down before checking on the remaining customers that lingered about the area. Once they all had refills of drinks or food, she bussed a kiss across a beautiful brunette's cheek, who surely must be Marty, then disappeared out the door.

Meg, the carriage racer, was an enigma, he would give her that. And should he ever require diverting conversation, he knew exactly where to find her. But that was not why he was in Woodingdean. He had one month to dedicate to himself before his father required him to return to London and begin the life of a duke's heir. There was a wife to procure, a wedding to plan, and little heirs to beget to ensure the continuation of the title. Oliver frowned at his last sip of ale, suddenly disinterested in the peaty brew.

His time was swiftly ticking away, counting down the hours, and while he adored his father, and understood the process of succession, there was a bitterness that chewed at him. For this was not the life he was meant to lead. This was not the life he had been promised. He was the second son, the spare. His path was supposed to be one without the constraints of the dukedom, of the aristocracy, much like Meg's, and the resentment that threatened to overwhelm him warred with being the dutiful son. A battle that silently waged each day as he tended to his plants, the pendulum making another swing, striking another minute of his freedom.

Better to worry about that when the eventuality of it came to be. For now, he would let the salty sea air and his unwieldy greenhouse soothe him and hopefully allow him to heal. Future dukedom worries be damned.

CHAPTER THREE

OLIVER NEEDED SHIT. Well, horseshit, to be exact, seeing as how he had already procured fecal matter from cows, sheep, and a goose, which had been a rather unfortunate experience all around. While horses should have been easy to come by, he had made the rather poor decision to send his carriage and team to an inn in Brighton, a fairly rough distance away from the less than modest cottage, Bellawink, where he was staying. The cottage, inherited from his mother, was modest, nothing like the immaculate country estates and hunting lodges of the aristocracy. Its cream brick exterior still stood solid even three decades later, and while the home still employed servants, the number had dwindled to less than a dozen as Oliver had decreased its acreage to a more respectable amount while Christopher was still alive. But that had been before. And now...

Oliver shook his head. No nonsense in dwelling over that. Especially when one was now forced to carry manure for the monstrous length between the two, but his need could not wait. His spinach experiment residing in the greenhouse would never get off the ground until he had gained all the required materials, thus his evening trip to the neighboring estate.

Baron Manor, a dilapidated property not far from

town, had become the eyesore of Woodingdean, an errant child that could never pull its act together. At least, that was, until its new owner had arranged for its repair. The once stately home had sat untended after the previous dowager's passing, and time had taken a hard toll. The brick exterior had become overrun with vines, their massive bulk consuming the structure, and two of its regal chimneys had collapsed under the weight of the vegetation, the pile of broken bricks looking like a burial mound. Oliver had become so used to its green draperies, that he had forgotten what color the brick had once been.

The town had been aflutter when it became apparent the Countess of Everly intended to rejuvenate the run-down home, and a multitude of people, from residential farmers to the local smithy, had flocked to the estate, attracted not only by its promise of work, but also intrigued by the gossip they might learn regarding the new owner. With the house still is disrepair, a camp of sorts had been set up in one of the properties fields, the assembly of tents appearing more like a makeshift caravan of travelers than workers, only lending to the town's chatter.

Oliver had been home for only a day before he caught snippets of gossip from the couple who cared for Bellawink, the Pettigrew's. Their conversation had been nothing but comments about the unusual woman who had taken over the manor and her rather peculiar ways, but he shoved the comments off. From one eccentric to another, he welcomed any form of oddity she planned to bring to their small corner of England. Given what he knew of the Everly estate and the former earl, he imagined the countess to be an elderly woman, hopefully, one given to lewd outbursts and outrageous attire. And so far, he had not been off. Mr. Pettigrew had taken it upon himself to report every abnormal item he had learned regarding the manor, and the Countess of Everly was high on his list of complaints. From trouser wearing to drinking with workers after the day's labor, the woman seemed determined to have not only Mr. Pettigrew, but the town, wonder at her sanity.

Rounding the road to the stables, Oliver pulled up in amazement at the image before him. A brilliant black stallion ran its paces around the ring, its coat a mesmerizing blue-black in the dappling sunlight. His lead rope pulled taut as he was put through his paces, the other end held in the hands of Meg. Brown locks were pulled back into another braid that danced and swayed as she moved with the stallion, and as her hair hit the sunlight, the strands became ablaze, a fiery warmth the color of whiskey. Trousers covered her legs once more, and her boots hugged shapely calves like a second skin. How a woman could be so at home in a pair of trousers, let alone carefree at the thought of others viewing her in that state, was mesmerizing.

Meg never took her eyes off the horse as she guided him around the pen, her soft murmurings barely discernable over the slight breeze and the horse's rough responses. Her attention never wavered even as he approached the stables, and he wondered at the concentration. No aristocratic woman in London would have given such an animal an iota of time and yet Meg seemed entranced by the stallion's dance, unaware of anything but the two of them inside the pen.

"Can I help you, sir?" a young boy said, his gaze pinning Oliver to where he stood.

"Yes, right. I'm Lord Greenwood, from the neighboring estate." The boy straightened and removed his cap at the title, and Oliver swallowed a groan. "I was hoping to speak with the stable master and see if I could procure some of his horse excrement."

The lad raised a brow at the statement but said nothing of the odd request. "Of course, my lord. I'll get Mr. Howell for you, my lord." The boy slapped his cap back on his head and scurried away to what could only have been the previous stable for the worn-down manor. While the framing of the structure appeared sturdy enough, a rather large portion of the roof was missing and the stable door lay propped against a tree some meters away. Mr. Howell had his work cut out for him if this was the state of the stables he was relegated to care for.

An older, balding man hobbled towards him, and Oliver had to catch his forearm to keep him from tumbling to the ground. "Easy there."

"Nearly met my maker," the man said with a chuckle. "What can I do for you, my lord?"

Oliver raised a brow. "You're Mr. Howell?"

"That I am. Felix said you had a need for horse shit. Lucky for you, I have a load of it for the taking and I don't ask questions." Mr. Howell shook off Oliver's arm and turned to head to the side of the perilous stable, his gait unsteady. The uneven ground made the trek to the manure pile an unnecessarily time-consuming adventure, with Oliver more concerned for the safety of his companion than in the actual manure itself. A large heap sat away from the stables; its newly added contents creating a potent stench. Flies danced around the hill and, for an infinitesimal moment, Oliver wondered if his experiment truly required the odious mixture before him. The thirty-minute walk from his greenhouse had seemed a rather simple trip, but the putrid smell before him, along with its obvious weight, would create a cumbersome journey home. But alas, science overruled his concerns, no matter how justified they were.

Taking the shovel that Mr. Howell attempted to wield, Oliver scooped the manure into the tin pail he had brought with him. His shoulders pulled at the weight, a sting of joy that could only be found in the work he loved. At home in London, manual labor was frowned upon, deemed an action that was relegated to the lowly, but here in Woodingdean, there was no one to frown at him as he got his hands dirty, no one to question if the future duke was in his right mind. After all, what sort of man found pleasure in menial labor and gardening experiments instead of opulent balls and refined clubs? If his father were to ever catch a glimpse of him handling fecal matter from an animal, he would no doubt question his youngest son's sanity. The idea sent a smile to Oliver's lips, pulling one corner up even as they pinched together in response to the weight.

"Well, if it isn't my husband," a sultry voice called out. "Come to fetch me home, darling?"

Oliver became stunned as he stood up and spotted Meg standing before him, a smile on her lips as she held onto the rope of the stallion beside her. He was up to his metaphorical elbows in shit and this woman was looking at him as if his presence were the moment she had been waiting for all day. His heart picked up its pace. From the exertion or the woman, he could not tell. "Hello." The words were stilted, and he wished he could recall them. Wished he could say something as pulse galloping as she. Alas, basic English escaped him.

"Hello." Her smile softened. "What brings you to Baron?"

Oliver waved at the bucket before him, suddenly unnerved that she had caught him at such a disadvantage. "It's for an experiment I'm working on."

"Truly?" she asked, handing the large brute beside her off to Felix. "What are you experimenting with?"

"The best source of fertilizer for vegetation growth."

"Interesting," Meg said, inspecting his pail and then the pile beside him. "And you think horse manure will work the best at helping to grow more abundant plants?"

"Possibly." God help him. He could barely form a bloody sentence as she stood beside him, a look of interest on her freckle-filled face.

"Do you know a lot about gardening?"

Oliver rubbed at the back of his neck, then immediately regretted the action. He reeked and heavens knew what foul substance covered his hands, and now, most likely, his neck. "Some." Jesus, say something more. "More than the average man." Fuck.

Meg laughed. "Probably more than the gardener. He's currently frowning at what he thinks to be a rosebush and scratching his neck. He's been at it for at least an hour."

Oliver chuckled at the image she painted. "Yes, probably more than him."

Meg leaned in. "Between you and me, he isn't really a gardener. But, he has a family of four rambunctious children with another one on the way, so he took the job."

"And the countess is all right with an inexperienced gardener?" Oliver raised a brow, surprised at the revelation.

Meg shrugged and glanced away. "She has a soft heart for those in need."

"Apparently." Oliver eyed the contents of his pail and frowned. "I can take a look at the plants if you'd like."

She blinked at him, seemingly as surprised by his offer as he was that he had made it. He certainly did not have time to be volunteering himself to an elderly countess and her inexperienced gardener, especially with the little time he had before he was due back in London. But something about Meg's quiet words and the knowledge that the countess had recruited an old man as her stable master and a young father as her gardener had him offering himself up to their needs.

She remained silent as she regarded him and Oliver filled in the silence. "If not, that's all right as well. Wouldn't want to step on the gardener's toes." He sighed and set the shovel back into the manure pile before picking up the pail of shit. Meg still said nothing, and the silence was deafening. "Right then. Well, thank you for the manure."

She put a hand on his arm, stopping his retreat. "If your offer is sincere, we would love the help."

Oliver released a breath he did not know he had been holding. "It is. Do you want to show me the areas he's struggling with?" He certainly did not have time to help an unknowledgeable gardener renovate an estate, but he could offer expertise where needed. Setting the pail back down, Oliver smiled at her. She nodded in response and turned towards the jungle that served as the manor's garden.

It was not a lot, as offers of help went, but it had to be enough. His time remaining in town was trickling down, the breath of responsibility blowing against his neck, a constant reminder that this life was now not his own. He had come to Woodingdean to prepare himself for his new future. He was the new heir to the Duke of Hedley, the new marquess, forced to take up the mantle that had belonged to his brother, Christopher. His best friend, now dead and buried.

No, Woodingdean was meant for healing. For his quiet greenhouse and contemplation, not for lending himself to other complications.

They stopped at a path that was covered in overgrown vines, a tangled web that belonged more in a Grimm fairytale than it did anywhere near Brighton. The bramble that stood before him in varying shades of green and brown mixed together, where one bush ended, another began. A wooden bench, surely once used to enjoy the surrounding area, now lay buried beneath branches and twigs like skeletal remains of days long passed.

A young man stood in the bramble, scratching at his neck as he examined the disaster before him as if uncertain where to begin. Oliver's hands itched to get to work, to clean the errant branches and discover the treasure trove of vegetation that no doubt lied below the rubbish and he bit the inside of his cheek, the sting of pain reminding him of his true purpose.

"Well," Meg said with a sigh, eyeing the same land-scape as him, "this is it." She turned to glance at him, her chocolate brown gaze sending his heart racing once more.

Blast, he was in trouble.

CHAPTER FOUR

I N THE LIGHT of day, her rescuer from the night before
was irritatingly handsome. Brown hair fell waywardly
across his brow, his patrician nose bracketed by long
eyelashes, with eyes she could not discern the color of. His
sharp jawline was speckled by dark stubble and his frame,
long and lean, in no way could measure up to the bulk of
the disreputable Charlie, but his forearms held strength.
Of that, she was certain. Veins had bulged as he lifted piles
of manure and his broad shoulders had flexed under his
linen shirt, hinting at a hidden force that made her inclined
to explore. But only for a moment.

Margaret shook her head as the man took in the disaster that was the gardens of Baron. Sam Hemmings, her
reluctant gardener, had taken one look at the landscape
and sweat had broken out on his brow. Margaret understood his distress, had even experienced it herself as she
examined the land that surrounded Baron Manor. But
what could be done? Sam desperately needed work and
Margaret was in even more desperate need of help, thus
their agreement was born.

Did it matter that neither of them had a clue what they
were doing? Possibly. Did that change anything? Absolutely not.

Like everything else she had confronted as she renovated Baron, Margaret had gritted her teeth, determined to make the best of it, and a jungle of vegetation would not be the thing that took her down. Given the way her rescuer sized up the landscape, Margaret had a feeling his knowledge was the saving grace she was searching for. His gaze danced from one indiscernible green lump to another, reminding her of a stray pup she had seen in London once. She had laid out a feast for the sad animal, and the beast had salivated as he eyed the options before him, so starved he was not certain where to begin. Anyone could see the task before him tempted him, and Margaret was determined to have him take it over.

"It's a bit of a mess," she said, a chuckle bursting from her lips at the understatement.

"Hmm," he said, and Margaret could not be sure if the sound was in agreement or contemplation. Sam had disappeared, no doubt overwhelmed at the work before him, and yet the man beside her stepped gingerly over the vines that littered what she assumed was once a pathway, before bending down to examine an overgrown bush. His brow furrowed, or at least she thought it did. It was hard to tell, given the length of his brown locks. He lifted what Margaret assumed was a branch before nodding his head and pushing to stand. "These are irises." He pointed to a group of flowers on the other side. "Black-eyed Susan's, and those large bushes down the way are hostas."

"Hmm," she said, echoing the noise he made earlier.

He laughed. "No idea what those are, huh?"

"No," she said with a laugh. "But if they're plants and not weeds, I'm thrilled."

"They are plants, rather hardy ones. If you have your

gardener clear back the vines on the pathway, those plants are in great shape and won't need to be replaced."

"Replaced?" Margaret stumbled at the words. "What do you mean, replaced?"

He pointed to the bushes that Sam had been staring at earlier and sighed. "Those roses are dead, as are the hydrangeas across the way. They take up a lot of the green space along the walkway and will need to be removed and have new vegetation planted in their place."

Margaret's stomach dropped at the potential coins that she would waste cultivating the garden into something beautiful and she groaned, rubbing at her brow. "That sounds expensive."

He nodded his head in agreement and turned to analyze the space before him. "Do you know if the countess has her heart set on restoring this piece of the property?"

His question was perplexing, for she was the countess. And yet, it seemed he had decided that she was not. It was an oddly satisfying notion, not being Lady Everly, and the longing to continue that possibility pulled her to ask, "What do you mean?"

He shook his head. "If she were open to having the garden look sparse for a bit, she could split the plants that are doing well in half and replant them in the spaces where the dead shrubbery is. I also know of some vegetables and herbs that not only grow beautifully but would serve as an additional food source outside of the vegetable garden that is probably in place."

"That's," Margaret paused and examined him, a smile taking over her face. "That's a brilliant idea. It'd save on funds and the surrounding laborers can use the additional vegetables and herbs, almost like a communal garden. Do you know of some fruit trees that can be planted as well for the same look?"

His brow furrowed once more. The look of concentration was breathtaking. "Blueberry bushes are rather simple and could be used to fill in the sparse areas." He raised a brow at her. "A communal garden? I've never thought of that before."

"The idea has merit."

"Do you think the countess will allow it?"

Margaret smiled as she eyed the area before her. Oh yes, the countess would approve of the idea without hesitation. She would have Sam start on clearing the vines along the pathway and once that was complete, they would take stock of the actual work that needed to be accomplished. Assessing the man next to her, she smiled. "Any interest in putting together a master plan for this area? The countess would pay you for the work." When he raised a brow, Margaret continued. "It may not be an astronomical amount, but she does have funds."

The stranger sighed, and she worried for a moment that he would decline, but he took in the landscape once more, then nodded his head. "I can make up a plan, but the countess can keep her money. That's all the help I'm afraid I can offer."

"We'll take all the help we can get." Anything was better than nothing at this point, and a guide was still one step ahead of where she was. Margaret stuck out her hand to the man. "You've got yourself a deal, Mr....? Goodness, for all our time together, I still don't know your name."

"Oliver Ludlow, Marquess Greenwood," he said, his voice flat as his hand enclosed about hers. Margaret swallowed the groan that habitually rose to her throat when the aristocracy was mentioned. Not that the individuals that made up the ton were terrible altogether, just that after her marriage to Everly, she wanted nothing to do with that species of human ever again. Convenient that her rescuer was none other than a member himself, and a marquess to boot.

Withdrawing her hand, Margaret curtseyed to the man. "I apologize, my lord, for not only requesting your services but insisting we pay. Thank you so much for your examination of the garden. I'll be sure to take your advice into advisement as we repair it." The words and tone slipped from her lips with ease, the daughter of a baron still fully engrained inside the woman she was attempting to become.

"Nonsense," he said, waving a hand and walking back towards the pail of manure. "It's the least I can do since you've granted me the use of your horse refuse. I'll have the plans drawn up and sent over in a day or two."

Margaret raised a brow at the statement. What an odd man. But if he insisted upon making good on his offer, she would not argue. Between the funds she had received from selling most of her dresses and all of her jewelry, along with the paltry amount she gained from the estate, money was tight as it was. Even the immense length of hair she had sold to the wigmaker, the quickest way possible to gain ready funds, had brought in a decidedly sad excuse for coins, and the resulting shear had left her brown locks shorn to just above her shoulders. It was enough to pay the workers for their time and materials, but if she were being honest, it left very little for her to survive on.

It was different, this life she had chosen. Lacking the finery she was used to, but the freedom that came with it was so intoxicating, she was not sure she truly even missed it. All the items she had sold, all the regalia, meant nothing when compared to the freedom Baron provided, even on the worst of days.

But, free was free.

"If you insist, far be it from me to decline. Thank you again, my lord. Your expertise will make the garden the highlight of Baron Manor." He raised a brow at her words, but said nothing more. Instead, the man bent down and picked a single iris bloom that clung to the stem for dear life in the autumn weather. The indigo petals showed slight wrinkles on its gentle flesh, but its beauty still shined. Without a word, he handed her the bloom, picked up his pail, and with a dip of his head, took his leave. "You're more than welcome to Siris' shit any time, my lord." Her words echoed, the booming of her voice unnecessary and only punctuating her sentence.

Margaret stared at his retreating back, stunned at herself. "You're more than welcome to our shit anytime," she said again, whispering the words to herself in disbelief. "Meg, you utter idiot. What could you have been thinking?"

"What are you muttering about?" a voice said beside her.

Spotting Marty out of the corner of her eye, Margaret sighed. The innkeeper's arrival did little to weaken how much the interaction with the man shook her. "Just making an arse of myself, per usual."

"Was that Lord Greenwood you were talking with?"

"It seems everyone but me knew he was an aristocrat." Turning back towards the stable, she motioned for Marty to follow her. "Lord Greenwood offered to help with the redesign of the gardens, and I took him up on it."

"Why do you sound irritated?" Marty placed a hand on her voluptuous hip, a black brow raised in question. In that pose, she appeared more like a Viking than an innkeeper, her dark locks flowing in the breeze as she stared Margaret down. The woman was built like an Amazonian queen, her tall frame and solid body only lending to her appeal. If Margaret ever thought herself strong, or her biceps impressive, she would only have to look at Marty's well-built form to realize how weak she truly was.

"I'm not irritated by his offer, just the opposite." Margaret picked up the discarded shovel with her free hand and placed it back against the stable. The tools necessary to take care of the horses sat piled up on one side of the structure awaiting the eventual day the shelter would be rebuilt and fully usable once more. "His plans will be useful, especially for Sam, who doesn't have the slightest clue what to do with the area."

"It's the fact that he's an aristocrat that's got you befuddled." Leave it to Marty to not only be blunt, but entirely accurate. After all, it had been Marty's honest opinion that had originally drawn Margaret to the intuitive innkeeper, her friendly demeanor and boisterous laughter creating a welcoming presence she had rarely known. It was as if she had sensed the desired comfort

Margaret had needed and effortlessly pulled her into the fold, adopting her as one would an abandoned puppy. Yet, it was rather annoying how often she was right.

Lord Greenwood had been a much safer individual when she had thought he was an average man who lived around the village, and the newly found fact that he belonged to the prestigious group of individuals she wanted to avoid made his involvement a complication. She could not fault Lord Greenwood for the world he lived in. After all, once upon a time, it had been her world as well. But it was a chapter in her life she had closed and she was determined to keep it that way.

"I'm fine, Marty. He only offered to make a plan for the garden, not become involved in the place's overhaul. Once his favor is fulfilled, he'll be out of my hair." She shook her head, forcing thoughts of the interesting man from her mind. "What brings you out here when you should be getting the inn ready for the night?"

"I brought you dinner and some staples." Marty motioned to the basket she held in her hands. Margaret's stomach growled at the mention of food, and Marty smiled. "I figured you hadn't eaten, and judging by that sound, it would seem I'm right."

"The day merely got away from me." Taking the basket from her friend's hand, she motioned for Marty to follow and headed towards the manor. The kitchen and its adjoining servant quarters were the only parts of the home that were entirely habitable at the moment, and while most would find the conditions unlivable, Margaret adored the tiny size of her current home. Its cozy interior had become her safe space. Within its walls, she had learned to mend a tear, boil water, and bake bread, albeit not well. But it was her own.

Setting the basket on the makeshift kitchen table, Margaret filled an empty cup with water and placed the iris inside before opening the basket and removing the treats within. A whole cooked chicken, some apples, a loaf of bread, and a peach pie soon covered the tabletop, their scents mingling in the air, and Margaret's stomach growled once more. Ripping a drumstick off the chicken, she took a large bite before pulling out a chair and sitting in it, her sigh filling the empty room. Her bones and joints ached from the labor she had put in for the past two months, but if all went accordingly, she would have a home that was not only her own but would be a haven for anyone else who needed it.

"Seeing you now, I would question whether you even knew where London is," Marty said, picking a piece of skin from the chicken and popping it in her mouth. "You're running around the countryside in breeches and boots and eating like an uncultured shipmate."

"If I belch like one, you're allowed to say something, but until then, let me be." Drumstick demolished, Margaret set it on the plate and reached for its twin. During her marriage she had barely been able to eat, her stomach tied in knots with anxiety, but here, she ate heartily, her appetite ferocious as if making up for lost time. Her period in Woodingdean had not only eased her mind, but her body as well. Her once sickeningly thin frame had filled out and muscles had taken shape, their appearance a source of pride. Should anyone she knew from London see her now, they would wonder if she had gone mad, not that she cared.

"Speaking of belching, Charlie asked about you this morning before he left."

"Ugh," Margaret said, swallowing the bite of chicken.

"The man is as educated as a bull, but he's a looker. I wouldn't judge you if you wanted to take him for a ride." Marty winked, attempting a saucy demeanor, but Margaret could only laugh at the woman's poor attempt.

"I certainly wouldn't pick that man to break my long-standing abstinence. I have standards, Marty. And even if I were interested, I have too much on my plate to add anything or anyone else." Marty raised an eyebrow. "The renovations take up all of my time during the day and I fall into bed at night exhausted. And if I get free time, I'd rather spend it having fun and trying new things."

"Bed activities are fun, Meg, especially with the right person."

"I wouldn't know." The words were mumbled and Margaret wished she could recall them. Her couplings with Everly had been minimal, and when an encounter did happen, it had been miserable. Her husband's body smothering her as he thrust his sex into hers, making guttural animal noises all the while. Each movement had burned as he thrust between her legs, and her sex ached for days afterward from the attention. If she had free time, she would certainly not fill it with that experience.

Marty nudged her. "It could have just been the wrong partner, Meg. Not every man is equal, nor talented. Half the fun is testing their mettle to see which fit the bill." Marty winked at her as she closed the basket and headed to the door. "I'm heading back to the inn. Will I see you tonight?"

Margaret shook her head. A quiet evening in her ramshackle home sounded more heavenly than the noisy inn. "I'll visit you tomorrow."

"Go to bed at a reasonable hour tonight," Marty said as she walked out the door.

"You can't make me," Margaret said, her voice a whisper.

Putting away the chicken and other provisions Marty had brought, Margaret filled the kettle and banked the fire in the large hearth that resided in the kitchen. After preparing a cup of tea for herself, she grabbed up the stack of letters from Harrison, and lit an oil lamp before taking her nightly walk through the manor, her steps echoing in the quiet home. Her feet pranced across a large beam she had placed along the hallway, the planks below creaking at the weight, a ghostly moan that left her feeling a little less alone.

The renovations inside the manor had started two weeks before, and thankfully, the foundation and walls were still solid and immovable. While the floors in some rooms had collapsed, the men she had hired from town had gotten to work repairing the joists and shoring up the stronger parts. Once the rooms were actually accessible, the actual work could begin.

While not overly large, as some familial estates, Baron Manor still had ten bedrooms, an expansive library, albeit its books had molded over time, and an office, as well as a ballroom and formal dining room. It was larger than she needed, certainly, but it was her own. And given the number of lost souls that had found their way to Baron already, Margaret had very little worry that the home would be empty for long.

Rumor of the manor seemed to have spread by word of mouth, and while its doors were open to all, she had a soft spot for women and children. But gaining residence at the manor was not a free-for-all. Members were required to contribute to its function, whether that be by helping with the repairs, making meals, or tending to the children while their parents worked. And there was the expectation that those who lived there treat the property more as a stopping point than a final destination, the goal always being rehabilitation in some mode or form.

A worn winged-back chair sat before a large ornate hearth in the study, its fabric barely resisting the sands of time as it sagged in some spots while clinging to life in others. Moths had at one time had a field day on the skirt that used to cover the legs, revealing the shapely wooden dowels inelegantly to those who passed by. It was rumored the former earl's mother had adored the spot, and that she would sit in it nightly with her cup of tea and stare into the fire. The villagers made the whole ordeal sound rather ominous, a ghost of the dowager floating about the manor, but Margaret chose to see it as a gift and willingly followed in her deceased mother-in-law's footsteps. If the woman had caused Everly to hate her as much as he did, she was a friend to Margaret and would be treated as such.

Sitting on the chair, Margaret set the lamp on the table beside her and wrapped the woolen blanket she had left on the chair around her shoulders for warmth. With a smile she sipped her tea and opened the letters from Harrison.

His correspondence since she left had been like clockwork, a letter every week detailing the ongoings on the ton, the renovations he had made to the home in Mayfair, along with any updates on her parents and sister. His words were a balm, soothing any fears she had regarding her decision to upend her life, as he repeatedly told her how proud he was of her and reminded her that he was always near should she need him. While her replies had been few and far between, what with Baron siphoning most of her energy, it sent a small spark of joy through her heart each time his post arrived. She would never admit it to him, but she had begun speaking to herself as he spoke to her, like an endearing friend who truly believed she was made for amazing things.

When the stack of letters was finished, Margaret examined the desecrated study that was hers. Barren of any furniture but the chair, some might call it sad. Meg called it the future. A blank canvas where she would create a new world, a new start. A new home.

Everly had severely underestimated his wife, it seemed.

Pity.

CHAPTER FIVE

O LIVER TAPPED THE pencil against his seventh sheet of paper. It was not that he was nervous at all about the plans he had so willingly offered to draw up. No, it was just that his bloody brain could not recall what the garden had looked like. Every time he reflected on the space, his mind conjured up the image of Meg. The setting sun frolicking behind her, casting beams of light upon her smile, her brown eyes dancing with pending laughter. His sketches became a muddle at that point, his fingers more inclined to draw the curve of her cheek than the paved pathway that lined the garden beds.

Throwing the pencil down, Oliver scrubbed his hands over his face, his stubble pricking his skin in a most unseemly manner. A rather poor image for a future duke, but Oliver could not drudge up the urge to care. With his worry focused on the plot outline, his spinach experiment had taken second-fiddle to Meg's request. All this bloody work simply to impress a woman who did not know him. His brain chided him even as he picked up the pencil once more and attempted another sketch.

When he finished, the light had all but disappeared from the room, the lone candle he had lit doing little to cast the shadows away, but he completed it. His body itched to head to Baron Manor right then and hand over the sketch to Meg. To pick up a shovel and get to work revitalizing the gardens. To see Meg's smile as she watched progress being made. Foolhardy at that. Traipsing about Woodingdean after a girl's smile was something poets did, not aristocrats on holiday. Still, his heart picked up its pace at the possibilities tomorrow held.

A quick check of his plants in the greenhouse confirmed that the entire experiment stunk, but one did not gain knowledge in a day. Walking the aisle of the greenhouse, Oliver talked to each of the spinach plants, giving them compliments on their hearty stalks and luscious leaves, and sounding all together bound for Bedlam, but it did little harm to whisper words of encouragement to the plants. If it helped them grow, it was all the better. And if it helped him feel less lonely, so be it.

For a moment, however briefly, he wondered if he should head to the Salty Siren for his dinner, but changed his mind. He would no doubt look like the fool he was, and all for a glimpse of a girl who more than likely could not even recall his name. Now that he knew where to locate Meg, and after having her smile and laughter directed at him, his befuddled heart wanted to surround itself with the sound.

A quick trip to the kitchen, and a buttered piece of bread later, Oliver stuffed the food into his mouth and made another. Anything to keep his hands busy.

The last piece consumed, he washed it down with a cup of lukewarm tea he had at one point made and never drank, then cleaned his dishes and headed to bed. While Mr. and Mrs. Pettigrew were entirely able to clean up the remnants of his dinner, Oliver did not wish to put any more work on the elderly couple. He already owed them more than enough as they cared for the place that had been his mother's haven.

When the morning light dawned, declaring the start of a new day, Oliver was certain of one thing. He could not simply foist off the plans for the garden and allow another to take over the enormous task of overseeing it. While it made little sense to interfere, and it was never asked that he physically help with the rejuvenation, Oliver knew that leaving the plans in the hands of anyone but himself would drive him mad. His spinach experiment was a relatively simple endeavor, and truthfully, what had he thought to fill his time with between measurements of the stalks and stems? A man could only say so many words to a plant before he went insane.

Decision made and leaving little time to second guess himself, Oliver readied for the day, made up another two slices of butter bread, grabbed an apple, and headed for Baron Manor, plans in hand. He left a slapdash note for the Pettigrew's relating them of his whereabouts, so they did not worry when they arrived later in the day.

People were already swarming the property when he arrived. Burly men carried stacks of wood into the house while women hung tapestries and bedding on every surface possible, attempting to air out the years of neglect the fabrics had seen. Unnoticed the previous day, a pile of broken furniture sat to one side of the manor, its height so large Oliver wondered if the intent was to make a bonfire of it. Mr. Howell and Felix had already begun their work, the black steed from yesterday, Siris, taking his exercise in the pen while they mucked out his stall, adding to the pile of refuse he had taken from before.

Meg was nowhere to be found and a pang of sadness hit his chest, but worry quickly replaced the feeling when he spotted Sam, the not gardener, wielding a large pair of trimming sheers in an unruly fashion. His aggressive clippings were aimed towards the vines, but either he had lost track of where the tangled limbs were coming from or he did not have a clue in the first place, as he took large chunks of leaves from a lush iris that Oliver intended to save. Searches for Meg were forgotten as Oliver rushed towards Sam.

"Oy!" Oliver said, his voice raised. "Put that down before you hurt yourself."

Sam turned at his words, large sheers slicing through the air like a saber and Oliver pulled to a halt to avoid their wrath. "What?" Sam asked.

"You're taking out a rather large portion of the plants we intend to keep," Oliver said, pointing to the iris that was missing half its head.

"It all looks the same, to be honest," Sam said with a shrug.

Oliver shook his head. While the countess seemed to have a rather soft heart, she had poor skills when it came to designating workers. Between Mr. Howell and his advancing age, and Sam's lack of knowledge, it was a wonder she thought to get anything done on the estate. Oliver picked up a smaller set of sheers that sat tangled in the bramble, then lifted a hearty stalk of vines from the pathway. "If you trim the ones along the gravel path first, you'll be able to get a clear idea of where the plants start," he said, clipping at the vines until a portion of the walkway appeared.

"Makes sense," Sam said, opening his sheers and doing the same on another portion of vegetation. Oliver sighed and turned back to the plants before him. These last few minutes had confirmed what he had already suspected. While Sam certainly could handle the job before him, it was going to drive Oliver crazy if the labor did not involve him. Taking the opposite side of the pathway, Oliver set to work, clearing the vines to the edge of the garden bed. The pile of dead vegetation grew beside him as he worked, the autumn sun and its rays' intent upon making the labor that much more arduous.

What could have been hours, though most likely mere minutes later, a boisterous laugh had him lifting his head from his work. In the distance, Meg stood with several women, beating out rugs and draperies that hung from a clothesline strung across the manor's main lawn. Meg's smile was brilliant as she wielded a racket, beating the tapestry with such aggression plumes of dust and dirt decorated the surrounding air. The woman beside her said something that sent Meg into peals of laughter, the sound melodic as it danced upon the breeze.

The pull that took over him as he watched her was a conundrum, her magnetic personality an anomaly he longed to learn more of, even as he questioned it. Oliver frowned as he took back up his sheers and trimmed once more, the repetitive nature of the work soothing the wayward thoughts of his mind. It was best not to dwell on his attraction to her, for that way truly only led to madness. Human laws of attraction made little sense, and what his mind could possibly find enamoring of this lively woman was a mystery he was certain could not be solved in a month. And her apparent lack of interest would only further depress him.

No, best to help Baron Manor where he could, grow his spinach, and prepare himself for his new position as heir to the Duke of Hedley. Those were simpler things, compact and easily explainable. And far less terrifying than a silly crush on a free-spirited woman who was more likely to summon a thunderstorm than have a curiosity in him.

When Oliver next lifted his head, Meg stood on a ladder, pulling rotted wood from the sides of the barn. Dirt smeared her cheek and sweat decorated her forehead, making the fine tendrils that framed her face coil into tight curls, damp with perspiration. The rolled sleeves of her linen shirt exposed the skin to her elbow, the veins of her forearms flexing as she pulled at the boards with a hammer. The sight was magnificent, so appealing he had to swallow the sound that attempted to rise from his throat. She was brilliant, her brow furrowed as she worked diligently, a small smile of triumph decorating her lips as each board fell to the ground, meeting its demise.

Oliver growled as he picked up the shovel and eyed the hostas before him. His plans would require him to split the plants in half and relocate them to the sparser areas of the gardens, and he was grateful for the spurt of energy as he set to work, the laughter that could only have been from Meg fueling his movements. Joy-filled smiles seemed to follow the woman wherever she went, her bright laughter given freely to everyone around her. Envy pulled at Oliver, sheer longing to have that delight sent his way, if only for a brief moment.

"Garden, spinach, dukedom," he said to himself, a chant. A prayer.

Garden. Spinach. Dukedom.

As motivation went, it was sorely lacking, but the words drowned out her laughter and silenced the reminder that she was out of his reach. A far more interesting human than a quiet, plant-obsessed man with as much excitement in him as a wooden pull toy.

"Hello," Meg said behind him.

Oliver dropped the shovel and turned, her voice a joy to hear, even as it surprised him.

She smiled at him, the same one she bestowed on everyone around her, and his heart fluttered. "I brought you some lunch," she said, holding up a sandwich and a mason jug. "Are you hungry?"

As if unaware of the situation, his stomach chose that moment to rumble indelicately, and she laughed at the noise. "It would seem the answer is yes."

Oliver regarded the spot Sam had been and was shocked to find it all but empty, a gigantic pile of vines the only sign someone had once been there. "Did Sam leave?"

Meg nodded. "His wife arrived with the kids and a picnic basket. They're down by the pond having lunch together."

"Oh." He rubbed his gloved hands on his breeches, aware of the dirt that had accumulated there as he had worked.

"Lunch?" she asked him again, a brow raised in question. Oliver nodded, and she smiled before leading him to a large tree that provided plenty of shade from the blistering sun. Even as autumn set in, its brisk breeze filling the day, the sun still had little trouble burning brightly. "It's only lemonade and a ham sandwich. I hope that's all right."

"It's perfect," he said, moving to sit near her while maintaining a respectable distance. "Thank you."

The ground beneath him crunched as he sat, the colorful leaves cushioning him beneath the large elm tree, his movement jostling them from their slumber as he took the proffered sandwich from her, amazed at the appetite he worked up.

"I wasn't sure I'd see you today," Meg said, her eyes closed as she leaned against the tree trunk.

Oliver turned himself toward her, the view of her much more fascinating than the ramshackle manor before him. "Why is that?" Oliver asked around a bite.

"Our band of misfits can seem like a lot to others. I was certain I'd scared you off."

Oliver laughed at her words. "You don't scare me."

A bright red leaf fell onto her head softly, her brown locks clinging to it like decorations. Leaning to one side, Oliver removed the intruder, his fingers slipping over the soft curls as he untangled the menace. Meg's eyes opened to meet his, and he smiled, showing her the leaf, before pulling away. "Thank you," she said, the words soft.

With a breath, Oliver released the leaf before removing the plans for the garden from his pocket. He set them down beside her. "I drew up some ideas last night and wanted to deliver them, but after seeing Sam nearly impale himself with the sheers, I thought perhaps I should work a bit as well."

"Mm," Meg said, opening her eyes and unfolding the plans. She scanned his work quietly and Oliver said nothing, happy to let the silence fill the void. His work was the one place where he found confidence, aware that when it came to plants, his anxieties and awkwardness faded away. Vegetation he understood. Vegetation did not have societal dictates and social niceties required to be considered worthy of acceptance. Christopher seemed to be the only one that had acquired that characteristic, one of the many traits that would have made him the perfect duke.

"These are really good," she said.

"If the countess is all right with it, I've already started halving the hostas for the barren parts of the garden beds and can have Sam start on the irises and black-eyed Susan's. You're lucky they are *Rudbeckia subtomentosa*." She frowned at him. "It's a perennial variety. It'll look sparse for a bit, but they should grow in and will cover the ground quite nicely."

Meg smiled at him and folded the paper before sliding it into her shirt pocket. "The countess thinks your plan is brilliant. Thank you for your help, my lord."

Oliver eyed Meg as he took a sip of lemonade from the jug. "Do you know the countess very well?"

Meg laughed, her eyes crinkling. "Fairly well."

Oliver frowned at her. "Why do I feel like I've missed the joke?"

Meg stood and brushed at her trousers before eyeing him and gracing him with her signature smile. "Because I'm the countess."

CHAPTER SIX

G IVEN LORD GREENWOOD'S silence, sandwich raised midway to his mouth, Margaret assumed she had summarily stunned him. Her title was unnecessary in Woodingdean. Here, she could simply be Meg, the odd eccentric who worked at Bitch Manor and occasionally raced carriages when the urge struck. Yet, something about Lord Greenwood's gentle tone and hand-drawn sketches had left her sensing that he would understand what a countess was doing hiding outside the wilds of Brighton.

She let the silence stretch between them. It mattered very little what he thought of her charade. She did not owe anybody anything any longer, and that included the knowledge of her title. And yet, the longer time went on she began to worry. "If you'd like to withdraw your offer to help, I'll understand. We wouldn't want word getting back to London that they've spotted you in the company of a newly made widow."

He set down the sandwich and brushed at the crumbs before meeting her gaze. "No, not at all. I was simply surprised."

"I don't meet the typical criterion for a countess, do I?"

"No? But in the best way possible," he said, standing.

"A countess who does manual labor in a pair of trousers is by no means ordinary, but that doesn't make you any less a countess." He laughed and rubbed at the back of his neck. "It explains how you were so familiar with the countess' thoughts regarding the repairs."

She smiled at him. "It does, doesn't it?" Shrugging, she examined the land that was now hers. "I'm more at ease just being Meg."

He watched her, his gaze so penetrating she was certain he could see to the very core of her, hear every thought that flit about her head. "Is it that uncomfortable being the countess?"

She frowned at his question, disliking the turn their conversation had taken. "It's all I've known since I was eighteen." Brushing off her hands, she motioned to the jug beside him. "Take your time. Sam will most likely be gone for a while if the size of the picnic his wife packed was any indication."

Margaret walked away, afraid if she turned back, he would see just how vulnerable his question had left her. Everly had stolen not only years from her life, but the opportunity to learn who she was, who she wanted to become. So yes, it was that uncomfortable being the countess, for that was a woman Margaret no longer wanted to be. No longer wanted to recognize. As the dust and dirt from Bitch Manor were scraped away, so too were the remnants of the docile creature she had been, and she was determined to find the beautiful layers buried far beneath.

The ruckus inside the house drowned out the musings Lord Greenwood's question had provoked and Margaret let the beating of hammers and murmuring of voices wash over her as she walked the home, peeking into each room. The restoration had become a labor of love and she reveled in the fact that each doorknob and mantle, each piece of molding and carved banister, were hers. While funding was tight, it only served to further provoke Margaret's desire to restore the home to its full glory. It would be a place of solitude for anyone who sought it. Its doors opened to nobility and poor alike, seeking relief from abusive spouses or parents. It would become the safe space she had desperately desired for herself all those years ago when the only option she had was to marry Everly or be tossed onto the street. A young woman would not have to resign herself to a loveless marriage with a bastard of a man, forced to deal with his tempest temper and brutal criticism.

With renewed determination, Margaret rejoined the group, taking apart the rotten exterior of the barn. Her hammer was heavy in her hand, her arms aching at the exertion she was putting them through, but she could only focus on the exhilaration that overcame her each time her own hands removed a board. This was her home, her land. She would rebuild it, renew it, and watch it flourish, just like she planned to do herself.

The next morning came early, the small crew of workers arriving with the rising sun, and among them, a single nobleman. This time, he came wearing an enormous hat that shaded his face from the sun and her gaze, and for a moment she mourned the view. The floppy monstrosity hid his squared jaw and chestnut locks, his green eyes now black in the darkness it created.

Not that Margaret was looking, no. It was simply that his facial composition was intriguing, that was all. Not that his toothy smile gave her butterflies, nor that she wondered what his bristled cheek would feel like cradled inside her hands. No. He was pretty to look at, but not for touching. Or smiling. Or laughing. Margaret growled as she picked up the garden hoe and attacked the vegetable beds near the kitchen door. The produce that had attempted to grow back was in a sad state, their lack of water and overall care apparent as they produced little crops. Under Lord Greenwood's master plan, the lot of it was to be gutted and started once more, and Margaret could not find a more apt way to start her morning. When a pair of gloved hands moved in beside her, shovel clutched between them, she knew she was in trouble.

"Good morning," he said, his voice still gruff from sleep, and Margaret closed her eyes, the images his voice conjured too intimate.

"Good morning, my lord," she said, keeping her head down.

"Oliver."

Margaret peeked up at him and found his gaze pinned on her, his green eyes just as bright as she remembered. "P-pardon?"

"I'm Oliver, and you're Meg." As if the words justified themselves, he took his shovel and attacked a dried bush she had not the foggiest clue of what it had once been. Oliver and Meg. Two human beings. She smiled at the notion as she took up her hoe once more and set to work. His name fit him, certainly much better than the title he had announced with such disdain, and the ease with which is rolled about in her mind gave a comfort she had not expected. The only other member of society she called by their given name was Harry, and only in private moments. A giggle slipped past her lips at the scandalous nature of calling him Oliver, and she felt another shackle break free.

Before long, the sun beat down on her neck and Margaret wondered if he had the right idea of wearing the hat. She was already tanned from her two months at Bitch Manor, and a cascade of freckles had begun to appear in the most peculiar places. She should have felt ashamed, her once fair complexion now a muddle of spots and no longer white as snow, but each new production of freckles had only served to fill her with joy. Their arrivals were marks of honor, badges she now wore as proof that Margaret Reedy, Countess Everly, was dead.

A jug of lemonade was thrust in her hands, and Margaret eyed the object before taking it from Oliver and drinking deeply. The sour liquid quenched the thirst she had not realized she had, and she sighed as she lowered the crock, relief flowing through her body. Not even noon and she had already sweated through her linen shirt, her hair no doubt an array of curls from the humidity, but she felt alive.

Her hands, however, were a different story. Calloused from the work she had done, they still seemed to blister at the most inconvenient times, its presence made apparent when a drop of lemonade rolled onto one, the sting causing Margaret to hiss. Oliver was beside her in an instant, his green gaze assessing the injury while gloved hands cupped her palm.

"What happened?" he asked, the words soft.

She shook her head. "It's just a callous," she said, trying to pull back her hand. "It looks much worse than it is."

One strong hand held her still while he used his teeth to remove one of his gloves, then the other, all the while, her attempt to withdraw and hide the injury behind her back remained futile as his much larger hands cradled her palm, his now naked skin against hers, stunning her with their gentleness and warmth.

He looked at her and Margaret attempted to smother her grimace with a smile, but his frown only confirmed how poor her acting skills were.

"We need to wash this. Do you have water and soap somewhere?" he asked as he turned her palm, his warm hands doing odd things to her breathing.

"Inside," she said, pulling her hand away from him. Turning to head into the kitchen, Margaret was stunned when Oliver followed beside her. "I can manage this."

He shook his head before opening the door for her. "How do you plan to bandage that on your own?"

He had a point. Choosing not to argue, Margaret grabbed the small slice of soap she had, along with the kettle of warm water she had used earlier that morning for her tea. Oliver took both items from her hand, grabbed a chipped ceramic bowl by the stove, and poured the water inside. "Do you have any linen to clean and wrap it with?"

"There's an older shirt that I washed outside on the clothesline. I was planning to have it torn into dust rags since moths got ahold of it. Would that work?"

Oliver nodded his head and left the small room, returning shortly with a piece of the white linen shirt. Using his teeth, he tore the fabric into smaller pieces and stacked them beside the bowl before taking the longer one and placing it on his shoulder. His hands returned to hers and he pulled her towards the table, submerging the blistered skin in the warm water. Margaret hissed at the sting. "It's all right," Oliver murmured as he rubbed the skin with soap. "I'll be quick."

The water clouded, a sudsy mess that made her hand disappear, and while she could see nothing he was doing, she could feel everything. Thick fingers gently scrubbed at the tender skin, circling the injury with soap before wiping away the bubbles. Heat took the place of pain, his movements entrancing her. When fresh water was poured over the clean skin, Margaret jolted, aware that her body had become firmly pressed against his while he tended to her hand.

She tried to pull her hand free from his, but he merely held on tighter, clucking his tongue at her as he pulled her towards the single chair and directed her to sit in it. His long fingers still held her while he examined the skin before blowing softly on it. Margaret's gaze narrowed onto his lips; his dusky pink cupid's bow puckered as he blew once more.

Christ, it was hot in here. She must have suffered heat-stroke as well, given the fire that was burning inside her as his lips came closer to the skin of her hand. "It's dry," she said, the words coming out in a croak.

"Right," he said, staring at her hand. "Good."

Oliver placed two squares of fabric over the wound before removing the long strip from around his shoulders and wrapping her palm. Margaret stared at the wall, certain that if she looked at him, she would do something utterly embarrassing, like cup his cheek, if only to feel the stubble that grew there. She swallowed and scrutinized the kitchen, noting the repairs that would need to be done, anything to distract her from the man that knelt before her, his sandalwood scent filling the air.

Her caretaker appeared so unmoved by the process, cleaning her hand with an almost sterile approach, as if tending to a mere dinner plate than a person, meanwhile, she was certain her cheeks were sporting an ungodly shade of red as she attempted to measure her breathing. From the pain or the man, she could not be sure.

"I have some salve at Bellawink," he said, tying the strip. "I'll bring it tomorrow. It'd be best if you didn't do any work that would require you to use it. That way, it doesn't need to be re-bandaged." He peeked at her, her hand still cradled in his.

"Okay," she said. His green eyes were more like a forest in the dark kitchen and Margaret searched them, aware of the tightness in her throat as she did. His sandalwood scent filled the air as calloused fingertips stroked the top of her bandage, so gentle she was certain she was imagining it, but looking to see would mean breaking the connection and she could not convince herself to do that. At some point in their journey to the kitchen, Oliver had lost his hat, his brown shaggy hair falling into his face, and Margaret lifted her uninjured hand, longing to see all of his sunning face. Before sanity could take over, she pushed the errant strand away, her fingers tangling in the soft wayward strands of his hair. His breath caught as her thumb slid against his stubbled cheek, the sound breaking the spell he had cast. Pulling her hand back, Margaret glanced away and cleared her throat. "Thank you for your help."

"Of course," he said, pushing to stand. "I'm going to head back." Without another word, he left the kitchen, closing the door behind him.

Margaret released the breath she had been holding and inspected both her hands, the one he had bandaged so carefully, and its twin, who had been graced with the feel of his skin. Her fingers retraced his steps, trying to reignite whatever magic he had created, but they were unsuccessful. Whatever that was, he produced it and him alone. She groaned at the knowledge, aware that she could do very little but avoid him at all costs, but her palms curled inward slightly, a poor attempt to retain the feeling he had ignited, trapping them within.

She did not have time for butterflies and soft caresses, damnit. But heaven help her, she wanted them.

CHAPTER SEVEN

OLIVER WAS SHAKING.

Fuck, he was shaking from merely a touch, but shaking nonetheless. Worry had kicked in fast when Meg gasped in pain, and the only thought he had at the time was to make sure she was all right. But once that bandage was on her hand, reality set in, and it took very little to realize that he was holding her hand, rubbing at the soft skin while he stared into her brown eyes. And that she was touching him, too. Her small hand pushing at his hair had been pure bliss, and he had to resist the urge to put it back when she moved away.

Bloody hell.

Muttering at himself under his breath, Oliver picked up his hat where it had fallen off his head and hit it against his leg, the sting bringing him back to earth. It was just a moment, something that could have happened to anyone who helped her. It had nothing to do with him, nothing at all.

Retrieving his shovel, Oliver pulled back on his gloves and attacked the overrun plants that took up the vegetable garden. It did not matter that the skin still tingled from the touch of her hand as it skimmed his cheek, did not matter that her spicy scent of vanilla lingering in the air. None of it mattered.

Meg remained scarce for the rest of the day and Oliver was grateful for it. While a part of him nagged that he should check on her, make sure she did not re-injure herself, he ignored it. She was a grown woman, perfectly capable of tending to herself given the life she had chosen, and she certainly did not need a man lingering around her, nattering on about wound care.

When the day ended, Oliver put up his shovel with the rest of the tools near the stable and set off for home, his forearms aching and his back throbbing from the labor he put them through. Stripping himself bare at his backdoor, Oliver snatched his towel from the clothesline and headed to the small pond beside the cottage. The water was frigid, but a good swim in the brisk stream would cool his ardor and loosen his muscles.

After an hour of exercise, and a quick wash, Oliver dressed in clean trousers and a shirt, pulled on his muddy work boots, and headed to the inn for dinner. The Salty Siren's plaque, a buxom mermaid perched upon a jagged rock, swung in the slight breeze of the evening, its creaking hinges a haunting melody that mixed with the soft chuffs of the horses nearby, but inside, Oliver was met with jovial laughter that quickly lightened his mood.

Two pints and three bowls of stew later, exhaustion ate at his bones, but he sat there, allowing the ruckus of the dining room to wash over him. The solitude at the cottage was nice, to an extent, the peace he found there unlike any other. But it was also lonely. During the day as he worked at Baron, it was easy to pretend like he was not alone in this world, but at night, the silence of the cottage was cloying, Christopher's memories like an errant ghost lurking around every corner.

As kids, they had played at the cottage during the summers, their mother preferring the countryside air to the stench of the city and their father only intent upon pleasing their mother. Her utter hatred of the city, and society, meant she allowed them ample access to the world that heirs to the dukedom would otherwise be denied. The pond and greenhouse were their playground, and they ran through Woodingdean feral, only returning home for meals. At night they slept beneath the stars, and during the day, they would pretend they were pirates, or explorers, or scientists.

It did not matter that sometimes Christopher would struggle to breathe from asthma. Oliver would simply stop their game until he could run again, but as Christopher got older, it became harder for him to breathe. His brother had been ordered to remain confined to his rooms as doctors had been uncertain of its cause, and the light that had once filled Christopher had slowly died away as he remained trapped in his apartments, never able to venture outside. Eventually, influenza had been what killed him.

This past year without him had been excruciating, made worse by the even quicker decline and passing of his mother. Within a brief span of time, he and the duke were the only ones that remained. And the weight of the dukedom now rested squarely on his shoulders, and it was apparent he had very little experience in what that required. It was because of the large duty before him that his father had agreed to his month-long trip, surely noticing the growing anxiety as Oliver reviewed task after task that he had very little hope of understanding.

Sipping at his ale, Oliver resisted the urge to drown himself in the brew and let the numbing feeling wash over him, but that way led to ruin, and he would have no one to hate but himself when the morning came. No, better to sit with the feelings, even though the knife was sharp and the pain still fresh.

A petite brunette with a long braid down her back weaved between the bodies of the dining room, and Oliver smiled as he watched Meg flit back and forth from the bar to the tables, certain that a countess working at an inn was the oddest sight he had ever encountered and frankly curious at what prodded her to do so. Her signature smile was present on her face as she delivered meals and ale, her hand still sporting the wrappings he had applied earlier. How she could put in a day's hard work at the manor, then come to the inn and wait tables at night was beyond him, but it would seem this woman could do nothing but surprise him.

When her eyes met his, Oliver smiled, giving a silent nod, before turning back to his meal. Removing the small notebook he carried with him in his jacket pocket, Oliver looked over the notes he had taken that morning on the spinach growth, jotting down hypotheses and climate conditions within the greenhouse. The plants were flourishing, their stalks and leaves thriving in the enriched soils, and he was content with their progress, although slightly more so by the goose fertilizer. Given its rather extensive collection method, the goose excrement was proving more effective than he had expected.

"Would you like company?" Meg asked, a tankard of ale in one hand.

"I'd love some." Oliver put away his notebook and watched as she sat in the chair across from him. "How's the hand?" he asked, motioning to the wrappings.

"A little tender, but not too bad." She took a sip of her drink. "Thank you for helping me bandage it. You were right, I would have been utterly useless doing it myself."

"Not useless. A bit more complicated, but I'm sure you could have managed. I'll bring the salve by tomorrow morning, and a pair of gloves as well. If you're planning to use tools, it's best to have them on hand to avoid injuries like that."

She shook her head and smiled. "It was rather silly of me to go after the yard work with such a vengeance, but after looking at your plans, I got excited. The notion of a functioning vegetable garden was too thrilling to pass up."

Oliver laughed at her words. He was certain his plans did not evoke that level of excitement, but it was kind of her to say so. His obsession with plant life and vegetation were topics hardly anyone understood, let alone attempted to join in, but there was something in the care and cultivating of horticulture that brought him peace.

"You were rather enthralled in your notebook. I wasn't interrupting anything?" Meg asked.

"No," Oliver said, withdrawing the notebook and handing it to her. "Just writing observations on the experiment I'm doing."

She raised a brow at him before opening the notebook and reading over his notes, the slow turn of the pages showing she was actually reading the words he had written instead of just glancing over them. "The fertilizer?"

Oliver nodded before taking a drink. He had learned over time to contain the rapid-fire information bursts that wanted to spill from him when he talked about his plants, and while his brain sought to detail every aspect of the experiment he worked on, he instead swallowed the words. It would be best to allow Meg to think he was entirely sane, unaware that he was a man who would happily lose himself to his greenhouse and the peace it provided.

"This is really interesting. No wonder you know so much about gardening," she said. "Are you sure you should spend your days at Bitch Manor when you're in the midst of such work?"

Oliver let out a burst of laughter. "Bitch Manor?"

She smiled. "The previous earl referred to the estate as such. Little did he know I would find it more empowering than demeaning." She leaned forward and rested her elbows on the table. "But in all seriousness, why offer your services at the manor when you are so busy with your own work?"

"The experiment itself is rather simple, and while I could certainly babysit it, I've found it can become rather quiet."

"I know what you mean. I'm so used to the noise during the day that at night, the manor can become almost too quiet. Thankfully, Marty lets me come here and work." She leaned forward and winked at him. "Plus, I get a free meal."

"So, everyone wins."

"Precisely. She offered to pay me once, but I renegotiated for hot meals. Her beef stew is worth so much more than a bit of coin."

"It is delicious." Oliver looked towards the bar where the innkeeper stood, a towel draped over her shoulder as she flashed a smile at a patron. "How can she offer to pay you for your work? She doesn't run this place, does she?"

Meg smiled, but the action did not meet her eyes. "She does, actually. Her parents sent her here from Marseille when she was ten. They wanted her to be protected during the revolution, and her father's older sister, May, seemed like the safest place. Her aunt and uncle owned the inn, and when her uncle died, she took over. Her aunt's health had started to decline, so Marty set her up in a nice house in town and has been running things ever since."

Oliver frowned. "How long has she been running the inn?"

"Twenty years?"

Oliver's eyebrows raised at Meg's statement. The innkeeper looked no older than thirty, and no matter which way Oliver did the math, his final conclusion was that she had been merely a child when she had taken over as proprietress of the Salty Siren. While the inn was not overly large, he knew it boasted several bedrooms, as well as a working kitchen and an impeccable stable. To imagine a young woman commanding it all was a feat he could not do, and as he glanced at Marty once more, he now saw her in an even more remarkable light. No wonder she had taken Meg under her wing.

Meg continued to flip the pages of the notebook and Oliver's heart skipped when she turned the page, revealing his drawings. The gardens of Baron sat before her, Sam in the background wielding a hoe, while Siris paced the training stall. "Goodness," Meg said, her eyes skimming the page.

Oliver cleared his throat. "It's just a sketch." Meg turned the page and Oliver's heart jumped to his throat as she revealed the picture he had drawn of her. "That's—"

Meg held up her hand as she took in her image on paper. Blood rushed to Oliver's ears, its swishing sound drowning out the buzz of the inn. She no doubt thought him disturbing. After all, who would draw a picture of someone they barely knew? "Meg," he said, unsure of what he could say to reassure her it was harmless.

She looked at him. "Is this how you see me?"

Oliver cleared his throat. "Yes, but you see—"

"May I have it?" she asked, her eyes back on the page, her finger tracing over the smile he had sketched. Her eyes had softened, filling with a sense of almost wonder as she took in her likeness on the page.

"Of course," Oliver said, taking the book from her and tearing the page out. "I'm sorry." He groaned. "I was drawing absently while formulating a plan for Baron and…" he gestured to the paper.

She shook her head, one corner of her lips creeping up in a smile. "No, you don't have to explain. I'm not mad, I'm…" she shook her head, "I didn't know I could look this way."

Oliver frowned. "You always look that way."

Meg looked at him, her brows raised. "Hmm," she said, the sound disbelieving.

She stared at the picture of herself for what felt like eons, and Oliver rubbed at the back of his neck, certain the longer she looked at the picture, the more she might see, not only of herself, but of him. "I think I'm going to head home," he said, standing.

"Did you walk here?" she asked. Oliver nodded, yes. "May I walk with you? I think your cottage is just beyond the manor."

"Of course," Oliver said, relief coursing through him. Perhaps she truly was not angry, or perhaps she intended to end him in the dead of night without a witness. Either way meant more time in her company.

Meg smiled before leaving the table with their empty tankards and his bowl, the paper tucked beneath her arm. Gathering his jacket, Oliver pushed in the chairs and stood at the door, watching as Meg said goodbye to Marty, grabbed an oversized frock coat from under the bar, and came towards him, a smile on her face. "Ready?"

Oliver nodded, and they left the inn, the quiet of the evening wrapping around them like a cozy blanket. The nighttime sounds of Woodingdean were comfortable, the crunch of gravel beneath their feet the melody as they neared their homes. Oliver stuffed his hands in his pockets and studied the stars that speckled the night sky, the moon so large and bright, it lit their path like a lantern. "This is nice," he said. To himself or her, he was not sure, but it needed to be said.

"It is," Meg said beside him. "It's as if we are the only two humans on earth." He could hear the smile in her voice as his mind painted the image, her eyes sparkling with merriment.

I think I'd be less lonely knowing you were with me, he thought, grateful the words did not slip from his lips. They were too raw, too revealing. Too close to the truth of just how isolated he was in a world that did not include his brother, his best friend. And this woman, she somehow called to that piece of him. Soothed it, understood it, for she too knew what it was to be alone.

As the road opened up to the path leading to Baron Manor, Oliver wondered at how a walk could end so quickly. Meg stopped beside him and eyed the road to her home, the moon's light painting her face in a milky glow. She peeked at him and smiled, but it did not hold her usual joy. The corners pulled up only slightly, and it never reached her eyes. The sadness he saw there filled him with an ache that almost had him reaching for her, if only to comfort. To take away whatever thought had brought such pain.

"If you ever find yourself overwhelmed by the silence, I'm just a short walk away. You're always welcome to stop by whenever you need," he said.

She nodded, standing beside him but saying nothing. Oliver racked his brains, desperate for an iota of conversation that might keep her by his side for a mere moment longer, but he could find nothing.

With a sigh, she looked at him. "Thank you for walking me home." She turned and followed the path to Baron Manor, disappearing around a corpse of trees, and Oliver stared at the spot where she had vanished.

With a frown, Oliver continued down the road toward the cottage, sleep sounding like just the solution required to fix whatever melancholy notion had lodged in his head, making him say nonsensical things to an interesting woman.

As he crawled into bed that night, his mind replayed

Meg's words and the touch of sadness that had stolen the light from her cheerful smile. Perhaps he was not the only one trying to escape something in Woodingdean. Perhaps Meg was just as lost as he.

CHAPTER EIGHT

A FTER A TERRIBLE night's sleep, met with a soggy autumn morning, Margaret was nearly ready to scream. They halted any work on the grounds and vegetable garden until the rain ceased, and exterior work was altogether nonexistent, opting for personal safety of the crew over roof repairs and chimney reassembly. What little labor that could be done in the house made the interior so loud Margaret had stuffed her ears with cotton, if only to maintain her sanity.

Oliver was nowhere to be found, not that she blamed him. If he had arrived, he would be forced to work on floor repairs or painting, and no matter how hard she tried, Margaret could not imagine the man with a paint-brush in hand. No, he belonged outside, surrounded by the greenery and flora he so obviously loved. But his absence was noticeable, his lanky frame one she found herself searching for without thought, even inside the darkened manor.

Wielding a paintbrush or hammer was also not an option for her, as each time she clutched the tool in her hand, the blistered skin throbbed. Blood had already tinged the wrappings Oliver had placed on her hand yesterday, the linen sticking to her skin, pulling at the angry flesh. Margaret growled at the thought of removing the bandage, certain she would injure herself further if she attempted to clean and redress the wound on her own. Besides, Oliver had said he had a salve that he would bring to her. She laughed at the expression she no doubt wore on her face. More petulant child than peculiar countess, no doubt. Forgoing the urge to work, Margaret instead collected broken and chipped crockery, wandering about the house and placing them beneath any leaks. It was nothing monumental, but it was something to keep her busy.

By noon, the rain had slowed to a drizzle, and what little workers that had showed up decided to head home before the next downpour, and Margaret could not blame them. There was little to accomplish because of the weather, so their time at the manor was pointless. Margaret's hand ached, and between the pain and the weather, she knew only a change of scenery would help with her sour mood. Grabbing a chunk of cheese, half a loaf of bread, and an unopened bottle of mead, Margaret threw the items into a cloth and wrapped the package tightly. Oliver had said she was more than welcome at his home anytime, and that was where the salve was.

The walk to the cottage took very little time, especially given that she ran for most of it. The rain had spurned her movements, its downpour picking up almost as soon as she left the manor, but her hand hurt just enough that she did not care if she got a bit wet, and her unusual urge to see Oliver had left her foregoing a jacket, a stupid decision if she did not say so herself. The cottage, which Oliver had called Bellawink, appeared beyond a grouping of trees that bracketed a small pond. Movement in the pond had

Margaret pulling to a stop, staring in amazement at the sleek body that cut across the water, his strokes measured and sure. "Dear God," she said, the words a whimper.

He was magnificent. The long frame she had originally determined to be lanky was in truth made up of solid cords of muscle, lean and sculpted so perfectly she was certain she was imagining it. His broad chest and wide shoulders moved with such fluidity it appeared as if the water parted ways for him, the motions so smooth barely a ripple was seen on the surface. He appeared unmoved by the storm that poured overhead, instead swimming lap for lap from one end of the pond to another.

Margaret's hands clutched at the parcel she held, uncertain of what to do next. She was a voyeur and an uninvited one at that. When she glanced back at the pond, Oliver had pulled himself from the water, a towel wrapped around his trim waist.

Turning her back from the delectable sight, she counted to one hundred, then started again. After ten rounds of methodically counting, Margaret turned back to find the pond empty, and Oliver nowhere in sight. Her hands shook, from the cold of the rain or the image she had just seen, she did not know. Naked men were not a common spectacle, even with her newfound adventurous side, and Oliver's lithe form did things to her stomach that she had never felt before. If that body paired with his remarkable personality was what she was forced to labor beside day in and day out, she was in trouble.

Praying he had gone to the cottage to change, she ducked her head against the downpour, determined to get the image of Oliver's body out of her mind. The sandstone cottage beckoned her, its pleasant gated entry and solid wooden door only adding to its charm. After a brisk knock, she waited, rocking back and forth from heel to toe. When a minute passed, she knocked again, then resumed rocking as footsteps came towards the door. When Oliver opened it, she thrust the package at him, dodging around his body and into the dry warmth of the cottage.

"Come in," he said, closing the door behind her. Oliver stared at her and it took Margaret a moment to realize that her clothes had become particularly soaked in the time she had waited for him to dress. Her linen shirt stuck to her chest like a second skin, her curly brown locks were no doubt a rat's nest on her head. "Did you walk here?"

"Of course," she said, pulling the thin white shirt away from her skin as his eyes flicked away from her chest. "I brought food if you're interested. Nothing fancy, but food." She looked at the floor, unable to meet his eyes. Margaret was certain he would know within an instant that she saw him swimming. Saw all of him, really.

"Forget the food, you're soaked." He grabbed her arm and steered her towards the back of the house, his grip firm. "We need to get you into something dry before you catch your death," he said, his voice surly. Inside a bedroom, he thrust shirt and trousers at her, along with a towel that was still slightly damp. Margaret's eyes crossed at the realization that the towel she held had been firmly pressed against his bare skin and she dropped it as if she had been burned. "Why are you standing there? Get out of those clothes and into the dry ones. I'll make you some tea," he said, closing the door behind him.

Margaret eyed the cloth, shivering as the cold from her clothing penetrated her skin. Decency be damned. She stripped out of her wet clothes and wrapped herself in the towel, wiping away the moisture that remained on her skin. Dried, she put on Oliver's warm clothes, rolling the sleeves of the shirt that were overly long on her compact frame, and tying the trousers tight with the ribbon that held her hair in its braid. Taking advantage of the brush he had placed on the nightstand, she sat on his plush bed and combed at the mess her shoulder length hair had become, wincing as the bristles found tangle after tangle.

A knock at the door had her lifting her head as Oliver returned, a large mug in his hand that had steam emitting from the top. "Tea?" he asked, raising the mug.

Margaret smiled and took the mug from him, cupping the ceramic, allowing the heat to warm her hands. A small sip had her sighing, and she looked up at Oliver. "Thank you."

He nodded and motioned to the brush she had abandoned. "Do you need help?"

She grimaced. "If you don't mind? I can't seem to find where the tangles begin."

Oliver picked up the brush and Margaret turned her back to him, sitting cross-legged on the bed. Smooth strokes raked across her head, thick fingers following behind and gently untangling the knots that had accumulated. Where she should have felt tugging and pain, instead there were only delightful tingles as coarse fibers met scalp. She shivered, unsure of whether she was still chilled or if it was the sensation of another person brushing her hair, and a soft sigh escaped her lips. It was a pleasure she had never known, her own mother uninterested in any sort of tender ministrations toward her child, and her maid's strokes had been so painful that Margaret had opted to do it herself instead of withstanding the potential hair loss that would occur at the woman's attention.

"Is this all right?" he asked, his deep voice filling the quiet room.

"Yes." It was all she could say, his gentle brush strokes releasing an uncomfortable sadness that could only have been found when touched with care by another. It was an act she had certainly never encountered in her years on this earth, nor did she think it would be one she would ever know again.

Oliver's motions were smooth, each movement met with little resistance as he pulled the brush from root to tip. Certainly, there could be no more tangles, and yet he continued to tend to her hair as if the act meant something more to him as well.

Margaret pulled away, the intensity of the moment too much, and uncrossing her legs, she moved to the opposite side of the bed, tea cup balanced in her hand. "Thank you," she said, standing and forcing a smile to her lips instead of the uncertain frown she felt. "Should we eat?"

Oliver nodded at her and set the brush back on the side table, motioning for her to follow him. A short hallway led to a neat but small kitchen, a table and chairs taking up a majority of the room. Herbs hung from the ceiling, drying, while on the stove, a pot of something boiled, creating immense amounts of steam. "The Pettigrew's made a stew for dinner. We can have it along with whatever you brought," he said, motioning to the parcel.

Her bundle of food sat on a counter, still wrapped and slightly damp, and Margaret hurried to it and unwrapped the parcel. The bread would no doubt be soggy and she was uncertain what had become of the cheese, but she was inclined to find out. The items were mostly dry, albeit a bit damp about the edges, and she smiled at Oliver. "Do you have a knife I can cut this with?"

Oliver brought over a scary-looking implement and scooted her out of the way as he reached for the bread and began slicing it into neat, even rows. The cheese met a similar demise only moments later and Margaret stood motionless at the awkwardness of it all. She had invited herself to a man's home and now he was taking care of her. "I'm sorry I intruded so suddenly. It was a rather poor day at the manor, what with the rain and all, and you said if I were in want of company that your home was always available." She looked at the food before her. "We missed you at the manor today."

Oliver set the knife down and turned to look at her, his face soft as he met her gaze. "I figured the rain left the garden a mess and didn't want to get in the way. And you do not need to apologize, Meg. I'm happy to have you here." He nodded towards a shelf that contained dining ware. "Can you fetch us two glasses while I open the mead?"

Margaret nodded, grateful for the errand. Glasses procured, she met him at the table and sat, watching as he filled each glass with the drink. Popping a bite of cheese into her mouth, Margaret reached for the bread and leaned back in the chair, taking small bites as she watched Oliver spoon the stew into two bowls before joining her at the table. "What herbs are those?" she asked, pointing to the drying rack.

"Lavender and peppermint," he said, taking a large bite out of the bread.

"What would one use them for?"

"I like to add them to my tea, especially when I'm sick, but I also use them for herbal tinctures." He shrugged. "Plus, they smell nice."

She laughed. "My tea tasted like peppermint."

"Yes, I put some in there to help in case you had a fever." His eyes focused on her bandaged hand and he frowned before pushing away from the table and fetching a small brown pot and a scrap of linen. "Give me your hand."

Following directions, Margaret placed her hand on the table and watched as Oliver unwrapped the old bandages, sighing as he saw the blood-tinged cloth. "Can't keep still, can you?" It was less of a question and more of a judgement, and she remained silent, certain an answer was unnecessary. He quickly cleaned the blister, the newly angered skin unhappy with the attention, and Margaret had to swallow her hiss of pain. It was her own fault, really. She did not know when to quit.

When the salve covered the wound, its cooling effect soothed the fire in her hand and she blinked, certain the potion was magic. "How?" she asked.

Oliver simply smiled before taking the new bit of cloth and wrapping her hand once more in efficient movements. When he finished, Margaret stared at her hand, still unable to comprehend. Oliver chuckled as he put away the salve and resumed his seat, making another piece of bread for himself as he chewed on a piece of cheese. "You're a wizard."

He laughed before taking a sip of the mead. "No, just a man who understands plants."

"What's in it?" she asked, looking at the clay pot.

"It's a mixture of turmeric and honey, along with lavender, which I've found helps soothe the inflammation of a wound."

Margaret looked at her hand again. "Brilliant."

"Science."

"It's still brilliant. And that you know about all of it makes it that much more interesting." Sipping at her mead, she watched as his cheeks pinked at her compliment. "Few men in the aristocracy have such knowledge, nor care to learn such things. It's impressive." When he did not reply, she chewed at her lip. Perhaps her honest opinion had overstepped their burgeoning friendship, but she found nothing useful in not telling the truth. "I'm sorry if my words embarrassed you."

He shook his head and looked at her. "They didn't. I'm just not used to hearing someone take an actual interest in my horticulture talk. It's nice." He smiled.

"How are your spinach plants faring?"

Oliver nodded his head, his lips pinched together as if in deep contemplation. "They're growing well. The goose fertilizer plant has taken an exceptional lead in not only growth but girth. It's unexpected."

Margaret laughed at the notion of Oliver chasing after a goose. "Goose fertilizer? That could not have been readily accessible."

"Oh, it wasn't. Thankfully, there is a family near the

pond that has taken up residence while they raise their young. The mother goose was less than pleased that I hung around their nest all day collecting samples. Geese are not amiable creatures."

"I don't expect they would be." She looked at him and they both laughed.

Oliver fiddled with his glass. "Would you be interested in seeing the plants?"

"If you're comfortable showing them to me, I'd love to see it. I've never seen a real-life experiment before, only read about them in stories."

"Finish your supper and then I'll take you. It's nothing exciting, a couple of plants in a glass room."

She took a bite of her bread and raised a brow at him. "Are you trying to dissuade me from seeing them or are you worried I won't think much of it?"

Oliver let out a large gush of air at her question and once more, she wondered if she had overstepped. Her newfound mentality of saying what was on her mind, no matter the circumstance, seemed to make him uncomfortable, but where the old Margaret would have rushed in to apologize, eager to make amends, now, she found she had very little time for those who danced around what they were truly saying. Life was much too precious to be wasted on useless societal niceties and uncertainty. The worst one could say in response was no, and once that notion was accepted, it really made being honest less terrifying.

"I don't want to bore you with a bunch of spinach plants and animal excrement," he said.

She laid her hand on his and waited for his eyes to

meet hers. "It doesn't bore me to hear you talk about something you love." She squeezed his hand before pulling back. "Plus, when you describe it like that, how can anyone find it boring?"

His smile returned to his face, and he nodded, signaling the end of that subject. "Were you able to get much done at the manor today?"

She sighed. "No. The rain made certain to ruin any repairs that took place outside, and what they accomplished inside created such a ruckus I thought about running away into the woods." He laughed at her words and she placed her hand on her chest, forcing dismay into her voice. "It was so loud I had to stuff cotton in my ears to get anything done." He seemed to find the notion hilarious as his laughter became louder, and Margaret joined in, certain the picture she had created was just as foolish as she had looked.

"You had cotton in your ears?" he asked between chuckles. "Tufts of cotton?"

Margaret nodded sagely, only further provoking his laughter. "What I would give to have seen that," he said with a smile as she finished her meal. "To the greenhouse?"

Nodding, Margaret followed him to the kitchen door and looked outside. The rain remained, although the downpour had changed into a slight misting that covered the landscape of Woodingdean in a dewy fog. She peeked around the door frame, certain she would spy fairies from a *Midsummer Night's Dream* dancing about in the haze.

"Ready?" she asked him with a smile.

He shook his head at her nonsense, but the smile that

flittered on his lips confirmed he found her action funny. With an excited squeal, Margaret ran for the glass structure that sat several yards away from the door. Oliver closed in behind her, his hands over her newly dried head to protect her from the moisture, and Margaret stumbled at the action. His arms caught around her, guiding her the last bit to the door before escorting her inside.

His kindness unnerved her, his thoughtfulness an oddity in the world she was used to. Her father had been nothing but a stern disciplinarian, the ever-present boogeyman that was used to threaten her should she make the wrong decision. And Everly, well, he was just an arse she had the unfortunate luck in marrying. It was understandable, really, that Oliver's gentle ways and thoughtful moments would disrupt her belief that men did not have a soft bone in their body, but to witness it in action, and for it to be focused on her, was altogether unsettling.

The warmth of the greenhouse sent gooseflesh on her arms, the heat a far cry from the damp chill outside. Margaret sighed as she took in the multitude of greenery that filled the glass house. Plants of all shapes and sizes took up every horizontal surface the area offered. Fragrant perfume tinged the air, released by the dozens of flowers inside, their spice sweetening the surrounding space. "I think I'm in love with this place," she said, meeting Oliver's eyes.

He laughed at her words and nodded. "I can understand that." He walked down one row, the ground filled with plants whose names she would never learn, and she followed him to the back of the hut towards a bookcase-type structure that held four similar pots. Green leaves sprouted from each pot, their stems hearty, but one noticeably growing faster than the rest, the soil almost covered by its large leaves.

Margaret expected the plants to stink, but there was no scent to be found. "Why doesn't it smell?" she asked.

"Instead of using the manure straight away, which would have been a time-consuming process, I made it into a tea-like brew and use that to feed them. A local farmer composted the cow manure, so all the samples were ready to use."

"You made manure tea?" she asked, her nose wrinkling.

"Would it make you feel better to know I have a special pot for it? I promise I didn't use the kettle I made tea for you in."

Margaret laughed, uncertain whether she was thankful that he had made her tea in a separate kettle, or worried that he felt the need to ease her mind on the matter. Placing her hand on his arm, she smiled at him. "I'm intrigued by the tea manure, not worried for my safety."

"Oh," he said, "Right, well…"

Margaret leaned closer to the plants. "So, manure tea helps to remove the smell, the cow manure is composted and the horse manure is from my farm. Does the horse manure need to be composted as well?"

He nodded. "It does. Thankfully, the pile you had seemed to be sitting for a bit of time, so I took from the lower portion of the manure instead of the fresher stuff to make certain that it had enough time to rid itself of anything that might harm the experiment. You should look into using manure for your plants as well. If you maintain it and keep it damp, it should compost over time and can be used all over the grounds."

"Should we separate the stuff underneath and use it on the beds we plan to keep?" Margaret's mind imagined the compost near the stables that could help the gardens and grounds flourish and excitement began as she put together a list of materials needed.

"Where it's at now is fine. Leave what is there to compost and when the time comes, we can separate it out and use it on the finished landscaping. No sense in making more work before it's needed."

"All right," she said with a frown.

He laughed as he peeked at her face. "Not enough work for you as the manor is now?"

She shook her head. "Is it that apparent that I'm slightly in over my head on the repairs?"

He smiled. "Only slightly. I'm not sure how you manage the chaos."

"I bask in it, truthfully." He raised a brow at her. "I was so used to the quiet, opulent townhome in London with the silent servants and the muted dinners. That monotone household was my nightmare, but the bustle of the manor, the noise and people, and the chaos is such a wonderful change. I think I flourish in it."

"You seem happy," he said. "That's all that is important."

Margaret looked at Oliver, uncertain why his words warmed her heart. He did not know of the docile woman she used to be, no understanding of the life she had escaped, and yet he saw her joy and it made sense to him. "You talk little of what's waiting for you in London," she said, the words soft so as not to spook him.

He frowned, inspecting a leaf of spinach with immense concentration before finally responding. "Life is waiting in London."

"A wife and kids?" she asked, hoping her joke would lighten the now gray mood, and in truth, anxious to hear him say it was not so.

"No," he said, one corner of his lips lifting in a half-hearted smile and her heart fluttered in relief, an emotion to be examined at another time. "An eventual dukedom, more than likely the hunt for a wife." He listed them off, nodding his head with each item, his lips pinched.

Margaret touched his arm with her hand, curling her fingers around his forearm. "Those are some large life moments." She rubbed her hand back and forth along his forearm, the prickly hairs where the shirtsleeve ended tickling her fingers.

He made a noise of agreement but said nothing more, his eyes watching her hand stroke his arm.

The moment was too tender, and she pulled her hand away. This connection to him was so comfortable, so familiar, that she longed to stay in it. To bask in the quiet moments as he tended to his plants, share a meal with him as they talked about their day. Revel in his soft ministrations as he brushed out her hair for the night.

It was too much.

He had just laid out his future to her, and the road he would go down was a direction she had no intention of following. London and high society had no place in her life any longer, and anything that came from following these budding feelings would surely lead to that path.

Margaret looked outside at the darkened night sky, the perfect excuse to get away from the unnecessary sadness that pulled at her. "It's rather late. I should go," she said, turning with a smile. "Thank you for the company."

Margaret left the greenhouse without waiting for a reply, her wet clothing forgotten as her mind urged her to escape. To run away from this cottage and its soothing presence. Run away from these feelings she yearned to learn more about.

Run away from the man who made her long to stay, even when she knew there was no future.

CHAPTER NINE

O LIVER WATCHED MEG leave, uncertain whether to follow. The rain had slowed to a misty drizzle. Even so, he wondered if he should make sure she returned to the manor safely. And yet, the speed with which she left had him thinking the answer was no. Something had spooked her, but he could not be certain what. He had thought their time together that evening enjoyable, and while he had known it would never go further than friendship, he enjoyed the moments spent with her. Her quick tongue and sharp mind kept him on his toes, challenged his thinking, forcing him to vocalize his thoughts instead of tucking them away for his own perusal.

Still, his hands had shaken as they brushed her hair. The act had felt intimate, something you would only do for someone you loved, but he knew things would never go further. Nor should they be forced to. Meg's friendship meant too much to muddy it with more complex emotions. So, if his arms longed to hold her, to feel the press of her body against his, he would ignore it. If his mind wanted to keep the image of her smile in his line of sight for the rest of his days, instead he would file it away, to be viewed at a later time.

Shutting up the greenhouse for the evening, Oliver headed into the cottage and tidied the kitchen, washing their dirty dishes and wrapping the last bit of cheese in a waxed cloth before dousing the candles and heading to bed. His room smelled of vanilla and Meg's still damp clothes hung across the wooden chair that resided at the foot of his bed. Oliver would fold them in the morning and return them, but he moved the chair closer to the hearth as he stoked the fire to help them dry.

Long brown hairs threaded his brush, and he pulled them out, throwing them into the flames, before setting it back down on the table. Readying himself for bed, Oliver doused the lights, but his gaze kept falling on her clothes, illuminated by the fire. Whatever had sent her fleeing in such a manner must have been terrifying enough to leave her things behind and he could not help but worry at the trajectory it would lead their friendship down.

When morning arrived, Oliver's apprehension had only worsened. Folding the now dry clothes, he brushed his teeth and ran his fingers through his hair before putting on his hat and heading to Baron Manor, Meg's trousers and shirt in hand, along with the salve for her injury.

The ground was still a soggy mess from the rain and shoveling mud was certainly going to be a much heavier task than dirt, but he itched to do something. Any sort of idle after the evening he had spent with her would only lead to him analyzing it once more, tearing apart every-thing he had said and done in an attempt to discern what had sent her away.

Meg was nowhere to be found, so Oliver set the clothes and ointment next to the kitchen door, grabbed his shovel, and worked on halving the black-eyed Susan's. The plants were hearty, their roots tangled in the mud, but

Oliver stuck with it, swishing the roots in a bucket of water, and carefully removing the dirt until he could chop the plant in half and transplant the new portion to another area. He went one by one, each bush requiring meticulous focus as he pulled them apart and readied them to be replanted. The sun was high in the sky when a jug and a sandwich were thrust in front of him.

Meg stood holding the food, arms stretched out like an offering. Oliver took the items and set them down, his eyes raking over her form. She seemed healthy, like she had made the return journey with nary a bump or scratch marring her tan skin, yet her eyes seemed hollow when she looked at him. "Thank you for bringing back my things."

He nodded and gave her a smile. "I set the jar of salve by the door as well. It's best if you reapply it daily since you seem to be averse to not working."

Her lips pinched, and she looked away. "Would you be able to help me change the bandage?"

"Of course," he said, picking up his food items and following her to the house and inside the kitchen. On the table was the jar of ointment and a fresh strip of linen already laid out awaiting his arrival. "Have a seat."

Removing his hat, Oliver washed his hands in the tub of water before taking her hand and unwrapping the bandage he had applied the night before. The blister already looked better, the skin a healthy pink. Washing it in the water, he dried it with a towel. Kneeling, he opened the jar and scooped out a dollop, setting it softly onto her palm. With slow motions, he rubbed the mixture into the skin, gentle as he neared the tender area. Reaching for the wrapping, Oliver wrapped her hand with sure movements before tying off the ends.

"All set," he said, looking up into her eyes. Meg stared at him, her brown eyes searching his while his hand still held hers. "Meg?"

She brought his hand to her lips and kissed his palm, and Oliver's breath caught in his throat at the touch. Soft lips trailed across his palm, her warm breath dancing on his skin, threads of bliss scattering at each press. She raised her uninjured hand and cupped his cheek. Sure fingers slid into his hair, nails biting against his scalp, as she leaned forward and pressed her lips to his. The touch was so soft, Oliver was certain he was dreaming, but her fingers tightened in his hair as she pulled back a bit to look at him. Her eyes were dark chocolate, and he wanted to drown in their sweetness. Instead, he whispered, "Again."

Meg wasted no time, pulling him close as her lips met his, her mouth parting to meet him. She shivered as he matched her pace, devouring her luscious mouth like a man deprived of his favorite treat, and when he pulled back to change course, she whimpered, her hands tightening as if to keep him close. He was drowning. His only saving grace was her sweet kiss, and he moved into her embrace, his hands sliding into her hair as her kiss consumed him.

She was fire and water, light and dark, heaven and hell all wrapped into one, and he was uncertain if he was nearing salvation or needing to be saved. All he knew was he wanted more. More vanilla-tinged spice tickling his nose, more chocolate brown eyes to drown inside, more sharp fingers and quick-witted words to keep him on his toes, begging for more. More of Meg, with her hands buried in his hair, legs bracketing his waist as she kissed him with a fervor.

When she pulled back to look at him, her gaze was penetrating, and as his heart thrummed loudly in his ears, he came to the startling realization that he truly could fall in love with this woman. He leaned forward and kissed her lips once more, wasting little time, letting her intoxicating taste overtake him again. His heart ached in the sweetest way as she met him, touch for touch, stroke for stroke, and all he knew was he wanted to stay in this moment with her forever.

Meg's arms slid around his neck, her fingers slipping into the strands of his hair, and Oliver growled, wrapping his hands around her waist and lifting her onto the table. His hands fell to her thighs, squeezing the muscles, and she shivered, her nails scraping his scalp, sending sparks of pleasure dancing down his spine. A kiss had never been this potent, this dangerous. It was remarkable.

Oliver pulled back, changing the angle. It could not be real, this unequivocal delight that sparked in his veins as her kiss destroyed him. It had to be an illusion. Heat exhaustion certainly must be its cause, but as her tongue tangled with his, her hum of joy singing in his ears as he pulled her closer, Oliver knew. He knew in his bones that in a lifetime of kisses, this one would leave an imprint on him that would never fade. This one would be the memory that would dwell in his mind until his final days.

A crash had them pushing apart and Oliver looked around the shadow filled room, dismayed to find nothing out of order in the small kitchen. Meeting Meg's eyes, the corner of his mouth tipped upwards at the sight of the smile that danced on her lips. Her laugh was soft as she looked at him, and Oliver cupped her neck with his hands and rested his forehead against hers, unable to contain the humor that overcame him as well. "That was unexpected," he said, his hand stroking the loose strands of her hair. "Must have been one of the workers."

He leaned forward to resume their kiss, but Meg's hand on his chest stopped him. "I should get back to work," she said, the smile still on her lips but not as bright. "It's only a matter of time before someone comes looking for me."

Oliver pushed to his full height and Meg hopped off the table, tucking the hair that had come loose from her braid behind her ears. She looked down at her bandaged hand and frowned before meeting his gaze. "Thank you for this," she said, raising it. With a nod, she turned and left the kitchen, the room so suddenly empty Oliver wondered if he had imagined their kiss.

With a sigh, he picked up his hat from the floor where it had fallen and hit it against his leg, the sting of the slap forcing him to snap out of the trance she had put over him. Yet even as he walked back to the garden and picked up his shovel, his mind replayed their kiss. The heady taste that could only belong to Meg, the hums of satisfaction as she destroyed him with teeth and tongue. And as time trudged on in that overgrown garden, Oliver became less and less certain he understood what the hell had just happened.

CHAPTER TEN

MARGARET DRESSED IN her still dark bedroom and slipped out of the house and into the vegetable garden. She had fallen asleep with ease, exhausted from the previous day's work, but hours later, jolted awake as her mind replayed her time with Oliver, the stillness of the room giving her permission to assess her decisions.

It was not that she regretted kissing Oliver, no. That had been a bliss she had never imagined. Kissing Oliver had been everything she could have wanted. But what if they had been caught? And where did they go from here?

They could not very well go back to how they were. A line had been crossed and it would only become awkward to pretend that they were merely friends after what had occurred. And surely, they could become nothing more. He was a lord, visiting Woodingdean to pursue a hobby before returning to his life in London, and she wanted nothing to do with what that entailed. But God, did she want everything to do with him.

Something about Oliver called to her, provoked her with his kind words and gentle touches, lured her in with his green eyes and lean strength. His presence had a way of lightening the chaos that surrounded her at Bitch Manor and their conversations were so easy, as if she spoke to an old friend.

With a sigh, Margaret picked up a pair of discarded gloves and a garden hoe and set about attacking the remains of a squash plant. It was just her luck, really, that the first man she had an actual interest in was a nobleman. If only he were not a lord, but a landowner. Or a villager. Christ, she would even take a highwayman over an aristocrat.

Blowing at a strand of hair the wind pushed across her face, Margaret frowned. It would be best to cut this off at the start and ensure no hurt feelings in the process, but how did someone tell another person that while you enjoyed kissing them immensely, it was best that they not take things further? It was certainly not a conversation they taught you in finishing school.

With a yawn, Margaret looked at the pitch-black sky and knew that sleep would be a necessity if she were to face her decisions when dawn approached. The winged back chair, while still dusty and no doubt uncomfortable, seemed the safest place in the home, and she could only hope the dowager's ghost and a toasty fire would keep away pesky thoughts while she tried to sleep. For sleep she must. Sleep first and fret over the worrisome man in the morning.

Yet, when morning came, Margaret had little sleep and not a clue as to how to handle the situation with Oliver. The only recourse she could think of was to act as they had before and pray he got the hint, but given the male species, she had little hope it would work. But it must. Fear drove her as she thought about the outcome a relationship with him would bring, and while her new mentality called for her to chase the things she feared,

Margaret could not convince herself that this path with Oliver would end in anything but heartache.

Commandeering an apple and a cup of tea from the kitchen, Margaret headed outside to the muffled tones of the workers arriving. After eating her breakfast, she settled into a comfortable rhythm, mucking out Siris' stall with Felix and Mr. Howell, before joining Sam in the garden as he transplanted the plants Oliver had marked in his plan. A few hours into her work, Oliver came to stand beside her, her heart stumbling at his presence. He said nothing as he worked, clearing out the brush from a rosebush that had not survived the years of neglect, and Margaret worried at the quiet.

When Sam joined his family for luncheon, Oliver finally spoke. "Did you have a nice evening?"

She gave a small noise of accord, avoiding his gaze. "You?"

"Yes."

Margaret pushed up from where she knelt on the ground and brushed her hands together. "I was planning to eat lunch out here. Marty stopped by earlier with some things for me to eat. What are your plans for luncheon?"

Oliver frowned at her before shaking his head. "I'm going to head to the cottage and check on the greenhouse. But thank you." He set his gloves down and left without another word and Margaret knew her carefree words had hurt him, but it was for the best. It would do neither of them any good to start something they could never finish, and even as she wanted to call out to him, to have him come back so she could try again, she kept her mouth shut and watched him leave.

Margaret did not see him for the rest of the day, and she chastised herself each time she searched for his tall frame among the men. When night fell, she returned to her room, exhaustion eating at every fiber of her body, but the sight that greeted her sent a smile to her face and a lightness through her bones. A single flower sat in a chipped cup on the kitchen table, more beautiful than any of the polished bouquets she had seen in London, and though she did not know its name, its beauty still made her heart throb even as her stomach churned. The brilliant man had done nothing wrong except to get involved with her, and it was clear to anyone that his intentions were pure. But the fear that gripped her when she thought of the future was primal, because there was no future. Not with him.

"Stay the course, Meg," she whispered to herself in the darkened room, but fell asleep to dreams of a day spent with a soft-spoken man who made her heart race. When morning came, Margaret awoke dismayed. Even in her dreams, Oliver's presence gave her so much serenity and joy that the lack of his company left her cranky. She had never once longed to share her every minute with some-one, let alone a man, and his gaping absence, albeit one she forced, only highlighted how much she wanted him.

Her melancholy mood followed her into the day and even as she smiled with Sam as they moved loads of fertilizer, it was as if she were an actor on stage, putting on a show so no one knew her true feelings. When lunch rolled around, Margaret headed over to the tree, desperate for seclusion, so she would not have to hide how unhappy she was.

"What's put that frown on your face?" Marty asked, sitting down beside Margaret.

The innkeeper's unexpected arrival did little to lighten her mood, and Margaret gave the woman a ghastly grin before sighing. "Decisions," Margaret said, her eyes straying to where Oliver worked. Sweat left his shirt clinging to his torso, molding itself to every ripple of muscle it could find, and when he took his hat off to wipe his brow, the fabric followed, revealing a small trace of skin above his trousers. They had avoided one another the entire day, and if he felt even an iota as dismal as she, he did not show it. "What brings you here?"

"Merely dropping off some staples for you," Marty said, following the direction of her gaze. "Would those decisions have anything to do regarding Lord Greenwood? Whether to pursue him?"

Margaret shook her head and looked at her friend. "Decisions I made previously regarding Lord Green-wood."

Marty sat up, her brow furrowed as she stared Margaret down. "Something has already happened?" Margaret groaned and buried her head in her hands, nodding to confirm Marty's suspicions. "Margaret Reedy, what the devil did you do?" she asked, the smile on her face showing sheer delight.

"We kissed." Marty clapped her hands as she turned towards Margaret, her blue eyes wide, and Margaret sighed, her head slumping against the tree. "He's so sweet, Marty, and kind and strong and thoughtful and... I'm afraid."

Marty scoffed. "Afraid of what?"

"Of losing myself to another man. I didn't intend to find someone I'd feel this type of pull towards. The only thing I know about relationships is that courting leads to marriage. Walter has barely been in the ground a year and yet here I am, befuddled by a member of the species."

"This is entirely different from an arranged marriage, Meg. Interest in someone doesn't mean forever. He himself said he's only going to be here for a short period of time. There are no expectations or requirements with this one, no marriage at the end of courtship." Marty shrugged her shoulders. "I don't think allowing yourself to have a little fun with a willing partner will send you down the path to marriage. What harm can truly come from it?"

Margaret nodded. Marty's words did little to dim the fear that still danced in her mind, but the truth that was contained within them pushed her melancholy away as she made her decision. This time, she would be in charge of deciding the path a relationship would take. "I have to go," she said, pushing to stand and brushing at her trousers.

"Now?" Marty asked, surprise in her voice.

Margaret smiled at her and the innkeeper laughed as she shooed her away. She took off for the spot she last saw Oliver, but pulled up short when she spotted only Sam surrounded by dead leaves. Her eyes looked at the open space around them. "Where is Lord Greenwood?"

"He headed for home at luncheon. Something about tending to his plants," Sam said, looking at her. "Don't know if he was planning on coming back or not."

Margaret barely heard the man's words as she ran towards the trail that led to Oliver's cottage. Her heart raced as her legs pumped, determined not to waste any more time on foolishness. She wanted Oliver. She wanted to be by his side as he grew his plants, wanted to watch the manor be rehabilitated so she could show him every room. Wanted to lie beside him in bed at night, the scent of sandalwood lulling her to sleep. London and the future be damned.

Damned about knowing where it would all lead, damn the fear.

She wanted him.

When his cottage entered her view, she picked up her pace, her breath escaping her lips in pants as she headed to the greenhouse, certain she would find him there. She pulled up short when he walked out of the glass structure and saw her, his stride pausing as she slowed. Bending over, Margaret rested her hands on her legs and waited for her breathing to slow so she could speak.

"Meg?" he asked, coming to her and bending down so he was in her line of sight, his hands cupping her cheeks as his eyes searched her face. "Is everything all right?"

Margaret launched herself into his arms and Oliver fell back with a soft oomph, his strong arm wrapping around her waist while his other hand protected her head as they landed in the grass. He rolled them over and looked her up and down as if checking for injuries, and Margaret smiled, cupping his cheek with her hand. Her eyes raked in the gorgeous features of his face, his sharp jaw covered in stubble, his green eyes framed by dark lashes. Long brown hair fell forward, covering his brow, while soft pink lips pursed as he looked at her. "Meg?"

"I'm sorry," she said, her fingers tracing his lips. "I'm

sorry for the way I behaved after we kissed."

Oliver shook his head.

"Can we try again?" she asked, her index finger sliding back and forth along his plump bottom lip, every nerve in her body chanting to nip it with her teeth.

"Are you sure?" He raised a brow as his lips puckered against the digit, bestowing a fairy soft kiss to its skin.

Margaret nodded her head emphatically, her eyes narrowing as he nudged her hand, his teeth scraping against her palm as his cheek settled against her fingers. "Yes, please," she said with a croak.

Oliver smiled, one corner lifting in a roguish manner that made her heart skip. His mouth moved lower along her hand, his nimble tongue swirling along the veins of her wrist, and Margaret's breath hitched as she watched him, her heart racing as she imagined the wicked attentions he could give to other places of her skin.

"Oliver, please."

"Tell me," he said, his voice a growl.

Margaret groaned, pulling herself up and nipping his lips with her teeth. "Kiss me."

It was a command, one he followed without hesitation as his mouth dropped to hers, the pleasure as swift as his tongue, its decadence only rising with each swirl and suckle. Margaret whimpered, unable to get close enough to him. She wanted to drown in his kiss, wanted to ignite in flames. His palm still cupped her head, his fingers cradling her skull while his other hand clenched her waist, flexing repetitively with every sigh that escaped her lips.

Margaret needed more. Her hands pulled his shirt from his trousers, baring the skin of his waist to her. Warm flesh slid beneath her fingers and she shivered, allowing her hands to wrap around him, her nails skimming his back. Oliver growled, the hand at her waist capturing the wrist of one arm and pinning it over her head. Her moan of complaint made him chuckle against her lips and she squirmed against him. More. She needed more.

Oliver pulled back from her and he whispered, "Come with me?"

Her body so inflamed she would follow him anywhere, Margaret nodded, taking the hand he extended to her and following him into the cottage and to his bedroom. Oliver lit a lantern beside the bed, the light casting a pale glow on his skin. Margaret closed the door behind her as he walked to her and slid his hands into her hair, bringing her mouth to his once more.

Need. It consumed her, made her body shake as he picked her up and she wrapped her legs around his waist. More, closer, everything. She needed it all. Oliver navigated them to the bed, setting her on the soft mattress before kneeling and removing her boots. Discarding his own, he crawled to her, lips searching for lips, fingers entwining as he laid her down on the pillow and Margaret allowed his kiss to consume her. Her knees bracketed his hips, and she arched against him, a sigh slipping from her lips as his chest brushed her own. How a kiss could be so explosive and yet comforting, she would never know, but she wanted to spend a lifetime finding out. She shoved the thought away, too afraid that examining it now would bring an end to a moment she wanted desperately to stay in.

Margaret shoved at his shoulders and Oliver sat back

on his heels and looked at her. Her braid had fallen apart at some point, and her chest rose and fell with each breath as she eyed him before pushing up to sitting. "Can… can you take off your shirt?" she asked.

Oliver unbuttoned the top of his shirt before reaching behind his head and pulling the linen over, baring his chest to her. His long fingers reached for her hand, placing it on his chest and she shivered as her hands danced along his skin, fingers skimming the outline of his abdominals, tracing his pectorals, swirling around his nipples before sliding down his arms and squeezing his biceps, committing his form to memory. It was the first male form she had ever seen, ever fully examined, and her heart quickened its pace as her hands moved over him, the twists and turns of his body exquisite and exciting.

Oliver slid his hand behind her neck and pulled her to him, devouring her mouth with a fever. Her tongue matched his as she wrapped her arm around his shoulders, his touch burning her skin, branding her as his. As she leaned back, bringing him with her, Margaret slid her hand between them, unbuttoning her shirt with measured movements, and he drew back. "Are you sure?" he asked, placing his hand on hers to stop the motion.

She nodded as she finished unbuttoning her shirt, more certain about this moment than she had ever been in her lifetime. "Yes."

Oliver squeezed her hand, and she smiled at him, guiding his hand to her breast. His fingertips were rough and warm and Margaret tried not to squirm as he watched her while those digits traced her from collarbone to the indent between her breasts. Her breath caught with his motions and she closed her eyes as she rocked into his touch, a moan escaping her lips.

Oliver cupped the flesh he had found, her nipple beading as his fingers played with it, and Margaret shivered beneath him, her teeth worrying her bottom lip. "Too much?"

She shook her head. "Not enough. More. I want more."

Oliver pulled his hand from the fabric and shifted the shirt higher, revealing her to him in slow increments as her breath hitched. He was beautiful in the lamplight, his gaze penetrating as it danced along her exposed skin. Removing the shirt completely, he returned to her breasts, plying them with his fingers, and Margaret moved beneath him, lost in the feeling. Her hands moved erratically, squeezing his arms, tracing his chest. He lowered himself so their skin touched as his mouth returned to hers. Her puckered nipples scraped at his chest and he growled into her mouth as he slid back and forth, her hands pinned above her head.

"Christ," he said, pulling back from her, before resting his forehead on hers. "We can stop here, Meg. I want you so badly I'm shaking, but we can stop here. Tell me no."

Instead, Margaret shook her head and, pulling her hand free from his grasp, let her fingers trail down the front of his trousers against the hard shaft that throbbed for her. Oliver hissed, pushing himself into her hand, and she cupped his length and squeezed.

"Meg," he said, her name a whimper.

They removed both sets of trousers with such speed Margaret barely registered Oliver's naked body against hers until the heat of her core brushed against his leg, the wiry hairs prickling her sex. Oliver slithered down her body, his broad shoulders separating her legs, and Margaret panicked. Her hand acted as a barrier, shielding her sex from his gaze, and Oliver pulled back and peeked at her.

"What-what are you doing?" she asked.

"I'm going to kiss you."

She raised a brow. "My mouth is up here."

He shook his head. "Not those lips, but these," he said, stroking the hand that hid her quim from his view.

"That's-that's not necessary. Can't we just—" she motioned to his sex and Oliver frowned at her. "Can't we just get on with it?" When he said nothing, she sighed. "Please."

Oliver's frown remained, but he headed back up and took her mouth with his, licking the seam until her tongue played along. He skimmed his hand along her thigh toward her sex, and his fingers played in her heat as he kissed her. Stroking his finger along the seam of her sex, Oliver growled as he nibbled at her lips. Margaret whimpered, her hands clutching his hair as he circled the nub of her sex. Her legs shook, but she fought her climax with each pass his thumb made, her breathing erratic as she squirmed against his hand. "Let it happen, love. Give in."

She shook her head; her moans muddled as she ground against his fingers. When a single digit slid into her sheath, the pad rubbing along the wall of her quim while his thumb stroked her nub in sure strokes, Margaret gasped, her body shaking with the ministrations. His teeth nipped at her lips before soothing them with his tongue, and she burst, light and sound, hell and heaven swirling into one colorful void as her body shook uncontrollably, her sheath squeezing his fingers with her pleasure. He muffled her cries with his kiss, as his nimble fingers brought her slowly back again.

When her body calmed, she curled into him, her breathing erratic as he wrapped his arms around her. What had to have been minutes later, Margaret stirred, stunned. "How can it be like that?"

He laughed as kissed her head. "Did you like it?"

"I-I...," she said, with a laugh, hiding her face in his chest.

Oliver pulled her closer and Margaret snuggled into his chest before pulling back from him. "But what about you?"

Oliver shook his head. "This was for you."

She propped herself up on her elbow and looked at him. "No. I want to take care of you as well." Oliver raised a brow at her and she leaned forward and kissed his lips, his taste reigniting her ardor. "Please show me."

Laying on his back, Oliver took Margaret's hand and steered it towards his hardened sex, his swallow loud as her small fist encircled the throbbing flesh. Covering her hand with his, he stroked up and down, setting the pace. When her motions were steady, Oliver let go, and Margaret pumped her hand up and down his cock, adding a soft squeeze as she neared the tip before lowering back down and starting again.

His climax came fast, and Oliver bit his hand to cover his growl as his hips lifted at the onslaught of pleasure. Bursts of seed covered his chest, each stream so impressive Margaret was sure it hurt. Finished, his body went slack, eyes closed as the breath swooshed from his lungs. A soft hum of happiness filled her body as she peppered light kisses along his shoulder, the smile on her face changing to a laugh as she felt him shiver. Dear Christ, she was in trouble.

Biting her lip, Margaret was not sure what to do, but moments later, Oliver pushed up from the bed and headed to the basin and poured water into it, dipping a cloth into the liquid and wiping his chest clean. Letting it fall to the floor, Oliver grabbed another and, after dampening it, returned to Margaret and though she gave a squeak of surprise, cleaned her as well. Once back in bed, Oliver pulled Margaret down beside him.

Their coupling had been cataclysmic, so jarringly different from anything she had known with Everly. Oliver's sweet words and gentle caresses were a glaring contrast to Everly's ministrations, her husband forging all attempts at her comfort instead opting for a few measly pumps of his sex into her before scurrying off to bed. That Oliver saw to her pleasure, cared for her wellbeing, and did not force himself inside her, spoke volumes about his character.

He tucked his head down to look at her, pushing a curl behind her ear, and when he met her gaze, he smiled, pulling her closer. He reached for the blanket, pulling it around them both.

"Do you want to have dinner with me?" she asked, running her thumb along the seam of his lips.

He frowned. "Is this another 'you have enough to share' moment?"

She shook her head, and he sighed before rolling them over, his warm body acting like a heavy blanket. His hand raked through her hair before he placed a soft kiss on her forehead. "I don't understand you," he said against her shoulder, "but I think that's part of the reason I like you."

Margaret smiled into Oliver's shoulder as he pulled her closer. She knew he would not ask any more questions about her sudden change of heart, and there was relief in the knowledge. How could you tell someone that you hated who you used to be, and that you feared being with them would weaken all the progress you made? You could not. Instead, she smiled and pushed those worries aside to be examined another day. Today, she was having dinner with Oliver.

CHAPTER ELEVEN

A CROCK OF stew and a loaf of bread that had been delivered by Marty turned out to be the dinner Margaret so thoughtfully wanted to share with him. The fact that they shared it snuggled upon a blanket overlooking Baron negated any implication that it was an invitation made out of pity, and no fault could be found in either the company or the food. Margaret had filled two bowls of the hearty soup for them and pulled out a bottle of wine she had tucked away for a rainy day, and together, they headed to the garden for dinner and a show. The sunset that evening decorated the sky in a kaleidoscope of colors more akin to a painting than real life, the purples and pinks a lucid dreamy end to a blissful day, and as they ate their meal and drank their wine, wrapped in the blanket Oliver had fetched, the stillness of the evening enveloped them in a calm rarely to be found at Baron Manor.

Leaning against a tree, Margaret rested her head on Oliver's shoulder. "This is nice," she said, taking a sip of her wine, her eyes perusing the striking scene before them.

"Mm," he said, reaching for her hand and entwining it in his. Margaret looked down at their interlaced fingers and her heart picked up its pace as he squeezed her hand. Never once had someone, let alone a man, shown any sort of affection such as he did, and never so easily. It was as if it were second nature for him, hell, for them both, to relax so fully into one another with little care of society's dictates. Here they were simply Meg and Oliver and nothing more.

"How are the renovations to the interior coming?" he asked.

Margaret sighed as her mind ran through the list of repairs still needed before the proper work could get underway. "The floors are almost sound, but some walls need to be repaired and there are still several windows awaiting new panes of glass."

He nodded his head before taking a sip of wine. "I'm in the garden all day, so I never know what goes on inside. It sounds like the disrepair is rampant there as well."

"It is, but I haven't given up hope yet. Baron is a stunning home that didn't ask to be abandoned, but she can be restored to glory again. I just know it."

"And you're certainly the lady to do it." It was not a question, but a statement, one that surely had to be made of sheer belief in her abilities, and Margaret smiled at the words.

"I think so."

As the sun disappeared behind a hill, leaving only bursts of light as proof of its presence, Oliver squeezed her hand before letting it go and pushing to stand. "I'll get the dishes started," he said, reaching for her empty bowl.

Margaret scrunched her nose at him as she dodged his outstretched hand and stood, bringing the bowl and glass with her. "Two people make for lighter work," she said with a wink.

He shook his head as he gathered the blanket and the

empty wine bottle and followed her inside to the kitchen. Marty had made quick work of teaching her the domestic skills required to live on her own, and while she had not become remarkably adept, she was very much capable. Two tin dishpans sat on a low counter under a window that overlooked the vegetable garden, and Oliver set the dishes onto the counter, then started rolling up his sleeves, exposing his powerful forearms. At the stove, he removed the large kettle of hot water and poured it into the first pan before heading outside to fetch water from the well for the second. Margaret scraped the last remaining bits of food into a tin pail before stacking them neatly beside the dishpans and retrieving the bar of lye soap she had, along with some towels. Rolling up her sleeves as well, she submerged the dishes into the hot water, allowing the heat to soak them. When Oliver returned, he filled the second dishpan with the cool water, then added a bit of the cold to the hot water pan so she would not burn herself. Throwing a towel over his shoulder, he smiled at her. "Ready?"

Margaret returned his smile, entranced by the image he created. "Ready."

Taking the soap, she set about scrubbing each dish and spoon until they shone before slipping them into the second tin. Oliver rinsed and dried the dishes beside her, the silence that filled the kitchen comfortable as they each worked. It made little sense, the dynamic that easily came, as if they had done the same task together for years, and Margaret was not sure whether to be enamored by it or frightened. Even her friendship with Harrison, a relationship that spanned nearly a decade, did not lend the same ease that she felt with Oliver.

"Why are you so natural at this?" she asked him.

He shrugged. "My mother wasn't very fond of the city, so the cottage was her safe place. My brother, Christopher, and I would come with her each summer before the season officially started and spend weeks getting into trouble all over Woodingdean. We kept very little staff at the cottage, so my brother and I easily picked up on the tasks that needed to be done."

"Dishes aren't a very regal chore for a future duke."

"I certainly never intended to be one," Oliver said, his brow furrowed, before he pushed out a laugh. "For two young boys, dishpans filled with water and soap can lead to endless hours of fun. We'd wash the dishes while having water fights and being chastised about the kitchen by Mrs. Pearson."

Margaret smiled, leaning over and placing a kiss on his bicep. "Naughty boys."

When the dishes were finished and put away, Margaret took the towels out to the clothesline to dry while Oliver dumped the dishpans into the yard before setting them down on the kitchen steps. Wetness dotted his shirt from the chore, his forearms bared to her perusal, and she could not help but walk to him and slide her arms around his stomach before burying her face in his chest. Strong arms wrapped around her shoulders as he pulled her in close, his scent of sandalwood and Oliver surrounding her in safety as he hugged her in return. "I should head home before it gets too dark," he said, his deep voice reverberating against her ear as he continued to hug her with little sign of leaving.

"Right," she said, forcing herself to pull back from him. But courage taunted her, and stepping forward again, she cupped his cheek, her fingers scraping against his bristly beard. "Or, you could stay? Everyone has headed home for the night and won't return until morning."

Oliver smiled, and Margaret's heart lightened as he dipped his head, his lips touching hers ever so softly. "Or I could stay."

Margaret took his hand and led him inside, closing the door behind them. Inside the bedroom, she took off her boots before unbuttoning her shirt and pulling it over her head. Tossing the garment onto the single chair in the room, Margaret took off her trousers before throwing her nightshirt on. Oliver still stood by the door, his gaze taking in the shabbily made bed and roaring fire, before moving to take in her, and heat rushed to her cheeks, warming them. "I don't have another nightshirt," she said, rubbing one foot against the other.

"I don't sleep in a nightshirt." The words were soft, his eyes still pinned on her.

"Oh." Margaret took out the scrap of ribbon that held her braid together and slowly unraveled it until her hair danced around her shoulders in disarray. Picking up the brush that lay on the nightstand, she sat on the bed, determined to find normalcy in her nightly routine.

She stroked the brush through her hair and winced as it caught on a tangle. Oliver clucked his tongue before stepping forward and taking the brush from her hand. "You'll become bald if you keep that up," he said as he pulled the bristles through her tresses, the strokes soft and sure. "Why so nervous suddenly?"

Margaret frowned at his question. "I've, that is... Well, I've never actually slept with someone. Walter would leave after our couplings and... I've only ever slept by myself. I want you here, I'm just not sure..." She paused and looked at her hands, which were clenched in her lap.

Oliver stopped his brushing and put his hands on her shoulders, pulling her into his chest. "I just want to be with you tonight, in whatever way you feel comfortable."

"Oh," she said. Her fingers lacing together, squeezing one another as she attempted not to fidget. Some men would have taken her hesitancy as a chance to convince, to persuade their partner into a physical intimacy they may not be ready for, but Oliver once more proved to be the outlier. The pressure to be intimate had been removed and the relief that enveloped her was sudden.

Margaret leaned back into his caresses, allowing the motions of Oliver and the brush to lull her body into a softness that could only mean sleep was near. She yawned, covering her mouth with her hand as the sound escaped, and Oliver laughed. "Into bed with you," he said, moving away from her and pulling back the sheet.

Margaret wiggled under the blankets, the pillow cradling her head as sleep called to her. Oliver walked around the room, extinguishing the candles before undressing and climbing in beside her. His arms reached out for her, pulling her into the cradle his body made, and she scooted against him, unable to get as close as she required. She wanted to wrap herself in his warmth, crawl inside his arms, and stay there forever, but this would have to do.

The wiry hairs on his chest tickled as she rubbed her nose against them, his scent stronger there, and his cock lay thick beside her thigh, its presence shaking the comfort she had found only moments before. Margaret pulled back to distance herself, but Oliver resisted. "Ignore it, Meg. It's a common occurrence around you, but it doesn't control me." He kissed the top of her head. "Sleep."

Margaret frowned, but closed her eyes as he instructed, the quiet hum of her body settling against his, filling her limbs with weight as sleep overtook her. Her final thought as she drifted off to dreamland reverberated in her head, following her into her dreams.

I wish it could be like this forever.

But that would never be possible.

CHAPTER TWELVE

WHEN OLIVER AWOKE, it was to find the bed empty, the embers in the hearth dying as the bite of cold touched his nose, its cool fingers a cruel way to wake. Worry pinched his chest for a moment at the thought of being abandoned after a night together. They had spent it in a tangle of limbs as they slept, Meg searching for him even in her sleep, wrapping her body around his as if afraid he would disappear altogether. But when morning came, she was the one missing. Oliver tried not to let disappointment overtake him, but it was hard not to. They had made such great strides yesterday, and he was certain they were becoming something more than just the friends she had claimed they were, but the harsh light of day dissuaded those notions.

Dressing in his dirty clothes from the day before, Oliver made the bed, folding back the top blanket and plumping the pillows as he would do at Bellawink, a simple task that removed one more item from the Pettigrew's list of to-dos. With a frown, he left the room, only to find Meg sitting at the kitchen table, a pot of tea before her, one slim hand wrapped around a chipped cup. "I was certain you were planning to sleep the day away," she said with a smile, pushing back from the table. She rounded the piece of furniture, coming towards him before sliding her arms around his waist and resting her head on his chest. "I missed you."

Oliver returned her hug, wrapping his arms around her shoulders and burying his nose in her braided hair, her vanilla scent filling his nose. "I missed you too." He scraped his fingers into her hair, cradling her skull as he pulled back to look at her. "What has you up so early?"

She laughed at him before pushing onto her tiptoes and kissing him on the lips. "It's almost noon. You nearly slept the day away."

Oliver frowned at her. That could not be right. He never slept in, his body waking him like clockwork every morning at five, so he could tend to his plants. Removing his timepiece, his eyebrows raised as her statement was confirmed. Luncheon was nearly upon them, yet the house remained quiet. "Where are all the workers?"

Meg removed herself from his arms and returned to the table, pouring another cup of tea before handing it to him. "I have all the work happening outside the manor today. You were so tired, I wanted to make sure you weren't woken." She kissed his shoulder before smiling at him. "Are you hungry? I have some bread and butter, and Felix brought some eggs from his chickens."

"Felix has chickens?" he asked around a sip of tea.

Meg laughed. "Mr. Howell has chickens and Felix tends to them. I guess they laid more than the pair could eat."

"Eggs and bread sound fantastic." Taking the single chair at the table, Oliver watched as Meg cracked and scrambled the eggs before cooking them on the wood-stove. Bread lightly smeared with butter joined the skillet.

His stomach grumbled at their delectable smell, and when she placed the plate of food before him, he picked up his fork and started eating without hesitation. Meg refilled his tea before pouring more for herself, and leaned against the counter, watching him eat.

"What?" he asked.

She shook her head, a small smile peeking out from behind her teacup. "Come here," he said, holding out his hand to her. Meg placed her hand in his and Oliver pulled her towards him until she was sitting in his lap, an impish smile on her face. Kissing her cheek, he ran his hands up and down her back, the feel of her next to him intoxicating as much as it was comforting. "Thank you for breakfast."

"I think I deserve more than just thanks, my lord," she said with a wink. She kissed his nose before moving her lips down to meet his. Her kiss was soft, a sweet agony that left a sharp pang in the vicinity of his heart. Cupping her jaw with his hand, Oliver deepened the kiss and like a firebrand she exploded in his lap, her hands tangling in his hair as her tongue joined the game, tempting him back to bed. But the day called, most of it already lost to sleep, and as much as lying in bed with this beautiful woman enticed him, he had promises to keep to her.

Oliver softened the kiss before pulling back entirely. The kiss left her lips swollen, her eyes unfocused and her breathing sharp. "I should get to work," he said, standing with her still in his arms, then turning sharply to deposit her on the chair. "Finish your tea and I'll see you for dinner." With a final peck on the lips, Oliver turned and left the kitchen, his stride light, and the annoying smile on his face surely signaling to all that he was a man besotted.

The day passed quickly, certainly because of his over-sleeping, but also in part because he knew he would fill his evening with Meg. He caught glimpses of her throughout the afternoon, working with Siris in the training circle or up to her elbows in the dirt as she reseeded the vegetable garden, and the knowledge that this woman was his only made him smile brighter. When the last workers left, Oliver rinsed his hands at the pump, put away his tools, and set off to find Meg. The exterior of Baron was empty, so he headed inside, certain she was hiding somewhere in the large home.

Past the kitchens, a long hallway loomed and Oliver walked slowly, the fresh timber boards filling the air with their woodsy scent. An empty dining room sat to one side and just past it lay what must have once been the study. A musty green chair was the only remaining piece of furniture in the room, its seat angled towards the barren fireplace, a petite brunette presiding over it. Her head rested in her propped-up hand, her stocking-covered feet tucked beneath her bum as she stared into the soot-covered cavity. Her face was soft, her eyes distant, as if she were in some far-off place he could not reach, and he wished he knew her thoughts. Wished he knew what her life before Baron had been like so he could better help with her subdued moods.

Not wanting to scare her, Oliver retraced his steps out to the kitchen and closed the door with a bit more force. "Meg?" he said, raising his voice.

"In here," she said, and Oliver followed his steps back to the study. She now sat upright, a smile on her face as she pushed her feet into her boots. "All done for the day?"

He nodded. "Just finished up."

She touched her hand to her chest. "And you came looking for me? I must mean a great deal to you, huh?"

Oliver laughed as he leaned against the door frame. "I'm going to head to the cottage to get cleaned up and check on the spinach. Do you want to come with me?"

She stood up from the chair and came to him, stopping only long enough to slide her hand into his. "Let's go." With a squeeze, she dragged him behind her, her steps sure as she walked towards the kitchen.

"What all is left to be done inside?" he asked.

"We finished the floors and walls today, so structurally, Baron could withstand a hurricane. We still need paper and paint, and the trim and doors need to be cleaned up a bit, but I think we're starting to see the other side."

Oliver followed Meg out the door, shutting it behind him, before leading her to the trail that led to the cottage. Their pace slowed as they walked, the quiet evening soothing. "Are you going to stick with the name Baron?"

Meg frowned. "I'm not sure. Walter called it Bitch Manor after he sent his mother to live here, and while it was once an insult, now I'm not so sure. But I can't very well go around England calling my home Bitch Manor, no matter how fitting, so I may just leave the name, and only those who truly know it will know the accurate way to address it."

Oliver laughed. "Like a secret code?"

Meg smiled at him. "Exactly. You must know the correct name of the home to be allowed entrance. Felix and his chickens will chase all others off the property."

The image she painted sent them both into peals of laughter. As the pond beside the cottage came into view, Meg spoke again. "I saw you swimming in there once." Oliver raised a brow at her and she quickly continued, "I didn't mean to see you and once I realized your state of undress, I immediately turned away to give you privacy."

Oliver nodded his head slowly, his eyebrows raised, and Meg scoffed at him. "I didn't look, truly."

He shrugged. "It's all right." He squeezed her hand. "I usually swim there once a day. You're welcome to join me sometime."

She shook her head. "The water looks cold."

"It is, but once you start moving, you hardly notice it." He winked at her and she laughed.

"I don't believe you."

"Your loss. It could have been fun." Oliver opened the door to the cottage, motioning for Meg to enter first. "The couple who takes care of Bellawink had to leave rather suddenly to visit their daughter, but I think there should be some provisions for supper. Why don't you head into the kitchen and see what you can find in there? I'm going to get cleaned up and I'll meet you in a bit."

Meg wandered off to the kitchen and Oliver hurried to his bedroom. A quick washcloth bath with the remaining water in the basin and a bar of soap was all he could manage, but once completed, he was decidedly more clean and smelled like himself again. The days working at the gardens of Baron were not only taxing on his body but had forced him to bathe twice a day, if only to ensure he did not smell like an animal. Clean clothes finished the job, and Oliver ran his fingers through his damp hair as he headed to the kitchen.

Meg stood motionless before the table and Oliver went around her, worried at what had her looking so perplexed. Two apples, both rather shabby looking, stood in the center of the table along with the small amount of mead leftover from their previous dinner together. "This won't do," she said, her eyes still pinned to the meager offerings of his kitchen. "I don't think either of us is qualified to make something even resembling a meal from this."

"We still have the stew and bread Marty brought over yesterday. Let's have the apples now to tide us over, then head back to the manor for dinner." Meg raised a brow at him and Oliver laughed, reaching for her hand. "Come on, Meg. Grab those apples and let's check on the spinach."

Meg picked up the small fruit and trailed behind him, muttering to herself about her need for nourishment. Unlocking the greenhouse, Oliver stepped inside, letting the warm air soak into his skin as he took a deep breath. The scent of earthy goodness filled his nose, and he sighed before closing the door. Throwing his apron over his clothes, Oliver tied it around his waist as he walked to the spinach plants to inspect them.

His leather-bound notebook and pencil lay beside the pots, his notes, and previous measurements filling the pages. A ruler sat beside the writing implements and, without hesitation, he picked it up and began measuring the height of each stem, writing the measurements in the notebook, then moving on to the next. He wrote about the thickness of the stalks, noted any additional leaves that had sprouted on the plant, and last, checked the soil composition. Squishing the dirt between his fingers, he noted the moisture density of the dirt, the familiar caress of plant matter and dirt lulling him into a sense of calm only found in the greenhouse.

Examining his previous notes, Oliver wrote his new observations, studying any drastic changes in the plant's growth rates and moisture retention, frowning as he flipped the pages back and forth to compare his previous remarks. The greenhouse was silent and warm, and Oliver wiped at his brow, startling a bit at the clatter of a pot behind him. Meeting Meg's eyes, she smiled at him sheepishly. "I'm sorry. You were so engrossed in your work, I didn't mean to disturb you."

Oliver set down the notebook and walked to her, kissing her head before pulling her in for a hug. "I'm sorry. I can get lost in here rather easily." He pulled back and cupped her cheek. "This must bore you."

She shook her head; the smile remaining on her lips. "Not at all. You become so engrossed in your tasks; it's fascinating to watch."

"Like animals on exhibit?" For certainly that must be what it was. That such a marvelous woman would find him intriguing, find his fascination interesting, was unlikely. No doubt, like countless others, she was merely being kind in her delight at such dull activities.

She wrinkled her nose. "No, like a painter creating a masterpiece."

Oliver laughed, still uncertain of her sincerity, but pulled her in for another hug, allowing her words to warm his heart. "I'm not so sure about the masterpiece bit, but thank you for finding me fascinating."

She pinched his side, and he jumped. "I didn't say you

were fascinating. I said your work was."

"Oh. What will it take to make me fascinating to you?" Oliver leaned down and kissed the delicate divot between shoulder and neck and she shivered in his arms. He worked his way slowly up the long expanse, lingering against each bit of soft skin before placing a kiss on the joint, scraping his teeth lightly against it, then soothing it again with his tongue. "What can I do to prove my worth?"

Oliver kissed along Meg's jaw, her breathing fast against his cheek. "I'll be whatever you want me to be."

Meg pulled back and smiled at him, the grin mesmerizing as much as it was seductive. "Just be you. That's enough."

She was the pied piper and lured by her song, he would follow her wherever she may go.

CHAPTER THIRTEEN

THIS MAN WAS lethal. A poison she knew would kill her plans and quite possibly break her heart, but she would happily drink it anyway. Margaret curled her fingers into his hair and pulled his mouth down to hers, his plump lips cushioning the kiss as she ran her tongue along the seam, her teeth nibbling on his bottom lip. Oliver growled at her antics and parted his mouth, consuming her with his kiss as his hands closed about her hips, lifting her onto the potting table. Their sexes met, still covered by clothing, but the feel of him hard against her core made her shiver and Margaret wrapped her legs around his hips, grinding against him, eliciting a groan from her companion.

It was painful, this want of him, but even with the sting of longing, pleasure coursed through her as his lips plied hers, his hands squeezing her thighs, the pressure only furthering her motions as she rubbed against him. Margaret pulled back just a bit. "More," she whispered.

The man wasted little time, his hands wrapping around her thighs as he picked her up off the table, his mouth resuming its destruction to her nerves. For a moment, Margaret wondered if she could ride him like this, and the thought made her quim pulse in want, the carnal image she had created so distinct, she wanted it. Craved it. When he let her legs slide down his hips, her feet returning to the floor, disappointment flooded her. "Turn around," he said with a growl.

Oliver spun her to face the table, grabbing her hands and placing them gently on the wooden top. The surface bit into her palms, but the sting was forgotten as he aligned his body with hers, his hard sex pushing against her bottom. Margaret pushed against him, whimpering at the need that took over, and he bit her neck, his fingers entwining with hers. "Shh, love. I'll make it better."

He removed his hands from hers, his large digits sliding over her stomach, brushing the underside of the swells of her breasts. "Yes?" he asked.

"God, yes."

Steady hands cupped her flesh, plumping the aching mounds as his lips placed fairy kisses along her neck. Margaret's breath hitched as his magical fingers kneaded her, her nipples straining for his touch. She could not focus, her core begging for the pressure she knew his sex would provide while her breasts ached for his attentions, desperate for more. A whimper left her lips as he tweaked the sturdy points, the pinch he distributed forcing her breath between her lips as he attended to her. It was too much. It was not enough.

She moaned as his teeth nipped at her shoulder while a single hand slid down her stomach before pulling the shirt from her breeches. "Yes?" he asked.

"Yes."

When his coarse fingertips touched her bare skin, she gasped, pushing against him. His hands skated over the front of her, tracing her belly button, then along the top of her trousers. Dancing just beneath the swell of her breasts, so close and yet so far. "Yes?" he asked.

Margaret nodded her head frantically. "Yes."

He cupped her, flesh against flesh, his hands repeating the same movements as before, but now his touch felt like fire. Margaret bit her lip to keep from crying out. He was masterful, his hands playing her as if she were his favorite instrument and only he could construct the sounds that fell from her lips. Margaret arched her back even as she pushed her sex against his, the need too much, the desire too high. She rolled her hips, gyrating, searching for relief only he could provide. "Please," she said, the word more plea than a command.

His lips returned to the juncture between shoulder a neck, his teeth scraping lightly before he bestowed a kiss on the injured skin. "What do you want, love?"

"More," she said, the words pulled from her lips as he ground himself against her.

"More touching? More kissing?" His hands left her breasts and intertwined with hers again, becoming an unmovable wall as she rubbed herself against him.

"Yes. All." It was too much. He was too much.

Oliver pulled his hands back and stepped away, giving Margaret space. "Show me where."

Margaret wasted little time, her hands falling to the top of her trousers unbuttoning the placket. She pushed them down a bit, then grabbed his hand and shoved it into the fabric. His growl as his fingers met her damp heat sent shivers coursing down her spine, and when those long digits traced the seam of her sex, she moaned, leaning into his chest and spreading her legs as wide as she could as pleasure overtook her.

His fingers skimmed the plump lips of her quim, swirl-ing in the dew she had created. He had created. Margaret spread her legs wider, giving him ample space to work, and the man did not disappoint. He traced and swirled, dipped, and danced along the outer lips of her sex, stoking the frenzy he had already created and Margaret panted as one long digit circled the nub at the top of her quim, her legs shaking as the fire inside her grew. That single finger became the tempest, pulling her closer and closer to the cliff's edge and Margaret closed her eyes squeezing them tightly as she was pushed, pleasure overtaking her, ripping a cry from her throat as her body shook against him, the pulses becoming brilliant flashes of light behind her eyelids.

Depleted, Margaret sank against the table, her cheek resting on the rough wood. Oliver's hand remained in her trousers, his finger coaxing last quakes from her and even as her mind screamed that it was too much, her body moved with him, undulating with each motion. "How?" she asked, her voice a gasp as she reflexively pushed into his hand, her quim throbbing.

"Let it happen again, Meg," Oliver said, his strokes sure.

Margaret pushed up from the table, her hands coming behind her back, searching for the fastenings of Oliver's trousers. "Not without you," she said, as she unbuttoned him, her hand gripping his thick cock. Oliver groaned, his hand faltering in its motions as she stroked him.

"Pull down your trousers," he said with a growl.

Margaret shoved the trousers down her legs, the fabric

pooling around her boots as Oliver pulled himself closer to her, his member pulsing against her arse. He tucked his sex between her legs, his thick length snuggling against her outer lips, and Margaret sighed, tightening her thighs around him. "Meg," Oliver said, his voice croaking. His hand grabbed hers and pinned it to the table while the other wrapped around to her front and resumed stroking her, his cock thrusting back and forth between the damp lips of her sex. He paused only once in his motions to lean forward, his hand turning her head towards him, and placed a soft kiss on her forehead before resuming his actions. It was such a gentle act given the circumstances and her heart pinched, but she brushed away the heavy emotions.

Their joining was raw. The table jolted with each thrust of his hips, his fingers covered in her dew as he played with her, and Margaret squeezed her legs tighter, the friction achingly sweet, but not quite enough.

But it was enough for Oliver. A curse rang out in the greenhouse as his hand stumbled, his seed spurting between her legs as his climax claimed him. Margaret whimpered, the fire he has so easily stoked still burning strong even as he found his bliss, but she bit her lip, determined to not disappoint him. She had already claimed her pleasure once before, and it was selfish to want more.

Oliver withdrew himself from behind her, and a hand-kerchief appeared between her legs, mopping up his mess. Margaret reached down to pull up her trousers, but Oliver's hand stopped her. "Not yet." He turned her around to face him, kissing her lips with aching tender-ness, before placing his hands on her hips and lifting her onto the table. "You didn't finish."

"I'm all right." The lie rolled off her tongue easily even as her sex pulsed, longing for completion. His hand stroked her between the damp folds and Margaret's eyes rolled into the back of her head at the touch, her thighs opening easily.

"Please." The plea was soft, the words sincere as he dropped to his knees and placed her still cuffed legs around his shoulders. His face was so close to her quim she was certain he could smell her, and mortification overtook her. Margaret placed her hand over it, humiliation eating at her. Walter had never dared to venture further than her breasts with his hands, let alone his mouth. Oliver kissed her hand, his tongue skimming the divide between each divot and the surety of its warm strength nearly broke her, but she shook her head. "Once. If you don't like it, I'll stop," he said, his voice muffled against her hand.

His tongue was a tempter, its surety and strength making her thighs shake with need, and with very little fight left, Margaret gave in, removing her hand and placing it on her stomach. Oliver wasted little time, his wily tongue licking up the seam of her sex, his growl carnal against her skin. "So good," he said, his voice vibrating against her.

It was exquisite. It was deadly.

What Oliver did with his mouth was most certainly a sin, and yet she could not find the urge to care. Her hands crept towards his head, her fingers sliding into the strands. To push him away? To pull him closer? She was not sure, only that the sensation he was creating inside her was stronger than any she had ever felt. Her limbs shook, her breath heavy as his tongue toyed with her, kissing that small bud that throbbed for affection with such surety

Margaret wondered at the skill. When his fingers joined the game, sliding into her with sure motions, she could take it no more.

The walls of her sex milked his hand as she screamed, thrusting her center into his face as she rode wave after wave of pleasure that did not seem to have an end. Her thighs bracketed his head, hanging on for dear life as she crested a peak, only to climb again.

When the storm finally passed, Oliver gentled his ministrations, his kisses making her jump from sensitivity. He kissed the inside of her thigh and looked at her with a smile. "I knew you'd like it."

She laughed, suddenly aware that he had her spread across his worktable like a feast. "If I had known that would be the result, I would have listened to you sooner."

Oliver smiled, his eyes hooded as he looked at her. "You look like a goddess strewn across that table."

"I feel silly," she said.

"You look lovely." He smiled at her, his finger tracing over the surface of her quim. "I think I could forgo dinner all together, for you are far more delicious."

Margaret's breath hitched as his nail scraped over the bud of her sex and her eyes narrowed on the man before her. "You can't mean that."

Oliver licked his lips and eyed her sex with sudden interest. "Want to bet?" He leaned forward, his tongue licking her thoroughly, and they both groaned, Margaret arching into his caress. He could definitely persuade her to remain here a bit longer. Especially if her companion with the very talented tongue continued doing that.

CHAPTER FOURTEEN

THE PAIN CAME swiftly, as it always did, and Margaret stifled her curse as another pulse tightened her abdomen. The honest crux of being a female was the monthly arrival of ones courses and it was truly ironic that a woman could bleed for five days straight and not die, yet still be called the weaker sex. Gritting her teeth and clenching the muscles of her nether regions, Margaret removed herself from the team that was refinishing the exterior of the stable and hurried into Baron. Inside her room, she removed the small package of cotton cloth she had tucked away in her trunk, along with a worn brown belt she had manufactured to hold up the fabric.

In all of humanity's amazing achievements and inventions; the wheel, the printing press, even recently, a steam powered engine that motorized a locomotive, women were still forced to wear the equivalent of a nappy during their courses. She would shake her fist at the indecency of it all if the aching in her stomach was not so monumental. Once the cloth was tucked and folded as best as it could be, Margaret pulled a much looser pair of trousers on, stomped on her boots, and headed back to work.

The first day of her courses were always miserable, the pains nearly crippling her as her insides twisted and turned, wringing themselves out like a used dishrag, but society demanded she continue on as if nothing occurred. And damnit all if it did not irk her that she be forced to perform as though her body were not attempting to remove its insides, all because she chose not to have a baby. There truly was no way to win at being a woman.

Rejoining the team, Margaret slipped on her gloves and retook her place, hammering pieces of wood to the exterior of the stable, forming what would be a solid barrier against the elements. She pushed on as if nothing occurred, and if she had to stop and take a breath as the pains threatened to make her cast up her lunch, she merely wiped at her brow, pretending to take a small rest instead.

As the sun dipped lower in the sky, the team dispersed, each heading home for the evening, but Margaret was determined to get the last few boards up. As if sensing her resolve, Oliver sidled up next to her, quietly picking up an abandoned hammer and began securing the boards to the frame. Margaret opened her mouth to thank him, the words on the tip of her tongue, but a slew of pains struck her, their tentacles spreading across the tops of her thighs and up her back, the agony so intolerable she let slip a whimper.

Oliver's hammer was dropped to the dirt as he hurried to her, his hands cupping her face as he searched for what caused her pain. "Are you all right? Where are you hurt?" he asked as his eyes inspected every exposed piece of flesh for injury.

Margaret waved him off, the pain lasting longer than it typically did, and her reply came out in a pant. "Fine. I'm fine."

"Bullshit you are." Without waiting for her reply, he

picked her up in his arms and carried her into the house, the stables forgotten under his chivalrous yet unnecessary concern. Yet, she allowed it, letting her head fall against his chest, his powerful arms creating a safe haven as her body rebelled.

At the manor, Oliver set her on her bed, his hands skirting her arms and legs as if looking for cuts or bruises. "I'm all right," she said, the wave of nausea passing as she made to get back up. "I need to finish the stable walls or we'll fall behind."

Oliver placed his hands on her shoulders, halting her movements as he sat on the edge of the bed. "Meg, you whimpered as if you had been stabbed. Your tenacity for finishing a job is commendable, but I don't think this is the moment to be dedicated. Now, please tell me where you're hurt so I can assess the damage and see what needs to be done."

Margaret's cheeks heated, and she looked at the wall, unable to meet his eyes. "I'm not injured." When he remained silent, she sighed and closed her eyes. "My courses have arrived, and I was merely struck by a pain. I'm sorry I frightened you. I'll do better to keep my outbursts contained so I don't worry you."

The room grew quiet and Margaret did not dare to look at him, certain she had crossed a line that lovers should never reach. Walter had declared the entire ordeal unhygienic and demanded that if she was partaking in such unfortunate circumstances, she should remove herself from his presence entirely.

"You little fool," Oliver said, the words whispered.

Margaret's eyebrows raised, and she turned to face

him, her arms crossing across her chest. "Excuse me?"

Oliver cupped her cheek, his thumb massaging the space between her eyebrows. "Why would you hide that from me?" The motion of his thumb was hypnotic, its strokes releasing the tension she did not know she held there. "Meg, it's a normal thing to experience, and if you're in pain, I want you to tell me. And you certainly shouldn't be apologizing for it."

"What?" She shook her head. "Absolutely not."

He raised a brow at her. "Why?"

"Because it will disgust you?" she said, the words coming out more of a question than a statement. When he shook his head, his thumbs now stroking the expanse of her forehead, Margaret closed her eyes. "And the only way it affects you is that we'll be unable to have any physical interactions for a couple of days."

The motions of his thumbs stopped and his hands disappeared at her words. Margaret opened her eyes to find him glaring at her. Without a word, he stood and left the bedroom, closing the door behind him with a resounding snap that told her in no uncertain terms that she should not leave the room. Releasing a loud sigh, Margaret took her boots off and laid back on the bed, the soft mattress cushioning her aching back. Her abdomen throbbed as a new pain scorched across the expanse and she closed her eyes to it, swallowing the whimper that threatened to break free. Her mind urged her to return to the stable, to finish the work that she had started, but every bone in her body hurt, her head throbbed from gritting her teeth against the agony, and she was utterly exhausted. Even the notion of brushing her teeth and combing her hair sounding grueling and with a groan, Margaret pushed herself up to stand to complete the tasks, albeit reluctantly.

With a new cotton piece secured and her nightgown firmly in place, she set about cleaning her teeth, the motions jerky as a wave of nausea hit. Of course, it was at that moment Oliver returned, his sigh of frustration only adding to her misery. "You don't know when to quit, do you?" he asked, setting a blanketed bundle down on the bed. "Your teeth will survive a night. Come on, into bed with you."

He waited as she rinsed her mouth before taking her hand and guiding her to the soft mattress, pulling back the sheets before she slipped inside. Once settled, Oliver grabbed the bundle and gently placed it on her abdomen, the warm heat it emitted soothing the pain that throbbed there. "Be careful where you touch it. The brick is still fairly hot."

Margaret sighed her agreement, letting the heated brick soothe the pains.

"Would you like me to brush your hair?" he asked, crawling onto the opposite side of the bed.

"When have I ever said no to that question?" she asked, her eyes still closed.

Oliver's soft chuckle as the brush slid through her hair was lovely, just as his strokes were, the motions a soothing focus that forced the pains to background noise as the stone and the man did their jobs. "My mother used to request something sweet during her cycle. Is there anything I can get you?"

"You don't need to do that."

The brushing stopped, the pause so long, Margaret opened her eyes to ensure he was still alive. His furrowed brow as he inspected the hair brush was worrying. "Why do you do that?" he asked.

Her heart, which had slowed to a contented beat, picked up its pace at his words. "Do what?"

Oliver sighed, closing his eyes and Margaret worried her bottom lip as she watched him. "That," he said, the word sad. "Why do you dismiss me anytime I offer to do something? Why do you assume that I'll feel disgust at your courses, or worse, anger at the lack of sex it might bring?" He opened his eyes and looked at her, his beautiful mouth pulled into a frown. "I know you've experienced things I can never understand and I know they've shaped how you view the world, but it hurts when you lump me into the same group as those monsters that creep around in your mind.

"I want to know you, Meg. I want to know when your courses arrive, not because of how it will affect our physical relationship, but because I want to take care of you. I want to bring you your favorite treat, and brush your hair, and warm a brick to ease your pain, because you've come to mean a great deal to me." Margaret's throat tightened at his words, the honesty in them unnerving as they stripped away her protective shell. "I know there's more that you've never told me, and whenever you're ready, I'm happy to listen. But until then, please, please don't assume those same qualities reside in me. I'm not like them."

Oliver met her eyes, and Margaret could merely nod her agreement at his request. "Warm chocolate," she said.

He nodded. "Warm chocolate it is."

Oliver resumed his brushing before leaving the room, only to return a bit later with warm chocolate and another heated brick. Setting the drink on the nightstand, he switched out the stones, covering it once again with the blanket, then handed her the mug. After finishing the sweet treat, Oliver took the ceramic from her and set it back on the table before tucking her hair behind her ear. "Are you tired?" he asked.

Margaret shook her head.

"How about if I read to you for a bit?"

"I'd like that."

The remarkable man removed his boots before picking up the book she had lying on the table and climbing across the bed to snuggle next to her. Oliver tucked his arm behind her head, his bicep cradling her as he stood the book against his leg and opened it to the page she had dogeared. A soft kiss was pressed against her head. "When this has passed, we're going to have a talk about how real men aren't afraid of a little blood," he said, before turning towards the writing before him.

Margaret's brow furrowed at the words, but when she turned to question him, he merely dropped another kiss on her forehead and began to read. His tenderness was foreign, but instead of allowing the confusion to overwhelm her, she decided to drown in it. Smother herself in his gentle ministrations and caring ways, a love so unfamiliar and yet so wholly longed for her entire life she could not be certain she was not imagining it. The soft timber of his voice filled the room, his words melodic and smooth and Margaret let the lullaby and the heat from the stone soothe her, lulling her to sleep.

When morning arrived, it was to find the water bowl on the nightstand filled with fresh warm water and a cloth to clean herself folded neatly beside it. The cotton under cloth she had used the day before was missing from where she had placed it on the trunk, and after cleaning herself and applying a new cloth to the belt, Margaret dressed and headed into the kitchen only to find the cloth in question cleaned and hanging across a chair to dry. The kettle was full of warm water for tea and on the counter, the chocolate Oliver had used for her treat the night before sat waiting in case it was needed.

With a large breath, and a thankfully less painful abdomen, Margaret went about making herself breakfast, all the while wondering about the chivalrous man who had taken care of her the night before. He said he wanted to know her, to know all of her. Perhaps it was time she did just that.

CHAPTER FIFTEEN

"DO YOU THINK a good marriage is like this?" Meg asked him, her head resting on his chest. It had barely been a fortnight since Oliver had run into Meg at the inn, saving her from Charlie, and yet, here she was, discussing marriage.

Oliver raised a brow at her. "What do you mean?"

"I mean happy. Comfortable. Like a warm shawl you wrap about yourself in on a chilly day." While their day to day had taken on a rhythm of familiarity, an almost marital feeling with shared responsibilities and physical connection, there had been little in a discussion of their feelings.

A smile tugged at his lips. "Is that how you feel?"

"Yes," she said. "It's different from how my marriage was, so I wondered."

"Different how?"

Meg sighed, her fingers brushing at the hand he had resting on her stomach. "My marriage was a transaction from beginning to end. I was bought and paid for with no real attachment or interest in my spouse, and if not for the marriage certificate, one would not have ever known we belonged to each other."

"That sounds lonely," he said, lacing his fingers through hers and giving them a gentle squeeze.

"It was."

She resumed reading the book before her, but Oliver could not get the notion out of his head. "What would it look like if we were married?"

"What?" Meg said, shock lacing her voice. "We haven't even said I love you yet."

Oliver frowned at her before picking up the book that rested on his chest and reading it once more. They lay in the middle of the field that stretched between their two properties; a blanket laid out on the crisp grass. The remains of the luncheon they had shared sat pushed to one side, happily ignored in lieu of their books. Meg's head was propped up on Oliver's chest while he lay flat on his back. His book, now summarily forgotten, was tossed to the blanket as he pushed up on his elbows and looked down at her.

"How did that question come about?" she asked.

Oliver shrugged. "It was just a thought." He looked at her and smiled.

She winked at him. "By the way, I love you." She said the words simply, yet their magnitude still hit him in the chest like a fist.

"Jesus Christ, Meg, you can't just go about saying that." He sat up with a frown, his movements rolling her off his chest.

Meg crawled towards him and sat in his lap, wrapping her arms around his neck. "Why not? It's the truth. Are you saying I shouldn't tell you the truth?"

Oliver shook his head, once more poleaxed by this woman. "No, but you could warn a man. You don't just throw out statements of undying love nonchalantly like that."

She raised a brow at him before kissing his lips. "And how should I have done it? Candle lit dinner, flowers? Sam serenading us on the fiddle as I tell you how much I adore you?"

Oliver chuckled.

"If I did it as you would, it would never happen. I'm surprised you didn't say it first."

He almost had. A million times in the past two weeks, the words had tried to slip out of his mouth, but he recalled them, terrified of what they could mean. Where they could lead. His father still required him back in London at the end of the month, and a respectable marriage and future dukedom still sat before him like the hangman's noose. Meg's words were everything he wanted to hear, and everything he feared.

Oliver cupped her cheek, the look of sheer joy on her face spurring him on. "I love you, Meg."

She smiled, her eyes crinkling. "See, that wasn't so hard." She kissed him, her sweet taste filling his senses as her tongue met his. She was lightning and thunder, the perfect storm all wrapped into one, and he could do nothing but stand beside her, absorb her beauty and chaos as it consumed him. When she pulled back, she brushed at the hair that had fallen across his eyes.

"What if we got married?" he asked.

Meg shook her head before kissing his nose and depositing herself back on the blanket. "I'm sure your father would have a few thoughts about that development. You're meant to be on holiday."

Oliver laughed. "You could win him over in time."

"I'm sure I could."

Oliver laid back down, book forgotten, as he inspected the clouds.

"Have you heard anything from him?"

Oliver shook his head. "No, the last correspondence I got from him was when I arrived, reminding me I only had a month to get my head on straight. There wasn't a word about his health or mental state, and between the two of us, he's the one I'm most worried about. So much loss in such a rapid succession." He shook his head. "A person needs time to grieve, but he's merely thrown himself into his work, as if afraid to allow himself to feel the true repercussions of their death. I worry that there will come a point where his body will not endure it for very long."

Meg set her hand on his arm, stroking it. "He's a good man to worry about you. Most parents in the aristocracy care little for their offspring. Their only requirement is to live long enough to continue the line. Outside of that, they could not care less."

"My parents eschewed the typical aristocratic mantra when it came to their children. Christopher and I were loved deeply as children, and it was apparent in everything they did. We went everywhere with them, ate dinner as a family. My mother was heartbroken when Chris died."

"I want to be like your parents when I have kids of my own." The words were neutral, but the look of pain on Meg's face was anything but.

"Do you want to have children?" Oliver asked.

Meg frowned. "I think so. Then again, maybe I just want to prove that I can be a better parent than my own were to me, and that is certainly not a reason to have children."

Oliver nodded. "You don't talk a lot about your life back in London." In truth, she had said very little beyond mention of the husband and parents. But from what she had said, Oliver knew it was nothing short of a nightmare. From a controlling childhood home to a controlling husband, Meg had not had it at all as he had.

"There isn't much beyond what I've already told you."

It was obvious she was putting him off, supplicating him, and while he longed to push the details from her, he knew she would only close up further if he did. "As long as you are not wanted for murder or theft of a priceless jewel, then you are correct. There isn't much to talk about." Oliver plucked up a strand of her hair and wrapped it around his finger. "So, if we were married..." he said, shifting the conversation away from the heartbreaking.

"Yes?" Meg said, laying down on the blanket beside him, a smile tugging at her lips.

"Hypothetically, where would we live?"

Meg pointed to an odd-shaped cloud that looked like a dragon, and Oliver grabbed her hand and held it, giving it a soft squeeze before pulling her into his arms.

"The manor is nearly habitable, although there isn't much in the way of furniture or window coverings, so perhaps the cottage at night and the manor during the day. Once it's finished, we can have a greenhouse built..." she paused as if thinking of the landscape.

"That clearing near the vegetable garden would be a wonderful spot. It gets plenty of sunlight and is within easy access of the home."

She hummed her agreement. "We'll build you a greenhouse there. That way you can work on your experiments and not have to trek all the way to the cottage anymore."

"But I like the cottage," he said, bringing her hand up to his mouth and kissing her knuckles.

Meg pushed herself up and looked at him. "I do too. Maybe we make that our secret hideaway. We let ivy grow on the outside until it all but blends in with the surrounding area. Let the road grow over with brush so people think it's haunted. When we want to be alone, away from the chaos, we go there, just us two."

"The villagers will make up stories about it if we do that."

She smiled, her nose scrunching. "Good. Let them. We'll forever be known in the Woodingdean history books as the ghosts of Bellawink cottage."

Oliver laughed, running his fingers into her hair. "I think I'd love being a ghost with you." Oliver swallowed at the painful bulge of sadness that threatened to well up as they pieced together their imaginary future. For that's certainly what it had to be. Right?

Meg rolled on top of him, peppering soft butterfly kisses along his jaw, the tip of his nose, his eyelids, and his cheeks. Oliver directed her mouth to his and deepened the kiss, utterly consumed by this radiant woman. When Meg pulled back, he frowned. "We haven't done it outside yet," she said, her words a whisper.

Oliver laughed before rolling her onto her back, his hand still buried in her hair. Her shriek of surprise filled the quiet meadow, and for an instant, Oliver could see them happily married, living at Baron Manor, escaping to

Bellawink cottage, and growing old together in their small corner of Woodingdean.

Kissing her lips, he rubbed his nose against hers. "I'm up for the adventure if you are."

They spent the rest of the afternoon in the field, muffling their sighs and groans of pleasure to ensure those passing by did not catch them. When the sun dipped down, they put on their clothes and headed back to Baron, going their separate ways as they entered the garden. As they parted, Meg's hand reached for his and squeezed it before falling away and Oliver smiled, his body humming in happiness.

Oliver went back to work, his eyes straying to wherever Meg was, a smile overtaking his face when he would glimpse her. They had transformed nearly half of the garden into what he had envisioned, the new greenery and cleaned walkways creating an inviting welcome almost as decadent as it surely had once been. Blueberry bushes from a local bramble had been procured and lay stacked together, linen bags wrapped around their roots as they awaited their turn to be planted. Meanwhile, the remaining rose bushes that had survived gave a lush appearance to some of the beds, and Oliver knew his next task would be to tame their thorny branches into submission.

Sam, surprisingly, was a quick study and had wasted little time in learning the method of transplanting the bushes that would flourish. Together, they worked fluidly, restoring the gardens to their former glory. All that remained was to complete the list of produce Meg wanted to grow in the vegetable garden, and they could begin those beds for spring planting.

Oliver lifted his head and wiped at his brow with his handkerchief, his eyes straying to where he last saw Meg. The stable, now sporting a brand-new roof and siding, stood flanked by a newly installed gate system and training pen, the compost pile, now a three-bin system, allowed for them to take from the more composted material, giving the newer refuse time to break down along with any food scraps and green material they discarded.

Meg stood with Siris, brushing the monstrous steed's black coat beside Mr. Howell. The stepstool she stood on boosted her almost to the horse's height, but she still raised on tiptoes to reach the upper expanse of his neck, her shapely calves and arse looking luscious as she leaned over the brute.

"I'll never understand her affection for that thing," Sam said beside him, smacking his work gloves against his pants to rid them of the remaining dirt.

"What do you mean?" Oliver asked.

"She won that beast in a bet. His owner was passing through and stopped at the inn during his travels. He left Siris outside, his flanks covered in sweat and his shoes caked in mud. Meg has such a soft spot for injured creatures and suggested to the man that he switch horses for the rest of his journey, but the man simply laughed at her and told her a woman had no place making decisions regarding animals." Oliver could already see what happened next, and he laughed. Sam looked at him and smiled. "Aye, Meg wasn't too fond of that. She told the man she'd play him a round of ving-et-un. If he won, he would get her company for the night, and if she did, she got his horse and he would not be allowed to take any other steed from the stables."

Oliver gaped at him, but Sam continued, unaware. "She knew she would win. Said she played cards regularly with some lord and she knew a few tricks. When the man lost, he attempted to renege on the deal, but Meg had already had Siris sent to the manor." Sam laughed. "I've never seen a person angrier, but she handled it as if she were the queen and he a mere peasant. Poor chap walked to his destination as far as I can tell, and that lucky brute of a horse became her pet. The beast eats better than any animal I've ever seen and is bathed so regularly he smells more like strawberries than straw."

Oliver's eyes fell to Meg and the stallion, his emotions a jumble. Anger and fear, along with a ridiculous amount of pride, filled him as he watched the pair. Siris leaned into Meg's scratches, his lips snuffling the loose strands that danced around her head, and Oliver wondered if she had seen a piece of herself in the stallion. Broken, they both had come to Baron to heal their scars.

When the day ended, Oliver headed to the pump to wash his hands and face. The pond would be a more efficient cleaning, but he missed Meg. Wanted to see her brown eyes sparkle when she smiled, hold her hand and ask how the rest of her day had gone.

A folded piece of paper lay on the table inside the kitchen, and thinking she had left a note for him, Oliver picked it up and read. Swooping letters covered the page, informing the reader of the author's experiences at school, a terribly strict headmistress, and a domineering mother who insisted upon weekly status reports of the author's education on how to become a suitable wife.

"There you are," Meg said, her voice filling the kitchen.

Oliver jumped, aware that he held a missive he had no business reading. Instead of shuffling his feet and hiding the letter like he longed to do, he handed it to her and smiled. "I'm sorry. I thought this was from you. I didn't realize it was personal."

Meg smiled and took the letter from him, folding it along the creases. "It's all right. My sister is at finishing school and has taken it upon herself to inform me of all her doings while there."

Oliver raised a brow. "You talk very little about her, or your parents, for that matter."

She shrugged. "My parents are the typical aristocratic archetype. I was a tool for the betterment of the title and was used as such. They arranged my marriage to Walter and when he passed, demanded I return home to be married off once more. It would seem Daphne might be destined for the same fate."

Oliver pulled her into a hug. "That couldn't have been easy."

"It wasn't, but it's all I knew. I went from their household being the dutiful daughter to Walter's and became the dutiful wife." She sighed. "I hate that Daphne is facing the same path and that there's no way I can help her. I was lucky my settlement gave me Baron. What if she isn't as lucky?"

Oliver kissed her head as his hands stroked her back. "I'm sorry, Meg."

"It's all right," she said, her words muffled into his

shirt. "You didn't know."

"No, it isn't." She needed a distraction from the wound he so indelicately tore at. "Can you swim?" he asked.

Meg pulled back, her brow raised, but she nodded.

Oliver smiled and took her hand, pulling her along behind him as they left the kitchen and headed for the path to Bellawink. As he walked with Meg towards the water, Oliver was determined to chase away any spirit intent on casting a shadow on Meg's beautiful face. Perhaps that is what leads to an advantageous marriage? He pondered the thought before squeezing Meg's hand. Yes, a refreshing bath in a cold pond was just the thing to silence any ghosts that longed to linger.

CHAPTER SIXTEEN

THE WATER WAS brisk, turning her skin to ice the moment she touched it, and Margaret wondered for a moment what the devil she had been thinking. Yes, she could swim, but not in a frost-tempered pool in nothing but her altogether. The man had seen her naked before, but looking like a drowned blue rat was another story entirely and Margaret backed away from the water, suddenly uncertain. "I think I'll wait for you out here."

Oliver swam towards her, his long arms cutting through the water like a knife. "What's got you so skittish? I've never seen you shy away from a challenge."

Margaret frowned. He was right, damnit. If she let something as small as momentary discomfort hold her back from doing something so inconsequential, what would happen when it came time for something bigger? Screwing up her courage, she ran into the water, diving below the surface before she had time to think. The shock that struck her body was stunning, her brain sending messages of panic to her every limb as she broke the surface, her breath escaping from her lips in gasps. Oliver laughed jubilantly beside her. "That's my girl!" he said, wrapping his arms around her and spinning her in the water.

Margaret shivered, sliding closer to his warmth. "You

do this every day?"

"Exercise is good for you." He hugged her close, his legs kicking slowly, keeping them afloat.

"This isn't exercise, it's torture." Her teeth began to rattle and Oliver rubbed her arms.

"You just need to move around. Come on, I'll show you." He released her and began swimming to the other side of the pond, his movements sleek and effortless. She treaded water, her feet kicking with desperation to keep her head above the surface. Swim. She should swim. With a groan, Margaret took a breath and headed in the direction Oliver had gone. Her muscles protested at first, tired from the day's activities, but soon, they relaxed, the motions becoming reflexive as she stretched her arm forward, then pulled it back, propelling herself through the water. At the other side of the pond, Oliver floated, waiting for her. "Well?"

"It's not too bad," she said, reaching out for his shoulder. He pulled her in close and she relaxed against him. "It's terribly cold, but it's not too bad. Maybe we can try again in July when the temperature isn't anywhere near glacial."

He laughed, tucking her wet strands behind her ear. "One more lap and then we'll head to the cottage?"

Margaret nodded, kissing his shoulder. "Race you."

She took off, certain he would win, but not caring as the water slid past her with each stroke. She could see why he exercised here. The solitude he found in the dark pool was freeing. A hand reached around her foot, pulling her backward, and Margaret cried out as Oliver slid past her, his trick effectively giving him the lead. "Cheater!"

He did not respond, more focused on winning than taunting her, but Margaret could hardly complain. From her viewpoint, she could watch his fascinating body work, his arms slicing through the water while his muscular legs propelled him forward. He was a magnificent creature, and he was all hers. "Come on, Meg. Let's get you inside and warmed up!"

Margaret smiled as she swam the rest of the way towards him, coming up onto the rocky bottom and reaching for his outstretched hand, a large towel tied at his waist. He draped a soft blanket around her shoulders and hugged her into him, rubbing her arms briskly. "Thoughts?"

Margaret laughed against his chest, the wiry hairs there slicked to the still damp skin. "It was fun," she said, her teeth chattering.

He chuckled, kissing her head. "Let's get you inside before you turn into an icicle."

Wrapping his arms around her shoulder, Oliver steered her towards the cottage, the cool air quickly slipping beneath the blanket and piercing her skin. Shivers took over as they walked in the front door and Oliver wasted little time stoking a fire in the parlor and directing her to sit in the winged back chair he had situated close to the heat. He left, returning in dry clothes with an armful of towels, and set them down beside her. Removing one, Oliver dried her hair with a gentleness so achingly sweet tears pooled in her eyes.

Margaret blinked them back, not wanting to concern him with her display of emotions. His care and affection for her were still so unfamiliar, and yet she longed for his soft caresses and kind words like one longs for air. It was a craving with no end, and as he pulled her to standing, rubbing a new towel over the expanse of her skin, Margaret realized that each day she spent with him left her hoping their time would never end. She wanted to live this life with him for as long as she could. When he placed a heavy quilt around her, Margaret cupped his cheek and brought his gaze to hers. "I love you."

Oliver smiled at her, rubbing her nose with his before kissing her lips. "I love you, too."

Margaret shook her head, unable to convey to him with words just how much he meant to her. The past two weeks with him had been nothing short of a dream, and if it were reality, she did not think she could believe it. To have such a man shower her with love was the most terrifying yet delightful thing to ever happen to her, and she could not begin to explain to him how earth-shattering it was.

Oliver picked her up, stealing the chair she occupied, before depositing her on his lap, his arms wrapping around her, warming her like bed stones. Margaret settled against his chest, breathing in his sandalwood scent, letting the beat of his heart against her ear soothe her like a lullaby. "I should feed you before you fall asleep," he said, his voice muffled against her ear.

"Don't want to move. Too comfortable." Margaret yawned and snuggled in closer to Oliver.

He laughed, kissing the top of her head. "If you insist. Sleep, love."

Margaret let the blackness claim her, sleep dragging her beneath its realm like a siren, the press and smell of

Oliver acting as a lure to the land of dreams. When she awoke, the room was dark but for a small glow from the fireplace, and Margaret startled when the pillow beneath her head shifted, its softness still smelling of Oliver, but decidedly less Oliver shaped. Pushing upright, Margaret examined the bedroom she was in, the quilted blanket still wrapped around her firmly. Everything was just as it had been, except for the man who had held her securely as she slept. "Oliver?" she said to the quiet room.

Beside her, the man moved, his hand snaking out to take hers. "I wondered when you'd wake up," he said with a yawn. "You've been asleep for a while."

"How is that possible?" she asked, glancing at the shuttered window. "What time is it?"

"Nearly morning. Between the work you're putting in at the manor and our late hours afterward, I'd say you were due for a long nap." Oliver sat up beside her and tucked a strand of hair behind her ear. "Are you hungry?"

Margaret nodded, her stomach aching with emptiness. Oliver kissed her forehead, then pulled his naked self from the bed, thrusting first one leg, then another into his trousers. Buttoning the placket, he smiled at her. "I'll make you some eggs and tea. Your clothes are beside the bed. I shook them out so they shouldn't be in too rough of shape."

He left the room without another word, and Margaret stared at the door, her brow furrowed. Even after two weeks of his attentive care, his kindness still left her off-kilter. It did not matter how many plates of food he made her, nor how many kisses he brushed on her forehead, Margaret still wondered that a man such as he existed.

Dressing in her dirty clothes from yesterday, Margaret brushed out her hair, then made the bed, tucking the covers up on both sides just as Oliver had done every morning. Meeting him in the kitchen, she smiled as he stood shirtless before the stove, his utensil occasionally moving the eggs about the skillet. A tea pot with steam emanating from the spout sat on the table beside two cups, and two pieces of toast occupied a single plate.

Margaret slid her arms around his waist from behind, resting her cheek against the warm skin of his back. "Breakfast smells wonderful."

He turned from his work, lips puckered, and Margaret pushed onto her tiptoes and kissed him. "The tea should be brewed by now. Pour yourself a cup. The eggs are almost ready."

Margaret headed to the table and poured tea into both cups, adding cream and sugar to hers, and a single lump of sugar to Oliver's. Pulling out the seat, she crossed her legs and rested her cheek on her palm, watching as he finished cooking. His back flexed as his arm pushed the eggs around the skillet, his bare feet peeking out from the hem of his trousers. His hair stood like a rooster's comb on one side of his head, the brown tufts defying gravity. She smiled when he turned towards her, skillet and spatula in hand, and placed the finished eggs on top of the toast. "Eat while it's warm."

Oliver set the skillet back on the stove, then took the seat across from her. They shared the plate, their forks occasionally scraping against one another as they took bites of the scrumptious eggs, their slurps of tea the only sound filling the kitchen. When the plate was clean,

Margaret picked them up and headed to the wash bins. "You cooked; I'll clean. Go get ready."

Oliver reached around her and kissed her cheek. "I'll be back soon."

Margaret hummed her reply, leaning into his embrace before returning to the dishes before her. Scrubbing each dish, she rinsed them in the clean water before drying them with a towel and stacking them back on the shelf that hung over the bins. Rinsing the skillet with water, Margaret swiped it with a rag before placing it back on the stove. Wiping the table with the cloth, she pushed in the chairs and looked over her work. It still left her stunned that in only a short period of time she had settled into taking care of herself. Chores that had seemed terrifying mere months ago were now second nature. Within a few minutes, she had set his kitchen back to rights, allowing their day to begin. All that was missing was Oliver.

As if he knew she was thinking of him, he slid up behind her, his arms encircling her waist from behind, his lips finding the delicate curve between her shoulder and neck. He smelled clean, his jaw smooth against her skin, and she shivered. "Ready?" he asked.

Margaret nodded, and Oliver's hand reached for hers, leading her outside into the brisk morning. The sun had only begun to rise in the sky, its rays casting weak beams of orange over the hills, the light useless in guiding their way along the path to the manor. But they did not need it. They knew this route by heart, traversing it each morning to ensure they arrived at the estate before any of the other workers. Their relationship was not secret. No, Margaret did not care who knew about it, but it was theirs, a private thing just between them, and they preferred to keep it that way. Surely some workers knew, it was hard to stop herself from staring at him during the day, nor hide the smile she sent his way as their paths crossed, but if they did know of it, they kept it to themselves.

Margaret squeezed Oliver's hand as they reached the meadow, the clearing alight like a pile of golden straw as the sun hit each strand. "Wait," she whispered, pulling him to a stop. "It's beautiful."

Oliver stopped beside her, his gaze taking in the same terrain as she. Margaret watched as the wind whistled past, the plants swaying like a gilded sea before them, and she squeezed Oliver's hand, wishing she could save the image before her forever. Oliver slid behind her, wrapping his arms around her shoulders in an embrace as he set his head upon hers. They stood like that for a time, neither speaking as the sun worked its magic on the meadow.

"We should get married here," he said, the words a whisper.

"Pardon?"

Oliver tucked his head into her ear. "Marry me here? Now? Just us, you and me." He Smiled. "Oliver and Meg."

Margaret smiled and turned in his arms, cupping his cheek with her hands. It was a spontaneous request, one made fully by the heart with little interaction from the head, and while any other time, she might have stumbled at the question, she followed his direction and let her heart lead as well. "All right."

Oliver kissed her palm before taking her hand and

walking her towards a small clearing in the meadow. The sunlight created a halo behind his brown locks, and Margaret's breath caught as she looked at him. He took both of her hands in his, kissing her knuckles before looking at her.

"I will honor and respect you. I will share in your pain and seek to ease it. I will share the burdens so that we grow together. I will bask in your joy and search for your light in the darkest of times. I promise all of this, through whatever life may bring, until the end of my days," he said, his voice a whisper in the dewy morning light.

Tears clouded Margaret's vision as Oliver spoke his vows, his hands squeezing hers lightly when his voice cracked from emotion. Margaret wiped at the tear that fell down her cheek before repeating his words. "I will honor and respect you. I will share in your pain and seek to ease it. I will share the burdens so that we grow together. I will bask in your joy and search for your light in the darkest of times. I promise all of this, through whatever life may bring, until the end of my days," she said, as tears fell.

Oliver smiled at her, his eyes clouded, before pulling her to him and kissing her, his lips sealing against hers as his hands cupped her cheeks. "I love you," he said as he drew back.

"I love you."

Oliver pulled her into a hug, his hand burying in her hair as he held her close. Margaret wrapped her arms around his waist, unable to get any closer, but still not feeling like it was enough. "We just did that," she said with a laugh.

"We did. Legalities be damned." He chuckled into her

hair. "Hello, Mrs. Margaret Ludlow."

Margaret laughed and looked at him. "Good morning, Mr. Ludlow. Shall we head to work?"

Oliver smiled and nodded. "We're celebrating our nuptials tonight, Mrs. Ludlow, so be sure to be on time for dinner or you'll have a very irksome husband to answer to."

Margaret wrinkled her nose, laughing at Oliver's words. "I'll be on time, husband."

As they walked towards the manor, their hands still clasped, the joy of the moment eclipsing all other emotions, Margaret could not seem to wipe the ridiculous grin off her face. It surely must be sinful to be this happy. The bright horizon assuredly could only hold good things for them from now on.

CHAPTER SEVENTEEN

THE TOWN FÊTE held in Woodingdean that weekend created a bucolic backdrop for Oliver and Meg. Walking hand in hand to the village, Oliver could not help the smile that took over his face as he looked at Meg, her eyes alight with pleasure as she took in her surroundings. Stalls with townsfolk selling pickles and jams, along with cakes and puddings, lined the village green, and people mingled around a small stage where a man played a fiddle while a young boy danced.

Meg clapped her hands when they finished their song, sticking two fingers between her lips and whistling, the sound piercing. Oliver laughed and her cheeks flushed. "I've never been to a fête before."

"I haven't been to one in a long time," he said, taking her hand and kissing her knuckles. "Let's see what all the fuss is about."

They headed to a jam stall first, the proprietor a young mother with a babe on her hip while a toddler sat on a crate, their legs kicking against the wooden side. "Lila, please stop," the mother said, a pained smile on her face as she looked at Oliver and Meg. Meg wasted little time assuring the woman that the girl was no trouble at all, then asked about her three varieties of jam while shooting smiles and winks at the small girl.

The woman opened a jar of peach preserves, dabbing a small bite onto a piece of bread, and handed it to Oliver. The taste was astounding; cinnamon and clove swirling with the peach. It was almost as if he ate cobbler instead of bread and Oliver sighed, certain he had found heaven. Meg laughed at him as he devoured the bread, then looked at the young lady. "We'll have a crate of the peach jam sent to Baron Manor, please."

The young woman gasped, but Meg was already squatting down to talk to the young girl, Lila. "What jam is your favorite?" Meg asked.

"The strawberry," Lila said, her voice soft.

"Well, that settles it." Meg nodded and stood. "We'll have a crate of the strawberry as well." Oliver smiled as he watched Meg coo over the small babe and give a kind smile to the woman before waving goodbye to Lila as they headed to the next stall.

"That was very kind of you."

Meg shrugged. "If my kindness helps one person, I'll call it a good day."

Meg proceeded to spread her kindness to every stall, purchasing a wheel of cheese from one and a shawl from another. They paid for two meat pies and a pint of ale and commandeered a tree to sit beneath, watching as the townsfolk mingled, the man and boy playing another sprightly tune on the fiddle.

Meg sighed and leaned against his shoulder, her hand seeking his and entwining their fingers. "This is fun."

Oliver smiled. It did not need a response. It was fun, spending the day with her, laughing as she made jokes with the stall owners, his chest swelling with pride as she gave bit by bit of precious coin to the people of Woodingdean. As she sampled a sweetmeat made by the local tea shop, Meg had done a small dance, her joy at the treat so overwhelming that her body required a way to show its delight, and Oliver had laughed, the movement making the woman altogether that much more adorable. She embraced life with enthusiasm, trying everything and laughing at herself when she found something she did not like.

Meg was a ray of sunshine. His ray of sunshine. His wife.

Even though they were both aware that their vows held little meaning in the eyes of the Church of England, Oliver could not help but feel that their commitment was just as valid as any other. He knew well that when his time neared its end, they would need to discuss what it all meant, but that was a worry for another time. Right now, their days had taken on a ritual so familiar it was as if they had been together twenty years instead of twenty days. It made little sense, even to him, but it felt right. It was right.

An older woman in a flowing pink dress stood at a booth, her trinkets catching the sun creating a rainbow of colors on the ground before it. Oliver kissed Meg's head and untwined his fingers. "I'll be right back."

At the booth, necklaces, rings, and bracelets sat on a red piece of cloth that covered the wooden surface. Each piece was exceptional, the designs uniquely their own, and Oliver smiled at the older woman. "These are beautiful."

"I made them myself, or used to." She held up her hands, the fingers bent at each knuckle. "My hands aren't what they used to be." She motioned to the pieces before her. "See anything that catches your interest?"

Oliver eyed the bobbles. The pieces were of excellent quality, but nothing like the exquisite jewelry he could purchase for Meg back in London. He wanted to cover her in jewels and diamonds, but the notion was absurd and Meg would no doubt tell him it was a waste of money. Oliver shook his head at her.

"I don't think—" His words trailed off. A necklace sat near the edge of the bright fabric, its stone glinting in the sunlight. The pendant was shaped like the sun, its rays made of gold, while the center contained a stone that looked nearly milky white in the sunshine. Along the chain, small beads of gold were spaced out evenly, as if stars that were meant to merely accompany the sun as it shone. "This one," he said, pointing to it.

"I made this decades ago. It's a wonder it caught your eye," she said, as she picked it up and handed it to him. The metal was warm in his hands, the stone glinting as he moved it back and forth.

"What is this called?"

"That's a moonstone. It brings the wearer good fortune, especially in love." She winked at him, and Oliver laughed.

"I'll take it."

Paying for his present, Oliver tucked the necklace in his pocket and walked back towards the tree to find Meg. The space they had sat in for luncheon lay empty and Oliver frowned as he turned toward the village green, his eyes scanning the crowd for a petite brunette in trousers and a shirt. Cheering and clapping erupted at the stage and Oliver made his way toward the sound, certain Meg would be among the onlookers.

The father and son played a spritely melody, the young boy now playing a fiddle as well and keeping pace with his father as couples danced amid a circle the crowd had created. Meg and Marty were one such pair, dancing with exuberance as they laughed loudly, their joy palpable. Hands on each other's hips, the pair spun in circles before switching directions; the crowd cheering their excitement as the two danced. Oliver stood and watched, a smile taking over his lips. How could he do anything but smile as the woman he loved danced with delight beside her friend? A push sent him forward, and he spotted Felix behind him, the young lad sporting a bright grin as he shoved at him again. "Dance with her, my lord."

Oliver laughed at the boy's antics and turned back to Meg, who held out her hand to him, his siren luring him to her. Oliver took her outstretched hand and wrapped his other arm around her waist, spinning her around as the crowd cheered. Her body sunk into his, allowing him to guide their movements, and Oliver thrilled in her trust. The hand around his shoulder crept into his hair, her nails scraping his scalp as she leaned into him, her laugh a melody in itself. "Did you miss me?" she asked.

"Always," he said beside her ear, placing a kiss on her cheek.

"We could do this all night. Dance here beneath the stars and moon."

"I think you'd eventually become cold, and I know you'd want me to feed you."

Meg pulled back and pouted. Oliver kissed her fore-head. "You know I'm right, but yes, let's do this all night.

Under the moon and stars, as the sun comes up over the hills. Until we're old and grey."

Her smile was brilliant, and she threw her arms around his neck before leaning into him. The crowd shouted, some even whistled, and Oliver could only laugh as he pressed a kiss to her cheek, uncertain if one human was allowed to be this happy in their lifetime. "I love you," he said, just for her ears.

"I love you."

The song changed, the young boy setting down his fiddle to dance once more and the surrounding people turned their attention to the pair, losing interest in the lord and lady who were so obviously besotted with one another.

Oliver took her hand and walked over to the tree they sat at before. Meg leaned against him, her arms wrapping around his waist from behind, her breath warm against his back. "This was fun," she said, smothering a yawn into his back. "A perfect day."

Oliver turned in her arms and wrapped her in his embrace, and Meg snuggled into his chest, her body soft and warm. "Are you sleepy, love?"

"Perhaps a bit," she said. "My husband kept me up late last night."

Oliver laughed and kissed her cheek. "You liked it," he said, his voice a growl as he remembered the night before. A tangle of limbs and whimpers of pleasure had filled their time while the world had slept, and though his body ached from lack of sleep, he would not change a second of it. "Let's get you home, wife."

Oliver tucked a strand of hair behind Meg's ear and

led her to the path back to Bellawink. They walked along, hands entwined. When the cottage appeared before them, Meg followed Oliver into the greenhouse as he watered and checked on his plants. The spinach was now over-grown bushes, their leaves nearly ready for harvest, and while each had done surprisingly well, the goose manure had won by a landslide. The plant had taken over the shelf where the rest of the spinach resided. Meg had taken to calling him Gilbert, claiming that something that large needed a name, and he secretly agreed with her. Gilbert was a force and would make for an eventually delicious meal.

When the watering and measuring were done, Oliver knelt before a sleepy Meg who sat huddled on a confiscat-ed armchair he had placed in the corner. "Bedtime," he said, cupping her cheek. Meg wrapped her arms around his neck and Oliver picked her up, her legs wrapping around his waist as she clung to him as a small child would. She snuggled into his embrace as he brought her to his bedroom, removing her boots and braid before tucking her into bed. "Are you hungry?" he asked, rubbing his nose against hers.

"Yes," she said, rolling over, the words muffled in the pillow.

Oliver laughed before dropping another kiss on her head and heading back to the kitchen. Throwing together a couple of rough sandwiches and a kettle of tea, he made his way back to the bedroom, Meg's light snores filling the room. The woman did nothing in half measures, eating and sleeping included, and Oliver chose to let her rest instead of waking her. Settling on top of the covers next to her, he watched her sleep, her breathing even, eyes fluttering as she traversed dreamland. A strand of hair fell across her face, her nose wrinkling as it tickled her, and Oliver tucked it behind her ear, smiling to himself.

"What are you smiling about?" she asked, her voice a croak.

"I thought you were sleeping?"

"I only needed a quick nap. Now I'm ready for anything," she said, rolling onto her side, her hand coming up to his cheek. "Why are you smiling?"

"Because I'm happy." It was a simple answer, but it was the truth.

"Me too."

He kissed her palm, suddenly remembering his gift. "I got you something."

Meg sat up as Oliver reached into his pocket and withdrew the parcel of paper the old woman had wrapped the necklace in. Handing it to Meg, he held his breath as she opened it, her mouth forming an O of surprise. "Oliver, it's beautiful." She shoved it into his hand and turned around. "Put it on me?"

Opening the clasp, he placed it around her neck, adjusting it behind her hair before pulling back as she showed him. The gold necklace was dainty against her chest, the sun settling right beneath her collarbone, its moonstone sparkling as it caught the last tendrils of light that filled the room. "Well?" she asked. "How does it look?"

"Beautiful. You look beautiful."

Meg launched herself at him, and Oliver hugged her close. "Thank you. It's perfect."

Her lips covered his, her kiss soft and sweet, and it said everything and more. When she pulled back, she smiled at him, her riot of curls falling forward across her face. Pushing the strands behind her ear, Oliver cupped her neck, pulling her forward and brushing his lips against hers. Meg's gasp forced a smile to his lips, and he did it once more, if only to hear the sweet sound again.

Hand on her hips, Oliver slid his fingers beneath her shirt, bare skin meeting his fingertips, setting him ablaze. Drawing back, Oliver looked at Meg, her eyes hazy as she watched him, a soft smile on her lips. "Yes?" he asked.

"Yes," she said, pushing onto her knees and kissing him, her tongue twirling against the seam of his lips.

Oliver wasted little time pulling the shirt over his head before settling back on his heels to watch her. Meg licked her lips as her gaze traveled over him and he trembled under her appraisal, his heart beating so fast he could hear it in his ears.

"Beautiful. So beautiful," she said, repeating his words from before and Oliver laughed as he slid his hands to her waist and lifted the shirt off of her. Bare before him, it still poleaxed Oliver the blow her beauty dealt him each time he looked at her. He needed to touch her, to taste her. His lips found the jointure of her neck and shoulder and he pressed soft kisses there, working his way along the expanse of skin leading to her jaw. She leaned backward, her hands wrapping around him as she drew him down with her, his body blanketing hers as he worshipped her.

Hands danced across his back, their touch eliciting a fire only she could create, and Oliver captured her lips in a searing kiss, attempting to convey the depth with which she shook him. Both pairs of trousers were removed with haste and Oliver settled back over her, his groan of appreciation as his sex touched hers eliciting a laugh from Meg. "You've never been inside me," she said with a whisper, her lips against his jaw as her fingers danced upon his cock.

Oliver moaned; his eyes closed as she stroked his hard length. "I didn't want to risk getting you with child. It's your body and your choice whether we take that step."

"Is there a way to prevent getting with a child when you're inside me?" Her hand stopped its ministrations and Oliver rested his head on her collarbone. "Marty said there's a sheath?"

Oliver shook his head. "That takes too long to prepare."

"Oh," she said, resuming her stroking, and Oliver's thoughts stumbled.

"I can pull out before my pleasure, but there's still a chance…" he said, the words trailing off.

Meg squeezed him. "Yes."

Pulling back, Oliver met her gaze, her chocolate brown eyes. "Are you sure?"

"Yes." Her hand left his sex and trailed up his chest before cupping his neck. "Yes."

Oliver took her mouth with his, his body returning to the cradle hers made for him, and he kissed her with everything he had, every breath in his body and drop of love in his heart. Meg whimpered beneath him, her nails scraping his back as she rubbed her sex back and forth across his cock, stimulating herself. For a moment he wondered if they could both find release this way, but the thought drifted as his hips pulled back and the tip of his sex nudged her damp entrance. His groan and her moan mingled together, the sound a beautiful symphony, and Oliver pulled back to look at her.

Curls spread like the tantalizing snakes of Medusa, brown eyes hazy, clouded with need. Dusky lips swollen from his kiss and pink cheeks flushed with pleasure. "Are you sure?" he asked once more, wanting to ensure the decision was sorely hers.

"I want to feel you move inside me." The words were liquid smoke, husky in the dark room, and Oliver swallowed, uncertain if he would survive this, let alone the night.

Notching the crown of his cock into her sex, Oliver slid inside Meg, her warm sheath enfolding him in tight, wet heat, and his eyes crossed at the pleasure.

"Oliver," she said, the words a breathy sigh as she clung to him.

"Good?"

She moaned her answer, and Oliver opened his eyes to look at her. She was gorgeous, laid out in his bed as she was and he wished he could save the image to his memory. "I need…" the words were gasped as he shifted his hips and he kissed her lips as he found a rhythm. "Oh," she said.

Lacing his hand with hers, Oliver let his other hand drift to where they were connected, his fingers playing at the sweet bud of her sex, circling it as his cock slid in and out of her, stoking the fire in both of them. "Yes?" he asked.

"Yes." The word was a gasp as her hips raised to meet

his, her teeth worrying her bottom lip as her sex tightened around him. Her moans grew louder as he moved above her and Oliver, who had never been a praying man, began to plead with an unknown force as his pleasure grew.

"Meg?"

"Oliver."

His fingers swirled and danced against the bud of her sex, his vision clouding as his peak approached. "Fuck, Meg?"

She screamed, her sex clenching and unclenching his cock as her pleasure threw her off the cliff and Oliver held on, desperate to see the full extent, but even as he battled through the exquisite torture of her climax, he felt his balls draw up and knew he was lost.

Pulling himself from her, Oliver pumped once, twice against the lips of her sex before euphoria took him with a shout of pleasure, his delight so great he was certain he would die. But die happy he would. With a sigh, Oliver fell to his forearms, bracketing himself over Meg as he caught his breath, her vanilla tinged spice filling each lungful, surrounding him in her.

She laughed against his chest, and Oliver looked down at her with a raised brow. "I know I've said it before," she said, "But, goodness."

The smile her words created did not leave his face even as he cleaned up the mess he had made. Even while he tucked them both in beneath the covers, and even as he drifted off to sleep with Meg in his arms.

When morning came, Oliver awoke with her still wrapped around him, her breathing soft against his shoulder. A new week of work would begin at the manor, the interior repairs nearly finished, with the outside close behind. Meg had spent her days indoors deciding on paint colors and furnishings, and this week would surely be no different. Oliver ran his hands through her hair, kissing her forehead. "It's time to get up, sleepyhead."

Meg groaned, rolling her head into the pillow, and Oliver laughed. His wife was not one for mornings. Once they returned to London, and their marriage became official, he would let her sleep to her heart's content, but until then, her ever present rooster he would be.

A sharp knock at the cottage door had him pulling out his timepiece from the pocket of his trousers. It was much too early for anyone to need either of them, but when the knock sounded again, Oliver pulled back the sheets and put on his trousers. A man in blue livery stood at the door, rocking from one foot to another while the horse behind him panted, blowing warm puffs of air into the cool morning.

"My lord, it was asked that I give this to you as soon as possible."

Blue livery. The Duke of Hedley had come calling a week early. "Does he require a response?" The man shook his head and stepped back, giving a bow.

Oliver closed the door behind him, irritation biting as he walked towards the bedroom, his fingers tearing open the note. His father had been so understanding of his need for solitude and yet dared to send a letter a week before he was due to come home. Opening the door to the bedroom, Oliver scanned the letter, the blood rushing from his head as he read the words repeatedly.

"Who was it?" Meg asked, her voice still husky from

sleep.

"My father." Oliver looked at Meg, the look of surprise on her face nothing compared to the dread that fueled his emotions. The devil had finally come to call. "My father is terribly sick, unresponsive. His doctor recommends that I come to London quickly."

CHAPTER EIGHTEEN

MARGARET'S STOMACH PITCHED at Oliver's words; the feeling so sudden, she was certain this was a dream. But the look on his face, skin pale, eyes solemn as he scanned the letter, only confirmed what he said. "Then you need to go to him."

It was the right thing to say, obviously, but the words were ash in her mouth. Their time in Woodingdean was ending far too soon, the dream-like realm they had occupied becoming little more than a memory.

"You'll come with me? I can't do this without you beside me."

Margaret shook her head. "I can't. Surely you must understand why. There's still so much left to do at the manor and we both know how it would look if we returned together."

Oliver frowned but said nothing and for a moment, she wondered if she had let him down. Determined to do everything she could to help him get off to London with haste, she stood, pulling on her shirt and trousers before going to him and wrapping him in a hug. "You need to go. Don't worry about anything else. Let's just get you there."

Oliver nodded, his gaze far off as if the shock had taken over. Margaret pulled him over to the bed and had him sit, then took up his traveling case and folded the small number of clothes that he had brought with him, before setting them inside. She placed his brush and comb on top and folded it closed before looking at him. "Get yourself dressed. I'm going to talk to the footman and see what is being done in terms of transportation to London." She frowned as the words left her mouth. It would seem the mannerisms of London were much harder to exorcize than she had expected.

After speaking with the footman, and learning that the carriage team at the inn had been alerted, Margaret went back to the bedroom. Oliver stood dressed beside the bed, albeit far less put together than she had ever seen him. "The carriage will be here shortly."

"Right," he said, nodding his head and picking up his valise.

Margaret took his hand and squeezed it, leading him out the door. The carriage pulled into the drive; the team moving with a speed that only lent weight to the sudden need for him to get to London. Oliver set down his valise and looked at her, cupping her cheek. "Are you sure you can't come with me?" he asked.

Margaret shook her head. "You know I can't. You need to focus on your father and I have a litany of things to do here." It was an excuse, and she knew it, yet it felt safe to hide behind the house and its tasks than confront what returning to London would mean.

"A week," Oliver said, looking at the waiting carriage.

"What?"

"Finish what you need to do here and come to London in a week." He took her hands. "Please. Please, Meg. Say you'll come."

Margaret bit the inside of her cheek. Now was not the time to have a conversation about her concerns regarding returning to London. She looked at the carriage; the horses prancing with anxious energy to get going while the footmen stood by, awaiting Oliver. Pinching her lips together, Margaret nodded her head.

"I love you." Oliver leaned forward and kissed her hard. Margaret held him close, aching to remember the feel of him, his taste. When he pulled back, she nearly cried out, but swallowed the sound as she let him go. Oliver jumped into the carriage, the door closing with a snap behind him. The window lowered as the horses moved. "One week. I'll see you in one week."

Margaret held up her hand, watching as the carriage pulled out of the drive, and then out of sight. "I love you."

Turning back to the house, Margaret walked through the rooms, tidying the items Oliver had left out, remaking the bed, and dousing what was left of the fire in the fireplace. The notion of returning to London, even with Oliver by her side left a tightness in her throat that became cloying when she thought too hard on it. Instead, she let the tasks take over. It was an act of mourning, walking through the rooms they had shared the past three weeks and closing them down, along with the memories they had made. The Pettigrew's would no doubt clean the home and cover the furniture, but Meg needed the movements, if only for self-preservation. Packing away the little food left into the cellar, Margaret shut the door behind her, the snick of it closing a sad last note of a beautiful symphony.

The greenhouse stood before her, and Margaret almost

convinced herself not to go inside. They had spent too much time within its walls, Oliver buried in his research as she wrote plans for the estate, but the knowledge that his beloved spinach plants resided within had her opening the door to check on them. She had watched him care for the plants multiple times and picked up the watering can, feeding each plant before taking the ruler and measuring their growth. His notebook sat on the worktable, and Margaret picked up the pencil and noted each piece of information. Oliver's chicken scratch filled the pages and Margaret's chest ached. He had left all of his hard work as he hurried back to London, but she knew how precious his father was to him, and a few plants were useless in comparison. Still...

Shuttering the greenhouse behind her, Margaret walked the path back to Baron, her heart heavy. Like a perfect holiday, their time in Woodingdean closed before she was ready for it to end, and even though a potential future together awaited in London, she mourned the life they had built here. Oliver's sudden departure had been a lightning strike, its reverberations felt in every nerve of her body. Even as their time together in Woodingdean had neared its end, they had still never specified what the future held and now, with its sudden arrival, she was not prepared to answer that question. It seemed that reality had come, whether or not she was ready for it.

Back at the manor, she walked the corridors of the home. The workers that remained were minimal now, the things left to be done trifling compared to when she had first arrived. Floors were now repaired and polished to a shine, the banister standing proudly in the foyer. The glass chandelier that had laid in a pile on the entryway floor now hung elegantly from a flowered ceiling medallion that Margaret had painted a robin's egg blue. And in the study, the winged backed chair that had stood like a soldier manning its post in the long-forgotten home had been reupholstered a rich forest green, the velvet a fitting uniform for one who had remained in the battlefield for far too long. The chair held a position of dignity before the fireplace, the gold and red tones of the room an appropriate backdrop to its new ensemble.

Margaret's desk was tucked into the corner of the room, its top filled with receipts and to-do lists of work yet to be completed, but they were all tasks left for her. They had restored the bones of Baron Manor, the dilapidated home now a shining beacon to all who needed it. Yes, it still required furnishings and household pieces, one could not eat soup with their hands, but it was a home. Yet, the space felt empty.

Without Oliver beside her, even just his presence within the space, the rooms stood hauntingly hollow. She had not realized how much space the man had taken up, not just in her home, but in her life.

"Goodness, why is it so quiet in here?" Marty asked from the doorway.

Her wonderful friend had offered to sew draperies for the master bedroom, but with all the disorder that morning, Margaret had completely forgotten. "I have drastically reduced the crew, since there are very few repairs left. It is rather spooky in here without them."

Marty smiled. "Afraid of ghosts, are we?"

Margaret laughed, the sound harsh. "I'd welcome

some entertainment."

"Is Lord Greenwood out in the gardens?" Margaret's mouth pulled into a frown and Marty stepped forward, her hand resting on Margaret's arm. "Meg? Is everything all right?"

Shaking her head, Margaret released a sigh. "Oliver has gone to London. His father is sick and requests him." Biting her lip, she looked at Marty. "He's asked me to meet him there in a week."

"What did you say?"

"I said yes, but…"

"But what? What is there to think about, Meg? You love this man and he loves you. Nothing is keeping you from being together."

Margaret rubbed her arms and looked at the green chair. Even with a new cloth draped around its frame, it was still the same chair that had sat in this manor for decades, withstanding the abuse of its owner and the eventual isolation as it was left alone to rot. No manner of fabrics and drapery could change that. Much like the chair, Margaret wondered if all that had been done in her escape from London was to cover herself with a new identity.

She had arrived in Woodingdean uncertain of not only who she was, but what she wanted out of this life of hers. The simplest solution had been to try on different traits to see what fit, her outlandish clothing choices and outspoken manner uncomfortable new behaviors that the old Margaret would have shuddered to see, but how can one be certain of what fits if one never tries it on? She was a blank canvas, attempting to discern what colors she longed to be, and amid that discovery, Oliver happened along.

He loved her, and she believed he did. The problem was, whom did he love? She could not even be certain of the person she wanted to be, the ending to the equation she had worked so hard on, so how was it possible that this wonderful man had any notion of her true identity when she did not know it herself? And what would happen if he realized that the person he fell in love with was a figment of his imagination? An experiment put on by a young woman with no notion as to who she was or who she wanted to be.

"I don't think I can go." The words were as loud as a shot in the quiet room.

"Why ever not?" Marty stared at her incredulously, and Margaret knew she could never explain it. How the fear of London and all it embodied made her break out into a cold sweat. How the notion of returning to that world, even with Oliver in it, sounded like a fate worse than death. Guilt ate at her as she thought about the repercussions her decision would have, how Oliver would come to hate her for abandoning him, but her fear was a bigger emotion. A larger monster. One she was not sure she would ever be strong enough to stand against.

Resigned with her decision, Margaret smiled at Marty. "Let's get started on the drapes."

Marty's mouth closed, her frown of disappointment doing little to ease the pain of Margaret's decision. "Meg, just-just promise me you'll think on it," she said, picking up the heavy violet fabric and carrying it up to the master bedroom with her.

The remaining days of the week flew by quickly, Marty saying nothing more as she arrived each morning to work on the draperies. But Margaret knew her friend wanted to interrogate her as the date loomed closer. It did little to help that Margaret's heart and head went back and forth on the decision, one day certain that when the time came she would go to him, the next terrified and changing her mind.

Exactly one week after Oliver had departed, a carriage arrived at Baron Manor, sporting the crest of the Duke of Hedley. The footman stood stunned when, instead of handing him her luggage, Margaret gave him a sealed letter asking for it to be delivered to Lord Greenwood with her apologies, then closed the door.

"All I'm saying is I think you'll regret this," Marty said with a shake of her head.

Perhaps she would. Hell, she already did. But she could do nothing of the terror that overtook her each time she imagined boarding a coach bound for London. Nor could she hide the uncertain truth that putting an end to their story would ensure Oliver would never come to regret falling in love with her.

> *Oliver,*
> *I cannot. I'm sorry.*
> *–Meg*

Meg,
Do you need more time? Take all that you need. I'll
be here waiting.
Missing you,
Oliver

CHAPTER NINETEEN

April 21, 1820
Six Months Later

D ANTE'S INFERNO NEVER stated directly that Almack's balls were one level of purgatory, but Oliver was certain it was merely a mistake made by its author. Certainly, Alighieri could not have known the intolerable pain one must face being crammed into a small, stuffy room, forced to suffer the attention of the Lady Patronesses' while swallowing lemonade so sour they surely made it of vinegar and not fruit.

No, Oliver would give Dante the benefit of the doubt. After all, no man can truly know everything.

But hell, it was.

"It's so warm I might as well be at a bath house getting my money's worth," Jamison Crenshaw, the Viscount of Averndale, said. "Why the devil are we here again?"

"Because it's what eligible young bachelors do when looking for a wife." Oliver scanned the crowd. "And don't curse. If Lady Jersey hears you, we'll no doubt be kicked out on our ears."

Averndale scowled at him before pasting a delighted smile on his angelic face and turning towards the crowd. "I'm not looking for a wife, Greenwood. That would be you. The devil knows why."

"Language," Oliver said under his breath. Not that Averndale was wrong. The man was far too young to be on the hunt for a wife, nearly five years younger than Oliver himself. Plus, the poor lad had some ungodly belief that the right woman would find him when the time was right. Oliver pitied the man his innocence, but would let age and experience teach him what love was really like. And while he certainly had no want to be at Almack's, or any other London society event for that matter, but title and lineage required it. His father had survived his illness, but the disease had left him bedridden, a shell of the man he had once been. So, while the dukedom remained entirely in his hands, the looming precipice of his father's end sat like a thundercloud on the horizon. So, a wife it was. And a real one this time. One who would show up when things became tough, and who would stand by his side, braced for the storm that no doubt would come.

Oliver pushed back the sadness and anger that threatened to overtake his evening and looked around the ballroom once more. Scads of young debutantes lined the fringes of the dancefloor, their doe-eyed faces alight with hope and disillusionment while their mothers stood stoically beside them, all too aware of what was at stake. Each eligible bachelor was a prize to be won, and they considered those who did not secure a proposal by the end of the season, the losers, forced to retreat until next year. The mama's eyed the men like prey and Oliver longed to pull at his cravat as they paraded daughter after daughter before him.

Each girl was stunning, their manners refined and their speech eloquent, but his heart was persistent. The useless contraption would not release the image of a petite brunette in trousers, her freckle-filled face alight with joy as she walked beside him along a meadow in Woodingdean. Miss Daphne Ramsey had the unfortunate timing of standing before him just as his lips pressed into a scowl, and the poor girl gasped, covering her mouth at the sound.

"I'm terribly sorry, Miss Ramsey. I was thinking of something regarding my estate. I hope you won't take offence," Oliver said, his gaze softening at the sight of Meg's sister.

"No offense taken, my lord," her mother, Lady Veerson replied, a courteous smile pasted on her face. "Daphne knows very well the trials a man must face when tending to estate matters, don't you, my dear?" The woman did not wait for her daughter to reply. "I hope this evening has found you well, my lord?"

"It has." Reminded of his place, Oliver introduced Averndale to Lady Veerson and her daughter, frowning as the woman angled the girl away from Averndale as if he contained an unlikeable smell. Mere moments in the woman's presence, and he could already see why Meg had such a distaste for her parents. "I hope you both enjoy your evening," Oliver said with a bow. "If you'll excuse us."

Taking Averndale's arm, Oliver steered the man away

to the refreshment table. "What a terrible woman," he said, the words a whisper.

Averndale laughed, reaching for a glass of lemonade before removing his flask and spiking the drink. "You cannot blame the lady, Greenwood. Of the two of us, you're the better catch for her daughter. A future duke would be the coup of the season."

"Yes, well, her daughter is far too young to be of any interest." The man did not need to know that Miss Daphne Ramsey was the sister to the one woman he could not get out of his head. A simple scan of Debrett's had given Oliver all the information he had needed about Margaret Reedy and her family, and Lady Veerson would have very little luck in trying to match her youngest daughter with him. Not after her eldest had left him with nothing but scorch marks in place of a heart.

"The daughter seems fine, but one would require a death wish to have Lady Veerson as a mother-in-law. That woman is a monster in human skin. I still get tremors when I think of the cretin she married her eldest off to. Thank God the bastard died early." Averndale shivered as he drank, from the lemonade or the terror of Meg's husband, Oliver could only guess.

"On that, we can agree." Removing his pocket watch, Oliver released a sigh. "I'm heading home."

Averndale frowned at him. "The least you could do is buy me a meal for making me come to this abomination with you."

"Have them put it on my tab at White's." Slapping Averndale on the shoulder, Oliver headed towards the door but pulled up short as he spotted a petite brunette with her back to him, talking with a group of young women. His heart thudded in his chest as he watched her turn and examine the ballroom, then fell as her face came into view. It was not Meg.

With a shake of his head, he left the assembly room. Inside his carriage, Oliver cupped his head in his hands. In the past months, there had only been a handful of times he swore he saw her, but his mind was always playing tricks on him. Meg was no doubt still in Woodingdean, living her life in that enormous home, surrounded by those she longed to help. How many times would it take for him to realize that it would never be her? That she would never come?

Oliver withdrew the letter he had always tucked inside his breast pocket. Her only note to him had become a worn piece of paper, its edges opened and closed so many times that they threatened to tear at the slightest mistreatment, but he could not leave it at home. It had become his talisman. His calling card. The last piece of her he had left. The only thing that remained, proving their time together had not been a figment of his imagination. When it had arrived, he was certain something had come up at the manor, that she merely needed more time before she could come to him.

But as his letters went unanswered, and time trudged on without a word from her, he knew. She was not coming, would never come.

Disbelief had hit him, blindsiding him, certain he had misread her words and actions, but no. Her silence spoke volumes into the void she had left him in. They were not enough. He was not enough. He wanted to return to

Woodingdean, to scream and cry, to beg her to explain, but all of that would lead to nothing but more heartache. She knew where to find him, knew he needed her, missed her. And she had made her choice.

It was this resignation that now filled the space she had taken up. A numbing quality that only throbbed when you poked it, so he left it alone. To carry her letter as a reminder of how stupid he had once been. A reminder that even the greatest love stories have sad endings.

When the carriage stopped at his father's Mayfair home, Oliver exited the carriage and headed inside. They had already dimmed the lights for the evening as he climbed the stairs to his father's room. He pasted a smile on his face before giving a brief knock on the door and heading inside.

Reginald Ludlow, Duke of Hedley, a man whose presence had once filled a room with joy and laughter, now sat diminished in his gigantic bed. His body took up little space, the sheets barely creating an outline of his frame. "Good evening, Papa," Oliver said, forcing a joyful note to his voice that he very much did not feel.

The sickness that had overtaken his father had left him weak and thin, his limbs more bone than muscle. Each meal was a daunting task, leaving him exhausted after only a few bites, and his doctor was not very hopeful that the duke would turn around. He warned Oliver to brace for a steady decline, and as the days passed and his father became weaker, Oliver feared the worst.

"Ollie," his father said, pushing up to sit. His valet, Terrance, set down his book and helped the duke, placing pillows behind his back to help prop him up. "How was the assembly room tonight, my boy?"

Oliver laughed, sitting on the bed beside Reginald. "The usual, I'm afraid. Poor excuse for refreshments and far too many bodies."

His father chuckled, the sound scratchy. "Almack's was always a terrible place to start a season." His father wiped at his lips with a white linen handkerchief, collecting the small bit of spittle that had accumulated there. "Anyone catch your interest?"

Oliver shook his head, taking his father's hand in his. "Not yet, but the season is still young. Perhaps the Mayberry ball will be different."

His father patted his hand. "Location doesn't matter, my boy. Love happens when it happens." With a sigh, Reginald leaned back, and Oliver grabbed another pillow and placed it behind his head. Sitting upright for long periods had become an exhausting affair for the duke, and Oliver's heart ached as his father's deteriorating body failed.

"I'm not so sure I'll find love," Oliver said, his words soft.

"Ollie, you are much too young to be this cynical."

Oliver laughed and leaned against the headboard beside his father, the man's hand still clasped in his. "That's the very reason I need you around. You're a fount of knowledge. Think of all the trouble I will get into without your guidance."

Reginald squeezed his hand. "I know, but your mother is calling to me. I hear her voice more clearly each day." Oliver's stomach plummeted at the words. "I'll go when the time is right. When I'm certain you won't need me any longer."

"Well then, plan to be around forever, as I'm sure I will always need you."

His father laughed and rested his head on Oliver's shoulder, stifling a yawn with his other hand.

"My lord," Terrance said, "it's time for His Grace to take his medicine."

Oliver sighed and placed a kiss on his father's forehead. "You heard the man. Medicine and then off to bed with you. No mischief tonight, or I'll disown you for good."

"Buggar off, I'll do as I please," Reginald said with a wink as Oliver stood to leave. "Goodnight, Ollie boy. Sleep sweet."

"Night, Papa. I'll see you in the morning for breakfast." With a kiss on his father's cheek, Oliver left the room, his heart as heavy as his steps. His father's deterioration was just one more reality life had forced him to face and when Reginald finally left this earth, Oliver would be truly alone. Putting on a brave face for his sire was never easy, but the last thing he wanted was to worry the man. If his father felt Oliver was unprepared for the future that lie ahead, it would only worsen the guilt he already felt at falling ill so suddenly, and that was something Oliver could never allow.

So, marriage it was. Marriage and a child to continue the line, hopefully before his father left this world. And if his future wife did not have uncontrollable brown curls or eyes the color of whiskey. If she did not prance about their garden in breeches, allowing the wind free design of her hair, so be it, even if the notion caused him immeasurable discomfort.

The ducal duties he had been so afraid of back in Woodingdean had been quickly thrust upon him with his father's illness, the attention required so sudden that Oliver had little time to worry if he was doing it correctly or if he should be doing it at all. Instinct had taken over, as if he had absorbed the knowledge watching Christopher learn it, and he seamlessly stepped into the role. Now, instead of greenhouses and errant gardens, his days were filled with parliamentary sessions and meetings with the solicitor, his nights filled with ton activities.

In his room, Oliver poured two fingers of whiskey and sat in a chair before the fireplace. The heat from its blaze did little to warm him, but the whisky did the trick, as it always had. During the day, he was the dutiful son looking after his ailing father and their estates, accepting invitations to social events, the impeccable lord on the hunt for a wife.

But at night, the flames called to him, their dance and sounds taking him back in time to a small cottage and the dark-haired woman who had broken his heart. In his dreams, she would cradle his face and kiss away the tears, her arms a haven from the chaos that surrounded him, and for a time, he would know peace. Then he would awaken and do it all again.

Meg,
What is going on?
I sent a letter to Marty, who informed me that all
was well at Baron.
Why haven't you replied?
—Oliver

CHAPTER TWENTY

May 2, 1820

"YOU WILL LIVE beneath my roof for the duration of your time chaperoning Daphne, and furthermore, you will display poise and elegance both inside and outside of this home, which means you will rid yourself of that scandalous outfit and wear something more befitting a respectable, widowed countess."

Lord Veerson's voice very much sounded like the herd of cattle that had taken over the north field at Baron Manor, their incessant mooing an annoyance, but one she gladly put up with given their fluffy adorableness. Lord Veerson, however, was neither adorable nor fluffy as he paced the sitting room of his London townhome, waxing on about Margaret's requirements and failures, his words no doubt an attempt to insult and anger her, but they did nothing instead.

As if removed from the conversation entirely, Margaret

watched as her father lamented on, his barbs doing very little to gain a rise out of her. And if his scowl was any hint, the smile that painted her lips was doing nothing but anger him more. It was odd, really, how little she felt as she watched his diatribe of his daughter's failings. Meanwhile, her mother sat on a plum sofa drinking tea as if she were at a garden party. Very odd.

Standing, Margaret brushed at her scandalous skirts, the merlot fabric framed by black lace trim quite lovely in her opinion, and laughed as her father sputtered at her audacity. "My lord, it seems you have been met with some confusion. I am here to help aid you, not requesting aid. If you feel that my assistance is no longer required, I am more than happy to see myself out." Lord Veerson scowled at her, his heavy grey brow lowering menacingly. "However, considering that mother is unable to chaperone Daphne because of her unfortunate accident," Margaret motioned to the cane that sat propped beside the sofa, "it would seem you are not the one who should be giving demands."

"Margaret," Lady Veerson said from the sofa, her mouth dropped open like a fish on a hook. "How dare you talk to your father that way? He deserves your respect."

Margaret raised a brow at her mother. "And why is that? What actions has father done to show he deserves my love let alone my respect? I owe you both nothing and require nothing from you. It's you that requires my help, so perhaps you should start acting like it." Taking up her gloves and reticule off the couch, Margaret nodded her head at her sire. "I'll have the carriage around at eight to pick up Daphne for the Mayberry ball. Do be sure to have her ready on time."

Inside the carriage, Margaret laughed, her entire body shaking as she recalled the stunned looks on their faces as she had taken her leave. It served them right, really. After all, they were the ones who wrote to her begging for assistance after Lady Veerson had injured her leg, and then dared to make demands of her? To require that she move back into his home? Absolutely not. His sheer audacity was humorous.

Leaning against the seat, Margaret watched as London rolled by. The air still smelled of rot, its musty haze serving only to remind her of one of the multitudes of reasons she had left the wretched town in the first place. There was nothing good to be found in London, and in truth, the only reason she had returned was to ensure that Daphne did not end up in the same disastrous marriage she had, and from what she had learned from Daphne's pleading letters, it would seem that her fate might be the same. Their parents had threatened to betroth the poor girl to a man fifty years older should she fail to make a match this season, and Margaret would be damned if she allowed that to happen. If one of them could receive a happy ending, it was better than none.

In the past six months, her fear of London had dissipated with the winter chill, the image of the woman she had once been a frail mirage that could not stand up to the woman she had become. Now, the only piece that kept her on edge was the potential of seeing Oliver once more.

The pristine walls of the Earl of Everly's Mayfair home came into view, and Margaret swallowed down the fear that arose whenever the carriage pulled in front of the home. It did not matter that the place now belonged to Harrison, nor that the man was one of her dearest friends. Like a looming specter, anxiety clutched at her throat as she spotted the familiar door, its brass lion head knocker gleaming in the sunlight.

"Oh, piss off," she whispered under her breath, to the house or Everly's ghost she was not sure. The carriage pulled to a stop, and the footman opened the door for her, forcing her from her maudlin thoughts.

Sterns, ever the epitome of butler standards, already held the front door open to her, his smile the only thing un-butlery about him. "My lady," he said, taking her gloves and reticule. "The earl is in the drawing-room awaiting your return for teatime."

Margaret smiled. "Thank you," she whispered, sending a wink his way as she headed in the direction he indicated. The drawing-room, her favorite place in the entire home, was painted a soft taupe, its white and yellow accents filling the space with childlike charm. It had been a room Everly had never renovated, and Margaret was grateful for his oversight.

"Am I late?" she asked as she entered the room, the scent of tea and cake overtaking her.

"Right on time," Harrison said, ignoring propriety and pouring tea into the two cups.

Margaret sliced the cake, placing a piece on each plate before handing it to Harrison. When they both settled back with their snack, Margaret smiled at him. "How did you know I would need something sweet after answering Lord Veerson's missive?"

"Intuition," he said, sipping at his tea. "How did it go?"

Scrunching her nose, Margaret picked up her fork and took a bite of cake, compiling her thoughts as she enjoyed its sweetness. "Typical? He demanded I move back into his home, adjust my wardrobe, and bend to his will."

"Goodness," Harrison said, a laugh alighting the words. "And how did he handle your response?"

Margaret smiled at the memory, setting down her plate on the gilded table before removing her slippers and tucking her feet beneath her skirts. "Not well at all. I don't think either of them was quite prepared for their daughter from Woodingdean."

"Can't say I blame them, considering I wasn't ready for their daughter from Woodingdean." He winked at her as she sent a scowl his way. "But I'm delighted to have you, nevertheless. I missed you."

Margaret smiled. "I missed you, too." Setting her cup in its dish, she said, "I've been meaning to thank you for the letters you sent to Baron. It was the perfect touch of comfort I needed."

Harrison nodded, his gaze leaving hers to inspect his teacup. "I'm glad you enjoyed them."

"I did," she said. "I only wish I had written you back as often as you wrote. Every time I went to form a response another disaster seemed to happen at the manor. They don't tell you that bit of advice when you begin renovating an estate."

"Perhaps you should write a book on it."

Margaret laughed. "I'm a novice at renovations. If you could have seen the state I was in each day, you would have doubted I was the same person. Covered from head to toe in dirt and filth," Margaret shuddered, "I was a sight."

"I'm sure you're charming in every state, Meg. A bit of dirt won't put me off. I'll stand by your side bejeweled or mud covered, just as I always have."

Margaret finished her tea and cake, allowing the sweet treats to calm her nerves. The ball that evening would no doubt be a daunting affair, the ton certain to gossip at her sudden appearance, but Margaret could handle them, especially with Harrison by her side. However, the possibility of running into Oliver loomed largely in her mind.

"What do you know about the Duke of Hedley's heir?" she asked, scraping her fork along the last bit of frosting.

"Greenwood?" Harrison asked. "Decent man on all accounts. In the market for a wife, from what the gossip says."

"Really?" The pang of pain that hit near the vicinity of her heart threatened to leave her breathless, but it was her own fault. It was selfish of her to expect that he mourned their parting like a widowed sailor's wife, vowing to never love again, as she had. And it should not have surprised her in the least that Oliver would look to marry, especially given the duke's failing health, but it hurt just the same. Yet, who was she to say anything? She was the wench who had abandoned him to the evils of London. By all ac-counts, her feelings regarding his marriage did not matter, and never would.

"He was at Almack's a week ago with Lord Averndale

inspecting the season's new debutants. No doubt your sister was among the pack."

Margaret's stomach turned at the thought of Daphne marrying Oliver, but she pushed it aside. Her goal was to ensure Daphne married for happiness, if not love, and that was all that mattered. "I'm sure she was, under the tutelage of my mother, no doubt."

Harrison sipped his tea and looked at her, his gaze analyzing. "Why the interest in Greenwood? Contemplating making a foray into the marriage mart once more?"

"Heavens no," she said with a laugh. "I'm far too content with my life to even humor the notion." She shook her head. "No, merely assessing the prey."

"You'll have me by your side, so calm your worries regarding that. I know the best from the beastly, and I'll direct you both in the proper direction."

Harrison said the statement with his usual enthusiasm, and yet the words held little of the joy Margaret was used to. "What about you?" she asked. "The title does need a new countess."

"The title has a countess," he said.

"Harry, I'm not really the countess. Don't you want to marry? I'll happily step aside if it means you'll be content." Harrison stared at her hard, brow raised, and Margaret sat back, wondering at the look. "What?"

He shook his head, his cheerful smile returning to his face. "Nothing." With a look at his watch, Harrison stood. "I've a few more things to attend to, but will be ready to escort you and Daphne to the ball tonight."

"Thank you, Harry," Margaret said, the words quiet. "For allowing me to borrow your home, for standing by my side."

Harrison smiled at her. "It's your home too, Meg, and I'll always be by your side. No doubt about that." Harrison leaned over and dropped a kiss on her head before taking his leave, returning to his old bachelor residence where he was staying while she visited. With a frown, Margaret looked at the cake and tea, uncertain of how the atmosphere had shifted so suddenly. Perhaps it was simply that she had not fully recovered from the journey to London. Chalking up the unease to travel, Margaret left the drawing-room and headed for her bedroom.

Harrison had insisted that she retake the countess' apartments, but Margaret had swiftly declined, opting for a guest room that held little memory. Even though she was still the countess, the title felt like a jacket two sizes too small. The woman she had been in this home, in this town, was a shadow of the person she had become, and retracing her steps left her off-kilter. There was little use in denying that Margaret Reedy, Countess of Everly, was dead and buried.

After a nap and a bath, Margaret felt ready to take on the London social season. Dressed in a midnight blue gown with silver slippers, Margaret pulled white gloves up along her arms, covering the tanned skin. A stop at the modiste, and Harrison's heavy pockets, had given Margaret the wardrobe required to tend to chaperone duties, but clothing could only hide so much. Her arms, once soft and white, were now corded with lean muscle, their coloring no doubt a result of her time in the sun, and her hair had developed a wild curl that no iron could tame. To the London beauty standards, she would be an enigma, but for the first time in forever, Margaret was at home in her own body. With a last glance in the mirror, she shrugged and headed to the foyer to meet Harrison.

"Ready?" she asked, draping a silver spun shawl over her forearm as she descended the stairs.

Harrison nodded. "Madame Laroché did a magnificent job with that dress."

Margaret smiled. "It's exquisite. A bit more daunting than trousers and a shirt, but I like the effect."

Harrison shook his head before holding out his arm. "Right then. Let's be off to fetch young Daphne."

Arriving at her parent's home, Margaret kept her sentences brief as she collected Daphne and escorted her to the carriage. Her sister released a sigh as she settled into the cushioned seat beside her. "Nervous?" Margaret asked.

Daphne shook her head. "Relieved. Mother has been pestering me since the season began, determined I try every tactic to win over any eligible lord available. I've yet to actually enjoy an event."

"We'll be sure you enjoy every minute of tonight," Margaret said. "But before we get to that, a couple of rules. Stay where I can see you, no disappearing to the gardens with anyone, and I must approve of your dance partners."

Daphne groaned.

"Daph..."

"Deal," her sister said. "I'm sure I won't have a very full dance card to begin with. Mother has bothered everyone so much nobody will ask me."

"That can't be true." Margaret set her hand on her

sister's and squeezed it. "Perhaps with mother out of the way, these men will be able to see you for the gem you truly are."

"Well, you can be certain you will have at least one name on your dance card this evening," Harrison said from the seat across from them. "Put my name down for your first waltz, Daphne."

"Really?" Daphne asked. "Oh, Harry, thank you!"

Harrison waved her praise off. "We're nearly there. Armor on tight and smiles bright you two. To battle we go."

Once their carriage made its way through the line, Harrison descended first, holding out his hand to help down Daphne, then Margaret. The onlookers that surrounded them stopped and stared as Harrison held out his arms for the women to take, escorting them through the line to greet Lord and Lady Mayberry. Women whispered behind their fans while the gentleman stared at Margaret, their beady eyes making her skin break out in gooseflesh. "Hold strong," Harrison whispered in her ear.

Finally, they were through the line and ready to be announced. "Lord Everly, the Dowager Countess of Everly, Miss Ramsey," the man bellowed. A hush fell across the ballroom as they walked down the steps, and Margaret forced a serene smile to her lips as her eyes glanced over the crowd. Men and women she had once thought of as friends gaped at her as she descended the stairs, no doubt scandalized to see a widow so soon after her husband's death, and Margaret pushed her shoulders back and held her head high as she met each of their gazes. But a pair of green eyes nearly sent her stumbling.

Oliver stood to the side of the staircase; his gaze unreadable as he watched her. Margaret was suddenly aware of how tight the bodice of her gown was, how out of control her curls were, and that her gloved hand affectionately rested on Harrison's forearm. It did not matter that the man beside her was nothing more than a friend, not when Oliver's passive eyes stared at them. Margaret squeezed Harrison's arm, desperate for balance as they took the last steps into the room.

"Meg?" he asked beside her, but Margaret shook her head, Oliver never leaving her sight, but his words shook her, reminding her of where they were, and Margaret broke the spell and turned to Daphne.

"Do you see any friends you'd like to visit with?" Margaret asked.

Daphne nodded and pointed to a group of girls that waved to her, but before she could permit sending her off, a familiar voice spoke from beside her.

"Lord Everly, Lady Everly," he said with a bow. Margaret turned, her eyes meeting Oliver's brilliant gaze, but instead of its usual warmth, they held nothing but cool reserve before turning to her sister. "Miss Ramsey, it's a pleasure to see you again."

Daphne dipped a curtsey before Oliver. "Good evening, my lord. I'm pleased to see you once more as well."

Oliver offered Daphne a smile that Margaret had never seen before, cool and calculated. "Is your second dance available this evening?" he asked.

Daphne looked at her dance card and nodded. "It is, my lord."

"Wonderful. I'll look forward to it." He bowed. "Enjoy your evening, my lord." He looked at Margaret. "My lady."

Margaret watched him leave. "That was odd," Harrison said. "You would think you'd done something to upset him."

"I did."

Meg,
It has been a month without a word from you.
Is anything amiss?
–Oliver

CHAPTER TWENTY-ONE

O LIVER HAD LOST his mind. It was the only logical explanation to what came over him the moment he spotted Meg walking down those stairs on the arm of a young man. It was jealousy, envy, pure and simple. She had returned to London to be with her younger sister, but would not return for him, and she did so in the accompaniment of the new earl. His reasoning did little to excuse his behavior and, as he danced with Miss Ramsey, he could not help but chastise himself. And yet…

"How have you enjoyed the season so far, Miss Ramsey?" he asked as they waited at the end of the set, the other couples making their way down the line.

"The season has been very delightful, so far, my lord," she replied.

"That's wonderful to hear." Oliver looked at his dancing partner. "Your choice of chaperone has changed since I last saw you. What brought your sister back to London?"

"My mother injured her leg in an unfortunate accident

and Meg volunteered to chaperone," Miss Ramsey said, her eyes assessing him.

"She seems fond of the new earl."

Miss Ramsey nodded. "She's known Harry since she was wed. They're quite close, actually. The best of friends, if anyone were to ask."

Oliver nodded, taking up Miss Ramsey's hand as they danced along the line. His mind scrambled at her words. Meg was close to the young man. Was that the reason she had rejected him? Did she harbor feelings for the new earl? Had she pledged her troth in a sun-drenched meadow to this man as well?

When they paused once more, Oliver sighed, opening his mouth to speak, but Miss Ramsey beat him to it. "I don't know what sort of history you have with my sister, my lord, but I must say it was rather childish of you to invite me to dance only so you could gather information."

Oliver turned to look at the young miss whose astute remarks were not only similar to her sister's, but wholly called for. "You're right. I apologize, Miss Ramsey."

She waved a hand at him. "Nonsense. A duke's heir dancing with me will increase my worth in the eyes of the other gentleman, so thankfully, this has not been in vain." She looked at him with pity. "My advice would be to speak with her, my lord. Whatever is between you both will only be resolved once you speak to one another."

Oliver laughed at the simplicity of the idea. "If only it were that easy." Holding out his hand, he smiled at the girl. "Ready?"

She nodded, and they danced the remainder of the set without another word. When the music ended, Oliver returned her to Meg who stood on the side of the dance-floor watching them. The earl was nowhere to be found, and Oliver wondered that the man felt so confident, leaving such a wondrous creature alone to the serpents of London. Not only did Meg look like a goddess, her gown hugging each exquisite curve, but her aura gave off such confident pulses that one was unexpectedly drawn to her. Or perhaps it was just him. What he would not give to see her in breeches, her hair blowing in the wind, but he was certain either form would bewitch him, as it had always been.

"A moment of your time, my lord," Meg said to him before turning to Miss Ramsey. "Daphne, why don't you chat with your friends for a moment? I need to have a word with Lord Greenwood before your next dance."

Miss Ramsey nodded to her sister, heading into the crowd without a word, and Meg looked at him, her eyes hard. "Follow me."

Oliver trailed behind her as they made their way to the dimly lit balcony, the cool air refreshing as it hit his face, but the relief lasted only momentarily as Meg turned on him, her brown gaze furious. "Have you lost your mind?" she asked, her mouth pinched as frustration flowed from her in vicious waves. "Is your intent to get back at me? To strike at me by dancing with Daphne as if I were so menial of a creature to be swayed by jealousy?"

"You're right. I'm sorry," he said, his breath catching as her anger stoked a passion in her, her beauty only highlighted by the energy.

"You don't get to apologize; you don't get to crush this before I've even started."

Oliver smiled. "You're right. I'm sorry."

"Oliver…" she said, her voice exasperated.

"Yes, Meg?" he asked, stepping closer to her.

"You should yell at me, berate me. Tell me you have every right to dance with my sister because that is what eligible gentlemen do." Oliver lifted her chin so her eyes met his. "You shouldn't be nice to me."

"You're right, but I made a mistake and should apologize for it. While I have every right to dance with Miss Ramsey, it was uncouth of me to do so if I did it only intending to make you jealous."

She looked at him, her eyes searching, a frown affixed to her face. "Don't be a gentleman."

He raised a brow at her. "Why not?"

She shook her head. "Because it only makes me that much more of a villain. If you were cruel, at least then…"

"At least then you wouldn't feel so bad for leaving me?" The words, once said, were a bucket of ice thrown over his head and he stepped back from her, allowing his hand to fall from her face. "Is that what you want? To not feel bad for abandoning me when I needed you most?"

"Oliver…"

"Because you should feel bad. You're not the villain in our story, Meg. You're the coward."

Her mouth pinched, but she said nothing, her gaze still assessing him.

Oliver sighed, rubbing his hand across his face. "You look amazing, and I hate it. I hate that you seem fine after everything we've been through." He shook his head. Their surroundings were not the place to have this conversation, but he could not keep the words from his lips. "Why didn't you come? I asked you to meet me in London and you said you would, and then you simply don't? Send a letter with no explanation, nothing more than I'm sorry? I waited. I hoped maybe you were just delayed, maybe you were working up the courage to return, but I never heard from you after that." He groaned. "I wrote to you for weeks, Meg, and you never responded. And now you're here, and you're smiling and on the arm of another man. It's driving me crazy that you're happy."

"You knew where to find me," she said, the words soft.

Oliver scoffed. "Why would I do that after a multitude of unanswered letters? Why would I disgrace myself even more?" He swallowed, his throat tightening as he held back tears. "Was it a lie? Because it wasn't for me. I married you. I pictured a future together, a life just like we talked about."

Meg's eyes shined in the light from the lanterns, a single tear escaping, and it only made his heart ache more. "I missed you. I missed you and I needed you. It was so hard, and I was so scared," he said, his voice cracking. Meg came towards him and lifted her hand to his cheek, brushing at the moisture he had not realized accumulated there. "But you left me. You left me all alone," he said as she caressed his face. "And I hate you for it."

She nodded, tears falling freely. "I know."

Oliver lifted his hand, tucking a curl that had escaped behind her ear, and her familiar vanilla scent drifted to his nose. He wanted to hold her, to take her hand and leave the ball, escape back to Woodingdean and the cottage. Back to where they were simply Oliver and Meg, but too much had happened. The rift between them seemed too large to mend, and in truth, he was not sure he wanted to. With a forced breath, Oliver let his hand fall, stepping away from her. The hand that had cradled his cheek moments before fell to her side, even as her tears continued.

"I'm sorry to have done this here," he said, handing her his handkerchief. Meg took it, dabbing at her cheeks while the moisture still flowed freely.

"I can't seem to stop," she said, her voice hiccupping. "How silly of me."

The handkerchief became a sopping mess in her hands, but before Oliver could reach for her, a voice interrupted. "Meg? Are you all right?" the Earl of Everly asked.

Oliver took a step back, all too aware of how the moment looked to an outsider, but Meg merely brushed the man off. "I'm fine, Harry. Just reminiscing with an old friend."

Everly looked at Oliver, his brow lowered as he took them both in. "I don't think that's the case," Everly said.

Meg dabbed at her nose a final time before glaring at the earl. "That's enough, Harry. I'm quite all right. If you misunderstand the situation, I'll make you regret it, so be careful regarding what you say next."

Everly frowned but smartly kept his mouth closed. "I should return to my sister, my lord," Meg said with a sad smile. "It was lovely seeing you." With a curtsey, she took Everly's arm and allowed him to lead her back into the ballroom.

Oliver's chest throbbed as if someone had struck him with an iron, and this woman had the temerity to return to the social event as if nothing had transpired. "Fuck," he said, rubbing his face with his hands. It was only the beginning of the night and already he wanted to flee, but even at home, he would not find relief.

He was miserable. Unhappy with every aspect of the life he led. He was a marionette, going through the motions of the day to day. Meanwhile, his heart slowly died, fading away into nothingness. Oliver took the steps down to the Mayberry's garden, praying that the budding greenery would revive him in some way.

The plants were only starting to rally, their buds still hidden at the probable chance of another frost, yet they seemed hopeful. Far more hopeful than Oliver felt at that moment. The gravel path veered off into several directions and Oliver laughed at the irony, his knees giving out as he fell to the ground. The laughter turned manic, tears and chuffs mingling in a symphony of the wounded and it took everything in him not to scream at the sky. Instead, he let his emotions run rampant, unleashed and unhinged, a chaotic storm with no end in sight.

When the tempest finally slowed, he pushed up from his knees and dusted off his trousers. His handkerchief was long gone with Meg, so he wiped at his face with the sleeves of his jacket. Exhausted, he left the ball through the side gate, the guests unaware of his absence.

As he made his way onto the street, Oliver released a sigh. He needed to find his happiness if he was to survive this life he was required to partake in. The dukedom required him to do so, and he could surely not go on like this anymore. Starting tomorrow, he was determined to find out just what that happiness could be.

Meg,
Have I done something to upset you?
Whatever it is, please allow me to make it right.
I'll come back as soon as my father recovers,
I promise.
–Oliver

CHAPTER TWENTY-TWO

SIRIS' STRIDES WERE agitated as he raced along Rotten Row, dawn barely peeking over the horizon. Margaret knew it was her own fault. The poor dear no doubt felt her energy and was determined to rid them both of it, but all his pace did was fuel the turmoil that spun inside her.

The Mayberry ball had been a successful endeavor for Daphne. Oliver's invitation to dance, along with Harrison's, gave the young bucks of London Society the courage needed to approach her sister. In the nearly two weeks since the ball, the drawing-room of her parents' home had been filled with eligible young men, each vying for Daphne's attention. It helped enormously that her mother and father remained carefully tucked away during calling hours as not to scare away the young men. It seemed her threat of turning Daphne into a harridan like herself worked wonders in negotiating with her parents.

And yet, while Daphne's popularity grew, Margaret's

own inner battle raged harder each day. The look of absolute agony on Oliver's face was an image frozen in her mind, his pain so apparent, so abject, that it seemed to almost overflow. And it matched hers.

Day by day, she had pushed through the anguish of missing him. Reminded herself that there was no possible way he could love her when he did not know her. How could he when she had barely known herself? Yet all of those mantras fell away the moment Oliver came into view. His face was gaunt, his body leaner, a shell of the man she had known, and it hurt. It hurt to see him in such shape, to wonder at the damage she might have caused. Perhaps none at all. It was egotistical to think that her absence had left a single mark on him.

Margaret pulled Siris to a halt, leaning against his broad neck and wrapping her arms around him. "I'm sorry, lad, I'm sorry. My mind is in a chaos you no doubt feel."

Siris chuffed at her words, and Margaret buried her face in his mane. "I'm a horrible woman for doing that to you, love." She could not tell if she meant the words for the horse or Oliver, but they felt right. She was a terrible human.

Dismounting, Margaret grabbed Siris' lead and walked him to the side. Hyde Park was empty, the citizens of London either still asleep or already at work, and while the quiet was lovely, it also emphasized how separated she was.

Around this time at Baron, she would have already fed Siris and the cows, check the chickens for eggs, and let them out to roam, before returning to the manor and watering the vegetable garden. Mr. Howell and Felix would no doubt already be at the stable, tending to the other horses they had gained while Sam and his wife, Betty, prepared breakfast in the kitchen.

Baron had become a community, a haven for those who were adrift. How terrifying it would be for the occupants to learn that its owner was just as lost as them.

Stopping to let Siris munch on some grass, Margaret sat on the ground, grateful she thought to bring her trousers and linen shirts. It would have been nothing short of miserable if they had forced her to ride in a habit and while she had the modiste put together one for her wardrobe, it would no doubt sit errant in her room unless Daphne ventured out during the fashionable hour. Until then, she would stick with what was comfortable.

Footsteps crunched on the gravel, and Margaret groaned. Perhaps it was simply a good citizen of London passing through the park on their way to their job. However, given that it was Mayfair, she knew the odds were against her. The steps came closer, and it became too late to save herself. Tucking her head down, Margaret pulled the cap that sat on her head lower over her brow. No need for the interloper to know she was a woman. Maybe a deep-voiced *morning* would be enough to will the man away. For it was no doubt a man. The footsteps were sure-footed and heavy, their crunch on the gravel path certain.

"Siris? Never thought I'd see the likes of you in Hyde Park," Oliver said, his booted feet coming into view beneath her hat brim.

Raising her head, Margaret frowned at him. "Why the

devil not? He's just as good as any other horse."

Oliver laughed as he held out his hand for Siris to sniff. The mammal gave a delicate inhale before chuffing happily, his nose pushing into Oliver's hand with enthusiasm. "I'm sorry, lad, I don't have any sugar cubes on me. I wasn't aware I'd be seeing you, but next time," he said, the promise soft as he scratched the stallion's nose. He looked down at Margaret. "It wasn't an insult. More regarding location than qualifications. We both know Siris would have the ladies' hearts melting were he to be seen in public."

In the light of day, Oliver's cheeks seemed more sunken, his once healthy frame so lean it was a wonder he could stand. The blue coat he wore hung off him, looking as if it had been made for an entirely different man, and grey strands peppered his brown hair, shimmering in the sunlight.

Heat pulled at Margaret's cheeks. The whole dratted season had gotten her druthers up, and she could not be certain what comments were intended as a compliment or an insult. "I'm sorry," she said, smiling softly at him.

Oliver nodded. "Apology accepted." He continued to scratch Siris as Margaret stood up from her spot on the ground, the horse leaning into his caresses, and Margaret was envious. The pair were so apparent in their affection for one another, and Margaret wished it were that simple for herself. Wished she could simply walk into his arms, lean her cheek against his chest, and allow his presence to take the anxiety away. But Siris had done nothing to hurt Oliver. She had.

"I assume exercising this brute is what has you out in

the park this early?" Oliver asked, scratching behind Siris' ears. The big baby leaned into the caress, chuffing happily.

"Yes. He's cooped up the rest of the day, so I've taken to exercising him when the crowds won't be a bother." She allowed herself to fully look at him, his disheveled state and exhausted appearance leaving more questions than answers, for there could not be a proper reason for him to be out at such an hour.

Oliver laughed. "I'm sure the fashionable hour is not Siris' idea of a good time."

"The chaos of the city does not mesh well with a country horse," Margaret laughed and scratched at the back of her neck.

Oliver raised a brow at her. "Are we talking about you or the horse?"

Margaret smiled, unsure how to answer. He was not wrong. London was overwhelming. The noise and stench, the constant need to be on guard so you do not unexpectedly disgrace yourself or your reputation. It was exhausting. "Both."

"Mm," he said.

Clearing her throat, Margaret gestured to him. "What about you? It's rather early to be out."

Oliver frowned, his forehead wrinkling as he stared at Siris. "Hyde Park is the only place in London that reminds me of Woodingdean." He nodded his head as if the statement were correct, but the answer displeased him. "The quiet, the trees. The way the Serpentine rushes past the banks. It's not Bellawink by any means, but it brings some peace."

"Do you have a conservatory at your home here?"

Oliver nodded. "It's not the same as the greenhouse, but it works, although I have had little time to putter around with plants. Between my father's illness, managing the estates, and now the hunt for a wife..." he shook his head, "It leaves little time to experiment with any sort of fauna, let alone spinach plants."

Margaret nodded. "They take a great deal of work. The ones from Bellawink have kept me fairly busy, although I'm certain most of that time was because of inexperience as opposed to actual work."

He stopped petting Siris, who grunted in protest. "You have the plants from Bellawink?"

With a smile, Margaret met his gaze. "Yes. Gilbert, Salazar, Sisco, and Guinevere," she said, listing the names off.

"You named all of my spinach plants?"

"When you've nearly brought them to the brink of death only to revive them once more, a name seems fitting, don't you think?" His slack jaw did not agree. "But they're all the perfect picture of health now. Matter of fact, their children are being used in the vegetable garden at Baron."

"They've had offspring?" His voice cracked.

Margaret pinched her lips. "It took me some time to figure out how to propagate them, but once I did, I got several seedlings that seemed to have found the will to survive."

Oliver stared at her, his brow furrowed. "Help me to understand this. Not only did my spinach plants survive, but they are thriving at Baron? All four of them?"

"Yes," she said, scuffing her boot in the grass. "Well,

no, not at Baron any longer. I brought them with me to London."

"They're here?"

"Yes. Harry thought I was insane when I took over the conservatory, but they seem to have acclimated well to their new surroundings. I've harvested them once already to make a fabulous spinach soup. Even Harry was impressed with their bounty."

Oliver laughed, shaking his head.

"I sound insane," Margaret said, laughing with him. "I understand why you were so fascinated with them. Each centimeter they grew, each new leaf they produced, a yellow spot appearing one day." She shook her head. "It's exciting."

"I'm more amazed that you continued it. You even measured their growth?" He shook his head. "I'm glad they have you."

Margaret took up Siris' reins and laced them between her gloved fingers. "Would you like to see them?"

Oliver stared at her, and Margaret wondered if she had overstepped. Even though their conversation was pleasant, there was still so much turmoil between them. So much damage, of which she was not certain could be repaired.

"Not today, no. Thank you," he said. "Perhaps another time."

Margaret nodded, her lips pinched. Anything she could say to convince him to change his mind would only make him that much more aware of how much she missed him. Of how much she longed to increase their time together. She was the calmest she had been since she had arrived in London and she would be stupid if she did not realize that it had everything to do with him.

"I should be off," she said, directing Siris back towards the path. "Daphne is set to attend the Chalford's tea this afternoon." Mounting the large steed, Margaret looked down at Oliver. His gaze was hard, his lips pinched as he looked at her.

"Get home safely," he said. With a bow, he turned and walked away, his departure a strike to the heart if she ever felt one.

"It's for the best, Meg," she said, guiding Siris to the Grosvenor Gate exit, her heart heavy. "This is all for the best."

Yet as her steed made his way towards Harrison's home, Margaret wondered if that statement were true. Even with all the success Baron Manor had seen, with the community that had developed around it, she still felt empty. Not that she needed Oliver, no, of that much she knew to be true. But she wanted him. And with all the damage she had wrought, all the destruction she had created, that aspiration was entirely futile.

Even if he could forgive her for her absence, he would never forgive, nor understand, that she was not the same woman he had known in Woodingdean. Their six months apart had rounded and sharpened the attributes of herself that she liked while eliminating the useless ones. Parts of her he may have adored quite possibly no longer existed.

The Margaret he had known was now a ghost, a shadowy figure in the outline of what had become her true self. So, even if he could be persuaded to forgive her for not being there in his time of need, she did not think he would ever forgive the possibility that the woman he loved no longer existed.

Meg,

I can see now that your silence was meant as an ending.

A period to mark the end of you and me.

I'm sorry that I disregarded it and am sorry to have bothered you with my letters all this time.

I wish you nothing but the best in your future endeavors and hope that if we ever meet again, we shall do so as friends.

My father has recovered from his illness, albeit not as well as I had hoped. I plan to remain in London for the foreseeable future while I take up the reins of the dukedom.

If you ever have need of me, you know where to find me.

–Oliver Ludlow, Marquess of Greenwood

CHAPTER TWENTY-THREE

M EG HAD SENT him the damn plants.

Four massive pots, much larger than the small clay ones he had begun with, arrived by delivery the next morning. She decorated each splendiferous plant with a placard, elegant script displaying each of their names, along with his notebook, which had developed some wear in the time he was away. The leather binding was worn and smudged and inside, pages were filled with haphazard writings, some sheets stained with indiscernible soot.

Oliver groaned as he rubbed his face, afraid to look at them. The spinach plants had become more like bushes than vegetables, their leaves large enough for an infant to use as a parasol if necessary. "Where should I have these placed, my lord?" the butler asked, accustomed to Oliver's inclination for green things.

"Conservatory," Oliver said through his hands.

"Of course, my lord." The butler directed four foot-men to deliver the plants to the conservatory and, using their moment of distraction, Oliver grabbed the notebook and slipped into his office. Setting the bound leather book on his desk, he went to the sideboard and poured himself two fingers of scotch. Frowning at the glass, he added another finger for good measure. Heavens knew what lay inside the journal beyond his own experimental musings.

Once settled in the chair, Oliver gulped his drink, then

reached for the notebook. Skimming past his own writings, he stopped at the first entry that was not his own.

November 15, 1819,
Gilbert measuring 18.6 centimeters
Plant A measuring at 16.4 centimeters.
Plant B measuring at 13.5 centimeters.
Plant C measuring at 12.7 centimeters.
Soil seems ok. Gave each plant ½ a watering can of
water, although I think it might have been too
much. Stalks seem healthy, I guess...

Oliver smirked. She over watered the poor things, no doubt giving cause for the plants to slowly develop root rot. A novice mistake. Turning the page, he found the same formation of notes for nearly a week before they lengthened.

November 23, 1819,
Plant A and C are starting to have yellowing leaves
with ugly brown splotches on them. Gilbert and
Plant B seem ok, but given that they have received
the same treatment as their compatriots,
I'm certain disease is just around the corner for
them as well. There aren't very many notes
regarding what to do should the leaves take such
a turn...
You would know far better than me. But you're
not here.
The soil seems rather damp and heavy. Maybe I
will cut down their watering to ½ a can every other
day and see if they improve?

There were no measurements to follow and Oliver turned that page, intrigued to see if she found the solution.

November 24, 1819,
No watering today, but as expected, Gilbert and
Plant B have joined the sick ward.
While Gilbert's spots are not as terrifying as A's
and C's, his rapid turn for the worse is worrisome.
I'm not sure what to do for them. Their soil is still
damp even without my watering and I'm not sure
how to help them dry up a bit.
I've moved their location from the wooden shelf to
a spot along the south window with hopes that they
will receive more sunlight to help their
drowning problem.

Oliver shook his head and set the book down. Somehow, his scientific journal had turned into the diary of four spinach plants and their caretaker. He could sense her concern as she wrote about the plants' symptoms and worried over what was to be done, but in truth, was flabbergasted she invested so much time over some measly plants. After all, he had left them for dead. Why should she care if they live or die?

Finishing the scotch, Oliver set the glass down with a click and picked the book back up again. She filled the rest of November with small entries, each one sounding more like a mother managing her child's sick bed than that of a woman and some foliage. She rotated the location of the plants several times, searching for the appropriate lighting to help their situation, fretted over whether to water them even the slightest on the chance that she killed them faster.

"They're plants, Meg. Plants die all the time."

When December 2nd appeared, its entry pages long, Oliver knew he would need more fortification. Refilling his glass, and removing his jacket and cravat, Oliver took the more comfortable chair before the fireplace and, book in hand, read once more.

December 2, 1819,

Talking with one of our local farmers, we've concluded that they have root rot. I've repotted all four plants in new, dry soil and changed out their pots to ones with a hole in the bottom so that the excess water drains away. Milo, the farmer, also mentioned trimming the leaves that were decaying, so I've taken to doing that, along with distributing the goose fertilizer to all four, as it seems that product works the best out of the lot.

Gilbert, Salazar, and Guinevere, which is what I've taken to calling Plants A and C, seem to have pulled through the worst of it and Salazar even had the appearance of a new stem, which leaves me hopeful.

Sisco, which is Plant B, however, has taken a turn for the worse. He is down to all but one leaf and while his stem appears green, I'm certain that it will be any day now that I arrive to find him no longer with us.

I wish you were here to help guide me through this process. There have been so many times I've almost written to you for advice. Almost asked you to come home.

Oliver blinked, certain he had misread, but the words still appeared as they had before. He turned the page with a flick, his gaze scanning past all the jumble of plants to any part where his name arose.

December 5, 1819,

… You'd be pleased to know that Sisco has rallied and has even sprouted a new leaf. I'm certain you will laugh at me, but I've taken to singing to them each morning as I water them. Mostly they are bawdy tunes I hear at the inn, and I can almost imagine you chastising me for not choosing something more appropriate. Yet, I know you'd be singing along as you did so…

His mind painted the image of Meg in his greenhouse, singing at the top of her lungs to their four spinach plants. Her cheeks would no doubt be pink from the warm air inside the glasshouse, her curls springing from her head in an attempt to escape the braid she had put them in that morning. The picture was magical. Wonderful. And the smile that bloomed on his face left him poleaxed.

This woman had gone quiet as a ghost, so much so, it would have taken a spirit board and a palm reader to contact her. She had ignored every letter he sent with little effort, and yet the notion of her singing to their spinach plants in the greenhouse was enchanting. It made no sense.

With a frown, Oliver returned to the notebook, baffled that his broken heart could still find joy in her.

January 15, 1819,
A visitor to Baron gifted me an orchid yesterday.
I'm both touched and terrified that I will kill the

poor dear like I nearly did the babies. I've named her Dorothea, and she has the most splendid purple flower blossoming from her stick-like stem. The babies seem all right with the interloper, although I have kept her isolated from them in case she has any pests she could pass along.

Gilbert, Sisco, and Guinevere are growing abundantly now that I've learned their water requirements and Salazar has developed round green balls beneath his leaves. Milo informs me it means that Salazar is female. Once she's ready, I'll harvest those leaves and perhaps we will have some new spinach plants for the spring.

I remembered today that your primary goal of this experiment was to learn about fertilizer and not about spinach propagation, and yet, here I am, learning how to keep these plants you cared for alive. We've had frost in the air, so I've taken the plants to the greenhouse I had built at Baron in the exact spot you recommended. You were right, it's perfect.

This dratted woman had taken a scientific journal, his scientific journal, and turned it into a damned diary about herself and their four spinach plants. Not that it was not interesting. Nor was it annoying to read about her discoveries as she took on other plants. But no. No. He had been swayed so easily by her once before, and heaven help him if a blasted diary be his grand reentry into another fascination with the Countess of Everly.

Oliver threw the journal down, and it landed on his desk with a slam. Slips of paper slid out from the last page of the notebook and his familiar handwriting caught his eye. Five letters, their edges worn, had been stuffed into the back fold of the notebook. He could not touch them. Did not dare to see the words that he had sent the woman; consoling her fear, pleading for her return, and ultimately accepting her departure from his life. But she had kept them, every last one he had sent.

Shaking his head, Oliver stared at the book, a frown on his face. None of this made sense. Not her tears at the Mayberry ball. Not her invitation to see the plants at her home. And certainly not the notebook and letters. The cold dismissal and disappearance she had so easily allowed did not align at all with her actions.

And neither did the fact that when she had pushed herself up to stand at Hyde Park, the moonstone necklace he had gifted her had fallen from the gap in her shirt, the pale stone sparkling in the early morning sunlight.

Their time in Woodingdean surely had been just a fantasy. Right?

But even as he thought back on their month together, her actions made little sense for someone intending to damage. She had been warm and open to adventure, hesitant before giving into the obvious attraction they both felt. One simply did not fake those sorts of emotions. And if she had, she was missing her calling to be on stage.

So why did she not come to London? Why did she ignore his letters, his pleas for her?

Whatever the answer, it would not come to him easily by any means. He needed a resolution to the mess that was their relationship, and the first step to gaining that was information. Standing, Oliver redressed and tidied his hair before calling for his carriage. Directing the driver to White's, Oliver sat back and stared out the window.

It was a puzzle that was missing far too many pieces for him to solve, and no matter which way he turned it, something did not seem right. Her words and actions did not align, and while his head told him to listen to what she said, his heart wondered if there was not something more to it.

If there was anyone in London who knew every last bit of gossip about the ton, it was Averndale, and thankfully, Oliver knew just where to find him. Inside White's, the man in question sat in an overstuffed armchair in the sitting room, holding court with two young bucks fresh on the season. A few other members sat in the curated room, but none of them gave Oliver notice as he headed toward Averndale.

"If you have a moment," Oliver said, raising a brow at the man.

"Excuse me, lads. Duty calls," Averndale said, shooting the boys a wink before grabbing up his drink and leaving. The boys quickly left the room, no doubt heading to the card room for much more interesting pursuits.

In a secluded corner, Oliver ordered a scotch for himself, then watched as the footman walked away to fetch his drink. The ornate fireplace roared, its crackling embers the only sound. Looking at Averndale, he pinched his lips together. "Tell me everything you know about the Countess of Everly and the previous earl."

Averndale leaned back in his chair, his eyebrows high as he took a sip of his drink. "Unfortunately, it's not my story to tell. Perhaps it's time you ask the lady in question?"

Oliver swallowed, his mouth pinched before he looked at Averndale and nodded. "Perhaps it is."

CHAPTER TWENTY-FOUR

Theatre patrons, each abuzz that Edmund Kean would once more play the stunning role of King Lear, surrounded the exterior of Drury Lane, and Daphne seemed to be a part of the chaos. Her darling sister, whom she adored more than life, would not shut up about how exciting it was to finally see Kean in a role he excelled in.

"Mother did not think King Lear was an appropriate production for a young lady," Daphne said to Margaret, again. "She thought Kean's insistence that they perform the original ending would cause women of good moral standing undue distress."

"Yes, dearest. You've told me that twice now," Margaret said, sending a gentle smile across the carriage to her sister.

Daphne smiled sheepishly. "I'm sorry, Meg. It's just that I'm so excited."

"I understand. I have revealed a universe of wonders to you now that mother is no longer your keeper. Just remember what I told you."

Daphne rolled her eyes, but she smiled as she did it, so Margaret forgave her dramatics. "Yes, yes. No disappearing with eligible young men, keep my more frivolous opinions to myself, and do what I can to not to muddy my reputation."

Margaret nodded. "As long as you do that, I'm more than happy to chaperone you anywhere you'd like to go. Covent Garden? St. Giles? Whitechapel?"

Harrison cleared his throat beside her. "Don't get too ahead of yourself, Meg. If you venture to those places, I'll no doubt have to come with you and I think we can all agree I am not the best choice of bodyguard."

Margaret and Daphne laughed. For all his belittling opinions regarding himself, in truth, Margaret had never felt safer than with him by her side. Well, almost never.

She had sent the spinach plants off to their original owner, and while their parting had been heart wrenching, she knew it was for the best. After all, she had merely cared for them in his absence. Little had she known how attached she would become to the beasts. Their time together had been the only thing keeping her from slipping into madness after Oliver departed, and she was grateful for their companionship. But perhaps it was best for them to sever every tie that bound them.

Daphne squealed as they pulled up to the theatre, the doors to the magnificent building open to allow patrons. Crowds of people already flocked to the place, no doubt making it a tight fit for those in the lower regions of Drury Lane, but thankfully, the trio would not be a part of it. Harrison handed them both down, then extending an arm to each of them, guided them inside and up to his box. The Earl of Everly's seat had held the same box for generations, but this was the first time Margaret had returned since Walter had passed, and it stunned her to find that the old anxiety returned as she climbed the red-velvet stairs.

A night at the theatre could either be a joyful affair or lead to a rage-filled evening, depending on how Everly thought she handled the night. She met each theatre outing with meticulous care of her appearance, a soft smile affixed to her face no matter the emotions that took place on the stage. But a simple word spoken in the wrong tone would be the only catalyst necessary to ensure the rest of her night would be a living hell, theater patrons be damned.

Harrison patted her arm and Margaret realized she gripped the fabric of his coat with such pressure her fingers had turned white. "I'm sorry," she whispered.

"It's all right. He's not here."

She smiled at him and released the pressure of her fingertips as they entered the box and took their seats. The round theatre allowed for audience members to not only view the show, but the other patrons as well, ensuring that ton gossip varied far and wide, and Margaret let her eyes wander the opulent room. Guests mingled in each box, their jewel toned gowns glimmering in the candlelight while the orchestra tuned their instruments for the show.

"I've invited a friend tonight as well. I'm hoping he and Daphne might develop an interest in one another," Harrison said, his words whispered.

"Playing matchmaker, Harry?" Margaret asked, shooting him a wink before propping her cheek in her hand. "Do tell me of our prospect."

"Lord Averndale is an old schoolmate of mine. Ran into him at White's earlier and invited him along. I'm not sure whether he is looking for a wife, but even if he isn't, Daphne being seen in his company will continue the intrigue and perhaps speed up the interest in some of the men who frequently visit, including Lord Winsome."

"Goodness, you're rather good at this," Margaret said. "It leaves me to wonder what a season would look like once you've joined the ranks of eligible bachelors in want of a wife."

Harrison shook his head. "That'll never happen. I'm happy to let this cursed title pass on to a distant relative."

"Come now, Harry, you can't mean that."

He opened his mouth with a reply, but closed it and placed a smile on his face. "Averndale! So glad you could make it."

"Everly," the viscount said with a friendly smile. The man was tall and lean, with expertly arranged blond hair and warm blue eyes, but it was not his figure that caught her gaze. No, it was the man who followed behind him that did. Oliver. "I hope you don't mind, but I brought along a friend?"

Harrison's smile froze as he spotted Oliver. "The more the merrier," he said, but his voice was cold. "May I present Lady Everly and her sister, Miss Ramsey? Meg, Daphne, this is the Viscount of Averndale."

"My lord," Margaret said, giving a small dip.

Averndale nodded his head. "And this is the Marquess of Greenwood."

Daphne smiled at Oliver. "We've met before."

Oliver smiled at her in return and nodded his head. Black tailored jacket and trousers adorned his person, his boots glistening in the box's candlelight, his cravat neatly pressed and tied. It made Margaret's fingers itch to muddy him up, to make him the person she knew in Woodingdean. "And it is a pleasure now as it was then. Good evening, Miss Ramsey, Lady Everly."

Margaret curtsied, her heartbeat thundering in her ears as she did so. When she stood, she met his gaze, but his green eyes were unreadable. The anxiety she had thought she put away reared its head as the three men congregated in the back of the box, the deep rumble of their voices doing little to calm the unease she felt.

It was to be expected they would bump into one another, but to do so at such an often frequency would surely drive her mad. It was rather hard to forget someone when they were everywhere.

Retaking her seat beside Daphne, Margaret twisted the playbill that sat in her lap, the paper desperately attempting to withstand the damage her hands wrought. "Are you all right?" Daphne asked.

Margaret forced a smile to her lips. "Yes, of course."

Daphne frowned at her before turning back to look at the stage. "I may be young, but I know what unease looks like. And Lord Greenwood seems to consistently be around whenever it occurs."

"Daphne…"

"Whatever is between you two needs to be sorted."

Margaret shook her head. "It isn't that simple. I've created some pretty devastating destruction."

Daphne nodded; her brow furrowed. "You could start by apologizing, especially if you want to mend whatever it is you broke."

Margaret looked at her sister. The young woman, for all her lack of experience, made it appear so simple. But she was right. The first step was apologizing and accepting the blame for the hurt she had wrought. "Thank you," Margaret said, reaching for Daphne's hand and squeezing it.

"We're sisters. It's what we do."

The lights flickered, indicating the start of the show, and the men gained the seats behind them as the house lights dimmed and the stage came alive. Kean took to the boards amidst a round of applause and Margaret smiled as the man nodded his head to the crowd before slipping effortlessly into the role of King Lear. Daphne leaned forward in the chair beside her and Margaret could not help but watch her sister instead of the actors on stage. Her face was alight with amazement, smiling as Lear's eldest daughters professed their love for their father and biting into her lip as he banished Cordelia from the kingdom. When the group paused for intermission, the girl leaned back in her chair, hand to her chest as if she had survived the entire ordeal alongside the king.

"What do you think?" Margaret asked.

Daphne smiled, her gaze never leaving the stage. "It's amazing. Meg. Why is it so amazing?"

"Sometimes art simply speaks to you."

Averndale approached them, taking the seat beside Daphne. "Are you enjoying the performance, Miss Ramsey?" he asked.

"Immensely," Daphne said, smiling at Averndale.

Margaret touched her hand. "I'm going to the ladies' retiring room. I'll be right back, dearest."

Daphne nodded and Margaret took her leave, navigating the full hallway until she found the ladies' retiring room. After tending to her necessities, Margaret dabbed at her face with a cool cloth before looking at herself in the mirror. "Daphne is right. He deserves an apology." With a deep breath, Margaret left the room. She did not know how, but she was determined to apologize to Oliver. He deserved that, and so much more.

As she neared Harrison's box, a hand snaked out from a hidden alcove and pulled her inside. A hand muffled her panicked shriek as she landed against a hard body, the scent of sandalwood filling her nose. "Oliver?"

"Who else would you be sneaking into alcoves with?" he asked, his voice low beside her ear.

"Only you," she said, the words whispered. Pushing away from him, Margaret allowed her eyes to adjust to the dark environment. "I was hoping to speak with you this evening."

"May I speak first, if it's all right?"

"Of course."

The room fell silent, and she wondered if he had heard her, but he filled the quiet. "Why were you at Baron six months ago?"

Margaret frowned. "What do you mean?"

"In all our time together, you never fully told me why you were in Woodingdean, of all places. Why you wanted to make Baron into a haven for those in need."

Margaret's throat tightened, and weight filled her chest. "I'm certain I told you."

"No," he said. "No, you never did. All I knew was that your husband had passed and left you the manor, but there's more to it than that, isn't there?"

Leaning against the wall, Margaret pushed air through her lungs. Swallowing, she gripped her reticule. "Walter was a terrible man, and I never wanted to marry him, but my parents..." she let the silence fill in the rest of the sentence. "My marriage... It wasn't just unhappy. It was vile. I was degraded and belittled from the moment we took our vows. Every word I spoke, every movement I made, every action picked apart with such malicious intent, but always spoken with such a kindness you'd thought you imagined it. And it wasn't just in the privacy of our home, but in public as well. At parties, with our family." She shook her head. "He would criticize and demean me; outline every flaw he could find in the most malicious ways, but he did it with such an astounding flourish it left you thinking his criticism was well meaning. But it wasn't. It was so he could break me, and he did. I couldn't eat, couldn't sleep. I was terrified I'd do something to provoke his attention. His hatred. When he died, I was happy. Relieved.

"My parents assumed after he'd passed, I would move back in with them, become a pawn in their game once more, but I couldn't let that happen." She let her head fall against the wall, its support desperately needed. "He left me Baron as a way to get back at me for being a terrible wife, so I sold everything that was mine and ran."

"You could have asked for help here. You have the new earl who obviously cares for you."

Margaret shook her head. "I had to do it myself." She closed her eyes. "You wouldn't understand, but I lost myself in my marriage. I'd become this shell of a person and I knew if I depended on anyone else, if I remained in London, it would never get better. I would never get better." Tears stung at her eyes and she let them fall. He would never know; never see how much damage the past had inflicted. "I'm so sorry, Oliver. I'm sorry I dragged you into this. I have no excuse for the damage I did to you, and I know the hurt I caused is irreparable."

"It was real, though, wasn't it?" His voice cracked, and it spurned her tears.

"It was. Even knowing what I know now, I'd do it all again. I'd fall in love with you just as deeply as I did before."

The alcove fell quiet and Margaret dabbed at her cheeks, her gloves absorbing the moisture.

"If you loved me, and I loved you... Then why didn't you come?" He let out a deep sigh. "Why did you take care of my plants and baby them like they were children? Why did you visit at the greenhouse and..." he paused "And why are you still wearing the necklace I gave you?"

Margaret swallowed, unable to put together the words to tell him everything.

"None of it makes sense, and it's driving me crazy. One minute I'm angry as hell with you and the next I'm wondering why I can't stay mad."

Margaret did not think. Did not dare. Taking a step forward, she slid her hand up Oliver's coat and onto his neck, bringing his head towards her. Her kiss was light, more of a question than a demand, but her breath caught at his familiar taste. Her heart whimpered at his closeness, begged her to close the gap entirely, but instead, she brushed her lips against his once more. "I'm sorry," she said.

Oliver's arm snaked around her waist, pulling her closer as his mouth crashed into hers, his tongue seeking with a surety that only he possessed. Long fingers slid into her hair, gripping her skull as he destroyed her with tongue and teeth, and instead of being frightened by his fire, she wanted to burn in it. Her arms tightened around him, urging him closer.

With sure steps, Oliver backed her up into the wall, her soft grunt as he pinned her merely fueling his attentions. His tongue swirled and danced, teasing, then consoling, and want pooled in her. Though time had passed, her body recognized him and demanded more. Wanted to be conquered, consumed. It was her whimper of need that shook her from his spell and with sure hands upon his shoulders; she pushed him back, his steps stumbling at her unexpected movement.

"We can't... This can't," Margaret said, covering her lips, which still tingled from his kiss.

"Why?" he asked the words a croak.

"Because that girl you fell in love with in Woodingdean wasn't real," she said, the words torn from her chest. "I made her up. I wanted to experience things, to be strong and brave and tell the world to bugger off, but I couldn't do that as I was." Margaret wrapped her arms around herself to ease the shaking that had taken over her. "She was a character. A mask I put in place to try to become someone other than scared, little Margaret, who was terrified of her own shadow. I despised the woman I was, wanted to tear her apart for being so weak. But Meg? Meg wasn't afraid. She took part in carriage races and sold all of her belongings to move out to the middle of Woodingdean. She wore trousers, and trained horses, and swam naked. She fell in love."

The words were pinched, pushed from her soul. "But she isn't real. That's why I didn't come to London. That's why I didn't reply to any of your letters. How could I when the woman you claimed to want to spend the rest of your life with was a fraud?"

Shaking her head, Margaret left the alcove for the safety of the ladies' sitting room. The plush cushions did little to console her as the tears fell freely. It was in this puddle of turmoil that Daphne found her. Without a word, she notified Harrison that Margaret was not feeling well, then helped Margaret pull herself together. With dry eyes, albeit a bit red and scratchy, Daphne guided her out of the ladies' sitting room and to their waiting carriage out front. She said nothing; her gloved hand gripping Margaret's tightly, reminding her she was not alone. And when they stopped at Harrison's home in Mayfair, Daphne put her to bed as one did a small child, with soft words and gentle touches.

For all their troubles, it seemed their parents had raised decent people.

CHAPTER TWENTY-FIVE

O NE WOULD THINK a story about a headless horseman would keep a brain occupied no matter what the chaos of their life looked like, but they would be wrong. Irving's *The Sketch Book of Geoffrey Crayon* was the latest in his father's literature endeavors, *The Legend of Sleepy Hollow* being the present story Oliver read to him that afternoon. But no matter how much Ichabod Crane and the devilish horseman attempted to draw his notice, Oliver could not stop his mind from replaying Meg's words from the previous night.

Their kiss had been an inferno, no doubt about it, but it was her words, the aching pain in her voice as she confessed her sins to him, that had broken him. While her love had been real, the woman he had developed feelings for had turned out to be a fantasy, an intricate mask that had tricked him with ease.

"*... ducks and geese are foolish things, and must be looked after, but girls can take care of themselves,*" he said, the words falling flat as he read them.

Reginald laughed. "That is certainly true."

Oliver set the book down in his lap and looked at his sire. "Is it?"

"Absolutely. Your mother was the most capable wom- an I know. Could handle herself no matter the situation, and she was a duchess." Reginald shook his head. "Damn near the strongest person I've ever had the pleasure of knowing."

Oliver nodded and picked the book back up.

"You ever met a woman like that?" Reginald asked.

Oliver frowned at the page before him. "I thought I had. Turns out I was wrong."

"How so?"

"She was pretending to be someone she wasn't." He shook his head. "No, that makes her sound malicious, and she doesn't have a malevolent bone in her body." Oliver thought about the woman he had known in Woodingdean. "She wore this persona like a piece of armor because events in her life had stripped away any last bit of self she had."

"And you fell in love with that persona?"

Oliver sighed. "Yes."

"I see," Reginald said. "Sometimes life can be so traumatic one loses every last bit of who they had once been. It can take everything within them to simply survive the day. What use do character and temperament have when you can barely keep yourself going?"

The book hit his legs with a thud. "What do you mean?"

His father, a frail shell of the man he had once been, looked at him with a brow raised. "Say you find yourself in the wilderness, only the clothes on your back. No food. No water. No shelter. Do you think it matters whether you like fish more than mutton if it's the only food you have? Does the scent of the soap really decide whether you will bathe if you have been covered in refuse for weeks?

The temperature of the water?" He shook his head. "If the events she dealt with left her to simply survive, it's no wonder she hadn't a clue who she was. I feel for the girl. Who is she?"

"Someone I knew."

"Someone you knew enough to love. And who's to say how well one knows another person? Look at everything you've been through this past year. Loss of family. The deaths of close individuals can cause irreparable changes in one's persona. You aren't the same person you were when you left for Woodingdean, and you certainly aren't the same man who returned six months ago." Reginald nodded his head. "People ebb and flow like water, Ollie boy. If they never change, they never grow, and how boring life would be if that were true."

His sire was right, as usual. Christopher's passing and their mother's untimely death had shaped him in ways he never would have expected, their absences creating a path to a life he never expected. Long gone were his days of quiet reflection and idle time, his newfound circumstances forcing him to be the face of the title and all its holdings. It was uncomfortable and disorderly, a way of life he was unprepared for, but had adjusted to it nonetheless. Could it have been the same for Meg?

Reginald motioned to the book on Oliver's lap. "We'll finish this another time. I think I'll take a nap before Terrance returns to bother me again about food."

Oliver sighed. "You have to eat, Papa. Food is nourishment and medicine for your body."

"You've become crotchety in your old age, Ollie. Perhaps you should change your future calling from duke to a nursemaid, what with all the worrying you've done over me these past months."

Oliver stood and set the book on the nightstand beside his father's bed. "I have no intention of becoming a duke anytime soon, which is why I require you to eat your meals with gusto. The quicker you are out of this bed, the more at ease I will feel and the less coddling I will do."

"I've told him the very same thing, my lord," Terrance said from the doorway, holding a tray carrying the duke's luncheon.

"Buggar off the both of you," Reginald said, but he had a smile on his face.

Oliver kissed Reginald's papery cheek, then smiled at Terrance. "Best of luck with him."

Terrance bowed with a smile. "Thank you, my lord."

Oliver left the room, Reginald grumbling about impertinent children the melody of his exit. Yet his father's words stuck with him the remainder of the day, echoing in the back of his head as he handled estate business, mumbling in his ear as he ate dinner in White's expansive dining room.

Meg's marriage, and no doubt childhood, had been turbulent at best, volatile at its worst. It had taken little for the ton to pick up on the previous earl's cruel ways. Murmurings had begun soon after their wedding of Meg withstanding the cruel remarks of her husband's temper, yet society had looked away, uncomfortable by what they witnessed, yet unwilling to become involved.

Averndale had willingly shared the gossip that had floated about the London social scene of the earl's malicious treatment of his wife. For years, Everly publicly chastised Meg for her appearance, her manners, hell, even her altogether presence, and yet the ton did nothing, choosing to turn a blind eye to his cavalier set downs and untimely outbursts. For a decade it went on until fate thankfully took the man to his grave. And that did not even begin to touch on her childhood, which had no doubt been an ordeal.

Judging from the interactions he had with Lady Veerson at the start of the season, Meg had incessantly been under someone's watchful eye, dodging barbs to her personality, her form, and a multitude of other trivial demands. It was no wonder she ran when she had the chance.

Oliver smiled as he thought about the woman he had met at the inn that fateful night. Clad in anything but a dress, drinking ale with a group of men after racing through the wilds of Brighton. She must have felt like a child given a free pass to experience life. Her joy and delight as she approached each day became crystal clear, her reasoning so understandable it was a wonder he had not noticed it before. All he had seen at the time was a fearless woman embracing the world around her. Little did he know that each day was a gift for her. What he had seen as strength had been courage. Courage to throw away the familiar, the safe, and risk it all for the chance to be happy.

With a shake of his head, Oliver put down his utensils and stood to leave. Dinner had tasted like air, his thoughts disorderly, rolling around his brain like turbulent waves with little sign of calming. He wished he could hate her. Wished there was a sure base for his anger to stand on, but that platform was now unstable and becoming rockier as time went on. She had hurt him, true, but what his father said made sense. Meg had been through events that he could never comprehend, and she had survived. It was understandable that she needed time to find out who she was. And people were constantly changing, morphing into a different version of themselves each day. It could be scary and uncertain, especially for someone who had been repressed for so long.

After checking in on his father, who was blessedly sleeping, Oliver made his way to the conservatory. The moon cast its milky light around the room; the plants playing hide and seek in the shadows, but he knew the space by heart. The spinach plants had been placed on a long wooden table he had built against the far wall, their gardener tending to their care in his absence.

"Hello, lads," he said to Gilbert and Sisco, before bowing to Guinevere and Salazar. "Ladies. I'm sorry for my lack of attendance as of late, but it seems you were well cared for during that time." Oliver checked over their leaves and stalks, noting the places where Meg had harvested, her cuts almost expert. "You all seem in rather a decent shape given the circumstances."

Their clay pots were damp, a sign they had been watered recently, and Oliver nodded. "Not much left for me to do for you lot tonight." His mind recalled Meg's note about singing to them, and he paused and looked at the vegetation before him. "I'm afraid I don't know any bawdy tunes, and knowing Meg, that was likely all she sang to you."

Oliver pulled up a stool that was tucked beneath the

table before removing his jacket and cravat. Rolling up his sleeves, he set his hands on his knees. "Can I interest you in a lullaby instead?" He was met with silence, thank god. If they had responded, he was uncertain what he would do. The notion caused him to smile. "A lullaby it is."

With a quiet voice, he sang the lullaby his mother had sung to him and Christopher as children.

> *Sleep, my babe, no ill betide thee*
> *All through the night.*
> *Guardian angels watch beside thee*
> *All through the night.*
> *O'er thy cradle stars are beaming*
> *Silver bright the moon is gleaming;*
> *You shall tread the land of dreaming*
> *All through the night.*
> *While the earth in calm reposes,*
> *All through the night.*
> *You shall sleep as sleep the roses*
> *All through the night.*
> *Hushed from sorrow and repining,*
> *Rest until the sun is shining,*
> *In my loving arms reclining*
> *All through the night.*

Oliver felt foolish as he finished the song, the plants not knowing nor caring that he sang to them. Unsure of what had come over him, and uncertain of what to do next, Oliver stood and reached for his discarded clothing. Tucking the stool back under the table, he frowned at the plants. "Well then, goodnight." With a bow, he turned and left, grateful no one but himself had been privy to his display of lunacy.

Yet, a lunatic he was, for certain, that had to be what had come over him. In the weeks since Meg's return, he had begun to edge toward bedlam a bit at a time, his mind and heart in a constant battle over what he was about to do next. But in truth, he already knew what had to be done.

It was time to finally close the chapter that was Oliver and Meg. Certainly, that was the only way either of them would eventually find the peace they sought. He would walk away and give her the space she required to find herself, and perhaps, in time, they would both be able to look back at their moments together as ones of happiness instead of sorrow.

With a sad smile, Oliver headed to his office and sat in the winged chair before the fire. Her entries in his notebook and the letters she kept were all clues, pieces of the intricate puzzle that he could never fully put together until now. He would not need the drink tonight, would not need its numbing relief. No, reality was doing the numbing well enough. She was his person, be she either Meg from Woodingdean or Countess Everly of London, but none of that mattered if she was not content with herself.

Maybe one day he would marry. Find a woman to care for with almost the same intensity as he felt for Meg, but he doubted it. She was the right woman at the wrong time, and the least he could do was grant her the autonomy she so eagerly sought.

CHAPTER TWENTY-SIX

T HE SOCIAL SEASON was undoubtedly the worst season of the year, Margaret thought with a smirk as she watched Daphne swirl by in the arms of a rakishly handsome earl. The Feathersbee ball was in full swing, complete with warm lemonade and little to eat, no doubt making it the highlight of the season, or so she was told. Lady Feathersbee had ensured the ton knew spring was upon them and her ballroom was decked from ceiling to floor in flowers, their pastel blooms adding color to the room but doing little to squelch the scent of sweat and perfume.

Smile firmly in place, Margaret tried with all her might to give the airs of delight and joy to those around her, but in truth, she was overheated and utterly exhausted. Sleep had gone missing, along with the last bits of sanity she had as she navigated the London season, and Lord Veerson's incessant nattering about Daphne's lack of marriage proposals had her contemplating patricide. All in all, a fabulous foray into the chaperoning profession. And that, of course, did not even touch on the emotional turmoil she was in.

She had not seen nor spoken with Oliver since their unfortunate interaction at the theatre, and it left her wondering what additional damage she had created.

"Your smile is terrifying," Harrison said, as he stopped beside her.

"Why didn't it work on you then?" she asked, turning it on him, her emerald green skirts swishing with the movement.

He smirked before sipping at the putrid lemonade in his hand. His grimace was a small speck of delight in her dreary evening and she laughed. "There she is," he said behind his glass.

Margaret eyed the dance floor. Daphne's dance partner, Lord Sebastian Winsome, had been a constant visitor at her parent's home, his attentions towards her sister endearing. Yet it seemed the poor dear was terrified of her parents, which led to his indecision regarding proposing. The man would need to gird his loins if her sister was to be his intended bride, no doubt, but once the marriage was completed, the pair would surely find nothing but happiness. Daphne had done little else but wax on about Winsome's handsome looks and intricate bouquets, which he had delivered daily, so surely her sister would be nothing less than pleased should he propose. Perhaps she should find a means to dispose of her parents for a few days so the boy could gather the courage to do the job.

"What do you know of hunting lodges in Scotland?" Margaret asked, tapping her lips with the tip of her finger.

Harrison sighed. "You cannot banish your parents to the wilds of Scotland to procure a marriage proposal. How would you even convince them to visit there?"

"One doesn't need to convince when the travelers are incapacitated."

"I'm going to pretend I didn't hear that," Harrison

said, setting his glass down on the tray of a passing footman. "Winsome simply needs to face his fears and do the deed. Once the proposal is agreed upon, the rest of the season will be painless for you."

Leave it to a man to state the obvious.

"Lord Greenwood, Lord Averndale," boomed a voice over the crowd.

Margaret's heart tripped, her eyes swinging to the staircase to watch as Oliver and Averndale progressed down the stairs. "I didn't know Averndale planned to attend this evening," Harrison said. "I've been meaning to ask him about the new horses he purchased at Tatter-salls."

"I'll wait for Daphne to return and then we'll join you." Margaret motioned for him to join his friend as her stomach twisted into knots.

Harrison nodded before making his way to Oliver and Averndale, and Margaret was thankful for the moment to gather her bearings. He looked well, less worn than he had seemed at the beginning of the season, his clothes fitting his long frame a tad snugger than they had before. And while she should feel pleased to see him on the mend, it hurt to know she did not have a part in it.

"Lady Everly," Lord Winsome said as he walked Daphne off the floor. "Miss Ramsey, it was a pleasure to dance with you this evening."

"My lord," Daphne said, batting her lashes at him before curtseying.

Margaret rolled her eyes at the display but smiled at the earl before taking Daphne's hand and steering her away. "Laying it a bit thick, dear."

Daphne squeezed her hand and executed a delighted skip as they made their way towards Harrison. "Meg, I do believe I'm in love."

"I believe so too, but perhaps you should keep that adoration contained until the man proposes." Patting Daphne's hand, they stopped beside Harrison.

"Averndale, Greenwood, you remember Miss Ramsey and Lady Everly," Harrison said.

"How do you do, my lords," Margaret said, dipping her head.

Her gaze met Oliver's, but she could not read his thoughts as he bowed to her and her sister. "Miss Ramsey," he said. "Lady Everly." He smiled, a soft curve of his lips that did not reach his eyes, but said nothing more before turning back to Daphne. "How are you enjoying this evening, Miss Ramsey?"

"I am having a wonderful time, my lord," Daphne said, shooting a brief look at Margaret before turning back to him. "And how are you?"

"I'm well," Oliver said, the smile still in place. "Is your dance card full this evening?"

Daphne shook her head and handed him the card that was tied to her wrist. Her brow furrowed as she watched Oliver scribble his name along a spot. "I look forward to our dance, Miss Ramsey," Oliver said, handing it back to her. "If you'll both excuse me, I see a friend of my father's that I must speak with. Miss Ramsey. Lady Everly," he said with a bow before leaving their circle.

Daphne leaned into Margaret. "I thought you had spoken?"

"We did," Margaret said.

Daphne frowned and shook her head. "That makes little sense. He didn't seem mad or happy to see you, it was almost... almost neutral."

Margaret nodded, the smile she wore as a mask nearly slipping as she watched him walk away. He was giving her space, just as she asked for. So why did it hurt so much?

"I don't understand," Daphne said.

Margaret patted her hand and released a deep breath. "There are things in this world you aren't meant to understand. Come, it's almost time for the next set and Lord Willoughby will be waiting for you."

"Meg..."

Margaret shook her head, silencing the girl. "Come."

For the rest of the evening, Margaret watched as Daphne danced with eligible bachelor after eligible bachelor, her thoughts swirling like the peach skirts that decorated her sister's gown. Whenever Oliver was near, either in conversation or as he came to escort Daphne for their dance, his smile was gentle. The knowing gaze of a friend from years past.

She hated it.

As their carriage made its way home in the wee hours of the morning, Margaret stared out at the passing scenery, her mind a million miles away. In their time together, Oliver had graced her with a multitude of smiles. His uncomfortable smile at the inn as she claimed him as her husband, his amazed smile as they toured Baron, looking over its repairs. The heady, sultry smile as he kissed her with a fervor, oblivion only moments away, and now this smile. The last smile. It was more of an acknowledgement of the past than an expression of joy, a gentle nod to what was and what might have been. A stark and painful reminder of the sudden finale she had placed on their story.

"Meg," Harrison said, his voice soft. "We're home."

"Right," she said, picking up her reticule and exiting the carriage, her motions instinctive. Walk to the door, hand Sterns her shawl and reticule. Smile and nod, then bid Harrison goodnight.

"Meg?" Harrison said as she climbed the staircase. Turning, she looked at him. "How about some warm chocolate before bed?"

Margaret nodded, her heart not in it, but unwilling to injure Harrison's feelings by declining. In the parlor, Margaret removed her slippers and tucked her feet beneath her skirts, before resting her head on her hand. With a sigh, she looked at Harrison and smiled. "Why the impromptu late-night snack?"

"It seemed like you could use a sweeter ending to your night."

Pinching her lips, she frowned at him. "What do you mean?"

Harrison looked at her before sitting on the sofa that sat across from her. "I've known you since you married my uncle. Hell, before that. I remember meeting you when you debuted." A corner of his mouth quirked up in an attempt at a smile. "You might not remember, but we danced at Almacks."

Margaret smiled. "I remember."

"I think I fell in love with you that night."

"Harry..."

His smile turned sad. "But you've never looked at me

the way you look at Greenwood. I don't think I've ever seen such abject longing on your face in the time that I've known you."

Margaret placed her hands on her lap as her heart dropped at his words. Her fingers tugged at the fabric of her gown as her mind searched for what to say.

"It seems I'm constantly missing my moment with you." He shook his head. "From someone who has had to love another from afar, don't you think it's better to take a chance and find out whether or not it will work?"

Margaret got up and sat beside him, taking his hand. "Harry, I didn't know."

He laughed. "How would you? You were married to my uncle and when he died, I thought it was best to leave you alone and let you heal." He patted her hand. "I take it you met Greenwood in Woodingdean?"

Margaret pinched her lips and nodded her head.

"Knowing you, I'm sure whatever you two are tangled up in is complicated. Anything I can do to help?"

Margaret sighed and rested her head on his shoulder. His admission had been wholly unexpected, and perhaps at another time, had she been a different woman, she might have returned his affection. But not now. Not as the woman she was. "You're a good friend, Harry. The best, if anyone were to ask."

"A fantastic review if I've ever heard one. I'll be sure to take out an ad in the paper so everyone is aware." He leaned his head against hers. "What are you going to do about Greenwood?"

"I'm not sure that anything can be done. The harm I did has left scars too deep to mend, I think. And even if they could, I'm not sure he'd like the person I am now anyway."

"That's utter nonsense, Meg. You're still the same person you were before, just a bit shinier. Perhaps a little rougher around the edges, but if anything, your finer points have merely been honed."

She shook her head at his words, their pronouncement unnerving. "No, it's best if we go our separate ways." She shrugged her shoulders, resignation taking over at her words.

"I don't agree, but who am I to advise about love?"

When their chocolate arrived, they drank it in silence, everything that might have been said dissipating as the hours gave way to the morning. Bidding each other goodnight, and going their separate ways, Margaret's heart nagged at her that she should have done more, said more to comfort Harrison, but she knew firsthand you could not force the heart to feel what it would not.

As the sun broke through the curtains of her bedroom, Margaret knew sleep was a lost cause. Her body was exhausted, but her mind would not stop replaying the neutral smile Oliver had graced her with the night before. She needed to grieve, needed to surround herself in something other than the abject sadness that threatened to wash over her should she allow it.

Dressing in trousers and a blue linen shirt, she pulled on her riding boots and tied her hair back in a braid. A ride with Siris would have to suffice. Perhaps between the wind and the horse's galloping paces, she could forget the man from Woodingdean. Her husband, her lover. Her friend.

CHAPTER TWENTY-SEVEN

M ARGARET'S JAW THROBBED as she sat in the corner of the sitting room, attempting to appear interested as Lord Tatham waxed on about his newest hobby, fishing. Daphne, thankfully, kept a polite smile and nodded enthusiastically as the man discussed carp, or bass, or whatever the hell species of marine life he had caught. The only fish Margaret cared for were sautéed and drizzled in a mouth-watering sauce with a basket of bread to soak up the delectable remains. Anything else was simply boring.

"Lord Winsome," a footman intoned.

"Oh, thank god," Margaret said, setting her teacup down with a click and pushing to stand. "Daphne, come, let us greet our guest."

Daphne politely excused herself from Lord Tatham before linking her arm with Margaret's, the girl's pale blue skirts swishing against Margaret's plum ones as they walked. "Meg, that was rather rude."

Rolling her eyes, Margaret sighed. "It was less rude than me running from the room if he described the gills of another fish he caught at his country estate. Weren't these men taught what polite conversation with a woman is?" She smiled as Winsome entered the parlor. "Lord Winsome, how lovely to see you," she said with a curtsey, peeking over at her sister below her lashes. Daphne's cheeks were a beautiful blush pink, no doubt from the excitement of her chosen suitor arriving, and her smile was wide as the pair made eye contact.

"Lady Everly, Miss Ramsey," Lord Winsome said with a bow.

"Would you care for some tea and sweetmeats, my lord? The chair beside Lord Tatham is available. He was just enthralling us with his fishing exploits."

"I'd be delighted," Lord Winsome said, smiling at Daphne.

"Wonderful!" Clapping her hands, Margaret had another cup fetched for their new guest before resuming her seat in the corner. "Now, Lord Tatham, back to your fish story. I'm perplexed. What was it exactly that the fish had inside its stomach when you cut it open?"

Lord Winsome winced at her graphic words. "Perhaps we should choose a topic more suitable to the delicate natures of the females present, hey Tatham?"

Lord Tatham blushed and nodded his head. "Of course, of course."

Lord Winsome smiled at Daphne. "Miss Ramsey, what phenomenal exploits have you been up to?"

"Meg and I visited the British Museum yesterday to view the marble sculptures they have from Greece. It was rather fascinating."

Lord Tatham's mouth gaped. "Is that an appropriate activity for a young lady?"

Margaret raised an eye at the young Lord. "Coming from someone who was discussing fish innards mere moments ago, I'm not certain you are in a place to judge, my lord."

"Uh, yes, um, you're right, of course, Lady Everly. I was just, I was merely asking… That is…"

"You were attempting to deem what is and is not appropriate for a young lady. However, as her chaperone, and the sister who cares for her very much, wouldn't you say that your chastisement of said activities not only insinuates that I am not doing my part as a chaperone, but that Miss Ramsey is thus an unacceptable candidate as the future Lady Tatham?"

"My lady," Tatham said with a stutter. "I did not mean to insult you in any way."

Margaret nodded. "I accept your apology, Lord Tatham. In the future, be sure to keep such patronizing thoughts to yourself, hmm?"

Lord Tatham nodded and stood. "Yes. Yes, of course. If you'll excuse me, I just remembered I have an appointment." He gave them a brief bow. "My lady, Miss Ramsey, Winsome. Good day."

When the door snicked shut behind him, Daphne looked at her. "Meg, was that truly necessary?"

Margaret sipped her tea. "He dared to disparage my chaperoning skills. I merely highlighted the flaw in his thinking."

Lord Winsome smiled. "Well, I for one am thankful for your set down as it gives me a chance to have Miss Ramsey to myself."

Margaret smiled and nodded her head to the man. "Happy to be of service. I will sit dutifully in this chair while you two discuss whatever it is young people talk about."

"What a ridiculous comment, Meg. You are still young." Daphne set her teacup down with a clink. "Have you any thought of marrying again?"

Margaret shook her head. "I have no interest in marrying ever again. I'll simply dote upon your children as their aunt and spoil them silly." Margaret winked at Lord Winsome. "Any notion when that might be?"

"Meg," Daphne said under her breath, but the smile on her lips said otherwise.

Lord Winsome cleared his throat and set his tea aside before taking Daphne's hands. "I am hopeful I may speak with your father today, Miss Ramsey, but if I were to ask for your hand." He swallowed and looked at their joined hands. "That is, if I were to ask you to marry me…"

"Yes," Daphne said, a smile taking over her face. "Yes, I'll marry you."

"Adorable," Margaret said into her teacup. "A bit cart before the horse, but that can be remedied quite easily." Looking at the footman, she said, "Please inform Lord Veerson that Lord Winsome has come to call."

The footman nodded. "Yes, my lady."

Margaret smiled at the young couple. "Well, let me be the first to offer my felicitations to you both."

They smiled at each other; their fingers intertwined as they looked deeply into each other's eyes. "Lord Veerson is awaiting Lord Winsome in his study," the footman said.

"I'll return as fast as I can," Lord Winsome said, squeezing Daphne's hand.

When the door closed behind him, Daphne stood up and squealed, the sound indelicate and altogether full of absolute happiness. Margaret held out her arms and

Daphne raced into them, jumping as if the joy within her could not be contained. "Oh Meg, is this real?"

"It's real, love. Let's hope father is accepting of the proposal. I'm sure he will be. After all, the man is an earl, but heaven only knows." She pulled back and smiled at Daphne, tucking a curl behind her ear. "I'm so glad you're happy."

"I wouldn't accept anything less," Daphne said.

Margaret pulled back. "What do you mean?"

Daphne smiled, but it was sad, the corners barely lifting. "I was ready to marry whomever they required, just as you had, ready to bite my tongue and do my duty as a daughter." She scoffed. "Hell, mother was halfway there. But then she was injured, and you came," Daphne smiled brightly, "And you were so fierce. A dragon slayer knocking father off his feet, and I knew I couldn't do it. I knew I needed to be fearless like you, to seize what I wanted."

"What?" Margaret's hand flew to her throat, her heart thumping at Daphne's words.

"You were so reserved when you were married to the earl, so scared, but when you arrived back from Woodingdean, it was like meeting an entirely different person. Look at how you handled Lord Tatham. Look at how you handle father and mother. You would have never done that before, never challenged their authority, but it's as if, I don't know, as if you've decided that the world can go to the devil." Daphne frowned. "The only time you've seemed like that old indecisive self is in your dealings with Lord Greenwood."

Margaret sank to the couch, the breath tight in her

throat. The racing of her heart became drumbeats in her ears, their pulses drowning out everything but Daphne's statement that broke her. "You're right."

"About which part?"

"I'm not the same woman, am I?"

Daphne frowned. "Oh. I thought you meant in your handling of Lord Greenwood."

That too was true. It was not simply fearing that Oliver could not love the person she was, but that she would somehow revert to the person she had been. "I've been such a fool."

Daphne sat beside her. "I could have told you that."

Margaret swatted at her sister playfully. "Brat."

Daphne took her hand and laced their fingers. "What are you going to do now?"

Margaret shook her head. "I don't have the slightest idea. If I were him, I'm not sure I'd be willing to give me another chance."

"The answer is always no until you ask."

Blowing out her breath, Margaret smiled at her sister. "Let's ensure your engagement is approved, and then we'll worry about my debacle." The door swung open at her words, Lord Winsome bursting inside with a brilliant smile on his face. "I may have spoken too soon."

Daphne stood. "What did he say?" she asked Lord Winsome.

Lord Winsome smiled. "He said yes."

Daphne let out a slight shriek before launching herself at Winsome, the man catching her expertly and spinning her around. Their joy was contagious if the smile on Margaret's lips were any sign, and she bowed her head so the pair would not see the tears that had unexpectedly sprung to her eyes.

Standing, Margaret cleared her throat and waited for the happy couple to look at her. "I'll give you ten minutes of privacy to celebrate your upcoming nuptials, but only ten minutes. When that time is done, a maid will noisily knock on the door and continue to play chaperone for the remainder of visiting hours." Margaret looked at Daphne. "Celebrate wisely."

Kissing Daphne's cheek and smiling at Winsome, Margaret readied to take her leave after notifying Daphne's lady's maid of the required time limit.

"I beg your pardon, my lady, but the baron requests an audience in his study," the butler said, his smile pained.

Swallowing the groan that attempted to escape her lips, Margaret smiled at the man before making her way upstairs to the dark cavern her father called an office. As a child, the room had terrified Margaret. Dark and depressing, it held very little light due to the heavy draperies the baron had covering the single window, and where one would have expected a cold like the hands of death, instead they found immense heat like the fires of hell due to the blaze that consistently burned in the fireplace no matter the temperature. It was amazing the man had not keeled over from heat exhaustion, let alone that he did not weigh less given the bathhouse like nature of the room.

Margaret rapped her knuckles on the door before opening it, a smile pulling at her mouth at the notion that her actions would cause her father undue distress. Heaven forbid they did not conform to societal expectations, even in the privacy of their own home.

"Seeing as how Daphne has become engaged mere moments ago, I'm not certain why you could possibly have need of me," she said, sitting in the seat across from his desk.

Baron Veerson collected the pieces of paper before him, tapping the stack on the desk until they aligned perfectly. "Seeing as how your sister has found wedded bliss, I think it's time we address your own unfortunate state."

"I beg your pardon?" Margaret sat up in her chair, a brow raised at her sire.

"You need to remarry. This nonsense with the home in Woodingdean and the misfits you've collected has gone on long enough. It is time we return you to respectable society, and seeing how the ton greeted you enthusiastically during your chaperoning duties, I feel it can mean only good things in the future." The baron cleared his throat. "I've taken the liberty of speaking with Viscount Milford. He has been on the hunt for a wife for some time now and is agreeable to the union."

Bile, hot and sour, crept up Margaret's throat. It did not matter that her father had no hold over her life now, did not matter that it would take little more than a quick set down to end this drivel entirely. No, his words eviscerated common knowledge, and Margaret was once more eighteen, sitting in this very room as the baron announce her marriage to Everly. The old fear wrapped around her like a blanket, its weight heavy as it attempted to pull her under, but a small voice inside cried out against it.

"No," she said, the word soft at first, but the voice urged her to use more power. "Absolutely not."

The baron bristled; his hands clenched as a stern frown took over his face. "The agreement has already been struck."

"How unfortunate, as I will not be participating in a marriage, nor anything else you deign to arrange." Leaning forward, Margaret placed her hands on the desk. "You no longer have any power to wield with regards to me and my future. Whom I do or do not marry will be a decision made by no one but myself, and those misfits, as you called them, are more of a family than you have ever been. They have supported and loved me through every trial life has thrown at me and celebrated when I've succeeded."

Standing, Margaret pointed to the door. "That union you're so proud of, the one you will no doubt boast about for decades to come, was arranged by none other than me. And while you'll sit placidly by, content that your daughter is engaged to an earl, I'll know that she married for love, and that had I not been involved, she quite possibly could have followed down the same path as I."

The baron scoffed. "You were a countess. You should have been grateful."

"Grateful?" Lacing her hands together so as not to strangle the man, Margaret raised a brow. "And what, pray tell, should I have been grateful for? Public humiliation by my own spouse? Anxiety that left me with a sickly frame that could barely stomach a cup of tea, let alone any actual nourishment?" She shook her head. "No, father, I am most certainly not grateful that you made me a countess, but I will let you in on a little secret. If not for that prison you sacrificed me to, all in the name of a title, I would not have become the woman I am today. And I most certainly would not have found the strength to tell you with the utmost capability that you can take that marriage contract and stuff it up your arse."

"How dare you—" The baron stood from his chair. "The viscount is expecting this arrangement to succeed."

With a large sigh, followed by a smile that she hoped made him fearful, Margaret headed for the door. "If you require it that much, father, then by all means, you marry the man."

Cool air met her in the hallway, its relief nearly as potent as the strength she felt flowing through her. Daphne's earlier words, along with her father's indelicate announcement, were a hard slap of reality. It was true; she was not Margaret Reedy any longer, but Margaret, Countess of Everly. Strength and courage now filled her as she dealt with her father, and her tolerance for absurdity had dwindled to such a pitiful amount that it felt easy to speak out on them.

She could never become her old self because she would no longer stand for it. She had priorities and standards that would never bend to the foolish rules of others. Daphne had found her happily ever after, and it was time for Margaret to go after hers. Fear of the future, of failure, of weakness, would need to become a thing of the past if she wanted Oliver to be a part of her life.

Inside her carriage, Margaret chewed on her bottom lip as the conveyance made its way towards Oliver's townhome. She had not a clue what she would say, what she would do, but she needed to do something. Even if his answer was no, even if the damage that had been done was irreparable, she had to try. Had to tell him how she felt before letting the sun set on another day.

If there was ever a time to make sure she was not the fearful miss she had once been, it was now.

CHAPTER TWENTY-EIGHT

"MY LORD, YOU have a visitor," the butler said, his voice breaking the comforting quiet as Oliver read to his father. "Countess Everly has requested a moment of your time."

"A countess?" Reginald said, pushing up to sit. "How interesting."

"Not that interesting," Oliver said, although his curiosity was peaked as well. "I'll meet her in the parlor in a moment."

The butler cleared his throat. "I beg pardon, my lord, but she asked to see her spinach plants, and I informed her we placed them in the conservatory. That is where she is currently."

"Her spinach plants?" Reginald asked with a chuckle. "This woman sounds like your soulmate, Ollie. Tell me she is of marrying age and I can die a fortunate man."

"No one is dying," Oliver said, staring hard at his father. "And no one is marrying as well. She is an old acquaintance, that is all."

"Is she an old acquaintance, or an *old* acquaintance? And you're thirty-five, Ollie boy, much too young to have old acquaintances."

"Papa..." Oliver said, the word a groan.

Reginald held his hands in the air in surrender. "All

right, all right. Go see your friend. Be prepared to tell me everything that happened when you return."

"I'll do nothing of the sort." Oliver left his father, who had begun interrogating their butler regarding their guest's appearance and probable age, and headed towards the conservatory, his heart beating loudly in his ears.

It had taken everything within him to remain passive at the Feathersbee ball, to respect the boundaries she had desperately required. For her to show up unannounced, well, it left him not only perplexed, but paralyzed. Forgetting her, forgetting Woodingdean and the cottage, their marriage in the meadow, would all be far simpler if they maintained their distance, but with her near, it only made the entire ordeal crueler. She would smile at a comment her sister made, and it transported him back to the gardens of Baron as she laughed with the workers. Small frown lines appearing on her brow would send him into a fit of worry, eager to ease whatever caused her frustration.

It was unfair, the entirety of it, but there was nothing he could do.

The warm air and citrus scent of the conservatory greeted him in a hug, and he knew without a word where to find Meg. Sure enough, she sat on the stool by the wooden bench, gloves, and reticule removed as she consorted with the plants.

"Gwennie, my darling, you've just sprouted beautifully since I last saw you. My gorgeous girls, you are growing so strong. Have the boys been courteous? We both know Sisco can be a bit of a bother if left unattended." Meg stroked a large leaf of the plant and frowned. "Now,

Sisco, don't think it means I love you any less than Gwennie. I'm simply stating a fact. You can be a bit particular when it comes to your requirements, and it makes for a rather exasperating time for everyone around you."

Oliver leaned against the wall and watched her. Her hair took on a riotous effect in the warm air, the curls springing from their coiffed positions, vying for freedom, but she seemed not to care at all as she chatted with the foliage, praising their recent growth with tender words.

Clearing his throat, he watched as her head raised, eyes jolting to where he stood. "Hello," she said.

"Hello. Come to check on the children?"

Meg laughed and stood, a single finger trailing down Gilbert's leaf. "No, just figured I'd wile away my time here with them while I waited on you." She smiled at him. "I needed to see you."

Oliver raised a brow at her. "Why?"

"Daphne got engaged today to Lord Winsome."

"Congratulations. I'll be sure to send around my regards to the couple."

Meg shook her head. "That's not," she sighed and looked at him, shooting him a half smile. "I can't seem to get my thoughts in the right order. This might take a while."

Oliver turned to leave. "Then perhaps it's best you come at another time—"

"I made a mistake."

The words stopped him short, his breath loud in the quiet of the room. "Pardon?"

"I made a mistake. Well, many mistakes. Many terrible, awful mistakes, and I hurt you because I was afraid. And I'm sorry. I'm sorry for hurting you, for abandoning you when you needed me most. I could give you a multitude of reasonings, explanations as to why I did what I did, but in the end, they would all point to the same thing. I'm a fool who let her fear impede quite possibly the greatest love of her life and I have nothing but regret for what my actions caused."

Her soft footfalls as she neared where he stood matched his chaotic heartbeat, and when she came to stand before him, it stunned Oliver to see tears in her eyes.

"Daphne is marrying a man who loves her dearly, and she says it is because of me. Because of my fearlessness, she went after what she wanted and I want to do that too."

"What is it you want?"

"You, if you'll still have me?"

He smiled, but his heart ached. "As much as I would love to be Oliver and Meg in Woodingdean, I think we've both changed a bit since then. I don't think I can go back to how we were before."

She nodded, her arms wrapping around her shoulders as if trying to self-soothe. "Right." She nodded once more. "Right."

"What are your thoughts on being courted?" Oliver asked, stepping closer to her.

"What?" she asked, her head shooting up and her eyes meeting his.

"Courting? What are your thoughts on it?" He smiled and rubbed his hands up and down her arms, mimicking the motion she had made moments ago. "It seems a bit backwards. After all, we are married, but given that you're now Lady Everly and I'm Lord Greenwood, perhaps it makes sense to learn about those individuals as well?"

"And what if you don't like Lady Everly? Meg blinked back tears and Oliver cupped her cheek, swiping his thumb across the rise of one and taking that moisture with it. "She's rather headstrong."

"Meg was a bit strong willed as well, so I'm sure I'll be just fine."

"She has a bit of a temper." She leaned into his hand, a smile pulling at one corner of her mouth. "And she's grumpy when she wakes up in the morning, and when she's hungry."

"Perfect. She sounds absolutely perfect." Tucking a curl behind her ear, Oliver smiled. "You are absolutely perfect."

"And what about Oliver and Meg?"

"I'm sure we'll see them again from time to time." Meg's arms wrapped around his waist and Oliver released a breath he had not known he had been holding. "They're pieces of us."

Meg nodded. "Courting sounds nice. When can we start?"

Oliver laughed. "Aren't you still a chaperone until Daphne gets married? It's not a good look for the chaperone to be courting a man while tending to her charge."

Meg blew out a breath between her lips. "She'll be fine. Winsome is a decent fellow."

"He is." The words were said with a smile, his eyes tracing over her face, searching for any changes that may have occurred in their time apart. A few new lines near her eyes, a couple more freckles across the bridge of her nose.

But still Meg.

Meg's hand drifted to his cheek and traced a line at the corner of his eye. "I'm sorry I hurt you. I'm sorry I put you through all of that." Tears returned to her eyes. "I should have been by your side, should have taken some of the load. Shouldn't have been so afraid."

Oliver shook his head. "It's over now. We'll start brand new, right here." He leaned his head down and rested his forehead against hers before pulling her into a hug. His arms wrapped around her shoulders as she buried her face in his chest, their bodies aligning perfectly as they had before.

Her fingers snaked into his hair, and she pulled back to look at him. "Would it be too forward of me to kiss you?"

Oliver laughed. "Absolutely not."

Meg pulled his head down towards hers, their lips touching in the softest of caresses, and she giggled against his lips. "If we are really courting, they would frown at this. They'd think I was a brazen hussy and demand we marry as soon as possible."

Oliver brushed his lips against hers with a laugh. "I won't tell if you won't."

Meg's smile against his lips breathed a second life into him and Oliver pulled her closer, sealing his mouth over hers.

It was home. She was home.

His body relaxed into her embrace, arms cradling her head as he deepened the kiss, searching for her familiar flavor. Her grip on his hair tightened and she pushed onto her toes, her body crashing against his. Oliver tightened his hold as he turned her towards the table and walked her back until she bumped against it. Lifting her, he stepped into the space her thighs created and Meg moaned into his mouth as their sexes aligned. "So good," he said against her mouth before pulling back and changing the angle of the kiss.

Time slowed inside the conservatory, the only sounds that of their breathing, the sharp sighs and moans filling in the gaps as their lips and tongues tangled with one another in a beautiful dance of reintroduction.

The clearing of a throat had them pulling apart, Oliver shielding Meg from the interloper. "Apologies, my lord, but your father wanted to know if I should be sent to your rescue," Terrance said from the doorway of the conservatory. "I'll return and tell him his concerns are unnecessary."

When the door shut, Meg burst into laughter, her face buried in his chest as her chuckles made her shoulder shake. "I think they caught us," he said into her ear, sending her into another peel of laughter that left him smiling as well.

Meg gasped and looked to her side before shielding her eyes. "We did that in front of the children."

Oliver licked the shell of her ear, making Meg shiver. "I've had my mouth on your sex in front of those plants. I don't think a few heated kisses will do much damage."

"Oh god."

Oliver laughed and stepped back, tucking an errant curl behind her ear. "Come with me. I have someone I want to introduce you to."

Helping Meg off the table, she shook out her olive skirts and checked her hair. "Do I look all right?"

Oliver kissed her nose before taking her hand. "Perfect."

Outside of his father's bedroom, Oliver hesitated. "My father still hasn't fully recovered from his sickness and he's bedridden most of the time."

"I can wait until he feels up to meeting me," she said, squeezing his hand. "There's no rush."

"Is that the woman from the conservatory?" Reginald shouted from the bedchamber. "Terrance said he caught you in flagrant delicato, Ollie boy."

Oliver covered his face with his hand to muffle the laughter that threatened to break loose. "I think he's excited to meet you," Oliver said.

"When's the wedding?" Reginald asked, his voice a shout.

Meg looked at him with a brow raised and a smile on her face before taking his hand and leading him into the bedroom. Heaven help him. Their life together was going to be one hell of a ride.

CHAPTER TWENTY-NINE

T HE WARM ARMS surrounding Margaret squeezed, their strength a comforting cocoon as she slept heavily. A bristled jaw and soft lips brushed against her cheek, and Margaret scrunched her nose at the feeling. "Come on sleepyhead, it's time to get up," Oliver said beside her ear. "You have a horse who will be very out of sorts if he does not get his exercise today."

Margaret groaned and rolled into Oliver, who shifted onto his back, bringing her on top of him. Squeezing her eyes closed, Margaret burrowed into his chest. "Oomf."

In the past two weeks since they had reconciled, they had found unending reasons for Oliver to be at the home. What had begun as transfer of visitation for the spinach plants turned into morning races through the park and quaint evening meals before bed. In society, they continued as usual, Oliver dancing with her on more than one occasion and joining their party on outings to the theatre or musicals, but in their own private time, they were Oliver and Meg, society be damned.

"Not a word, but most certainly an expression." Oliver kissed her head and rubbed his hands along her back. "Should I carry you to the stable like this?" he asked, pinching the loose linen shirt she wore between his fingers and giving it a gentle tug.

Margaret pushed off his chest, her hair falling like a curtain over her face. "I'm up."

Oliver laughed and left the bed, throwing on his trousers and shirt from the night before.

Harrison had departed London after the Feathersbee ball, claiming to have business up North, but insisted Margaret remain at the Mayfair townhome. Her heart still ached for Harrison, but knew he needed to reconcile his emotions in whatever way he thought right. The home that had once been a place of agony, a painful reminder of how much she was lacking, was now filled with happiness.

"Come along, darling, the horses await," he said, kissing her forehead before leaving the bedroom.

Once dressed in her conventional riding clothes, and slightly more alert, Margaret headed out to the stables and the already waiting and saddled Siris. Rubbing his nose, Margaret crooned to the beast. "Good morning, my love. Are you ready to run?"

"Greeting the horse before you greet me," Oliver said atop his sable mare.

"Jealous?" she asked with a smile.

"Perhaps," he said, winking at her.

"Try to keep up this time, yes?" Margaret climbed onto Siris and with a quiet *ha* sent the horse into motion.

Entering Hyde Park, she gave the stallion free rein, and he picked up speed beautifully, his blue-black mane dancing in the breeze. Margaret smiled as the warm sunlight of the spring morning hit her face, uncaring whether they left her with freckles in the wake of its appearance. The whole of London could go to the devil, for she was happy. Terrifyingly so.

The past two weeks had been like the pages of a fairytale, her mornings spent with Oliver, afternoons helping Daphne and her mother arrange details for Daphne's engagement ball, and in the evenings by the side of the man she loved. While not formally courting one another, Margaret was certain all of society could tell there was a link between the two. Matron gossips lifted their fans in discussion when they walked past, and even Lady Veerson, who was thankfully on the mend, felt inclined to ask about their relationship. Margaret simply smiled and said nothing, giving them a raised brow if they continued to pester. It was none of their business what she and Oliver did, and heaven forgive them if the town were to find out. The blushes these women would wear would certainly be news for the local papers.

The Serpentine's waters gurgled past as Margaret guided Siris along Rotten Road. The stallion seemed to have adjusted to the chaos of the city, and while he would never fully acclimate, the noise still a bit too much for the beast, but he seemed settled. His appetite had picked up, as had his attitude, and once again, the stubborn horse had taken his rightful place as king of the household. It seemed they both had adapted to their new setting, all in the name of love.

Pulling the brute to a stop near the footpath, Margaret turned and found Oliver and his mare almost on their tail. "She's getting better," Margaret said, hopping off Siris. "She'll be a country horse in no time."

Oliver laughed and patted the horse, whose name was Buttercup, on the neck, and the mare chuffed happily as she danced to a stop. Siris snuffled back and Margaret smiled at the pair. Siris, who only had a fondness for her and merely tolerated other creatures, had found a kinship with Buttercup and it was endearing, not that the old demon was softening any time soon. Grabbing Siris' reins, Margaret waited for Oliver to descend, then nodded at the footpath. "Want to walk?"

Oliver raised a brow at her but grabbed Buttercup's reins as well before taking Margaret's hand in the other. Kissing her gloved knuckles, Oliver let out a sigh as they walked along the footpath.

"Are you nervous about the engagement ball tonight?" Oliver asked as they meandered.

Margaret bit the inside of her lip and nodded. "There were so many details that I'm certain I missed one."

Oliver squeezed her hand. "I'm sure everything will turn out wonderfully. You and Daphne have everything well in hand." He chuckled. "I'm sure at this point, the only obstacle you have to deal with is your mother."

Margaret smiled. Lady Veerson had been a handful since they announced the proposal, claiming the pair to be the match of the century and demanding a party just as equal. Both she and Daphne had played a spectacular defense to their mother's demands, filling her time with tasks to keep her busy and nodding sagely when she began one of her tirades. Yet, behind the scenes, the pair had planned a simple, yet elegant affair that even surely their mother would not find fault in. Daphne's gown was a creamy chiffon masterpiece with pearls sewn into the bodice and hem and Margaret nearly cried at the last fitting. Her sister looked like an angel. No wonder Winsome had fallen for her.

"The number of times I nearly had her locked out of the room was astronomical." Oliver laughed at her words and Margaret looked at him. "Do you doubt me?"

He shook his head, brows raised. "Absolutely not. I was petrified of your mother even before we met."

"Does that make you hesitant about our future together?"

Oliver pulled her to a stop, releasing Buttercup's reins so he could cup her cheek. "I would brave your mother, the lady patronesses of Almack's, my father, and the king of England, if it meant I could be by your side."

Margaret smiled. "Truly?"

Oliver kissed her head and pulled her into his arms. "Truly. There is no way I'm ever letting this go."

Margaret released a sigh and let her body relax into his arms. This courtship of theirs was by no means easy, and there were still plenty of times her anxiety got the better of her. But Oliver was as sturdy as ever, standing beside her and reassuring her he had no plans to change his mind.

"When do you need to be at your parents' home?"

"Daphne asked that I arrive during luncheon," Margaret said into his chest. "She thinks mother will be on a tear today and asked that she not have to deal with it alone."

"Hmm," Oliver said, his voice vibrating against her lips. "Then we should probably make good use of the next few hours."

Margaret giggled, then paused at the sound. It was odd, peculiar. She smiled against his chest. She liked it. Pulling back, Margaret laced her fingers into his hair and pulled his lips down to hers. The kiss was searing, the heat and need palpable as their tongues mingled. Taking a step back from him, his green gaze hooded, Margaret smiled. "The last one naked is the loser." With those words, she turned and sprinted for Siris, jumping onto his back and urging him to a run, Oliver's smoky chuckle making her skin break out in gooseflesh.

They spent the next hours in a tangle of limbs, which was why Margaret arrived late for luncheon. Daphne frowned at her as Lady Veerson listed off items she required and Margaret mouthed sorry as she took the seat beside her. Her mother did not pause in her diatribe and it took Margaret one cup of tea and a roast sandwich before she had reached her level of tolerance. Setting her cup down with a clink, she looked at her mother with a smile. "Mother, may I see the list?"

Lady Veerson handed her the sheet of paper she had been reading over and Margaret took it and eyed its content. Half of the list was variable nonsense, all of which could or had already been handled by Daphne and Margaret, and she sighed and folded the paper into a small square. "This is very helpful, mother, thank you. Daphne and I will see to this. You should try to get some rest so you are refreshed and rejuvenated for tonight's affairs. Hosting is such a demanding position and it wouldn't do for you to not be in your best form."

Lady Veerson blinked, looking from Margaret to Daphne. Margaret kicked at Daphne's foot and her sister replied, "Yes, mother, please get some rest. I know how taxing hostess duties can be."

Lady Veerson smiled at them and nodded. "Yes, I shall do that. Be sure to take care of everything on that list."

When she left the room, Margaret tore the list into

small pieces before throwing them into the fireplace. With a smile at Daphne, she picked up her teacup and finished the last few sips before clapping her hands together. "Now then, shall we see where the staff are with the preparations?"

After checking with the staff, and ensuring they did, as had she thought, have everything well in hand, Margaret sent her sister upstairs to rest as she navigated the last few pieces of the ball. When eight o'clock sounded throughout the home, both sisters were dressed and readied, standing beside their mother and father as they greeted their guests. Lord Winsome, dressed in a dapper blue coat and black trousers, stood beside Daphne, his adoration of her sister obvious as he found any means to touch the small of her back or elbow. Margaret smiled to herself as she took small peeks at the loving couple.

"Lady Everly," Oliver said as he came to stand before her and bowed. His black breeches and charcoal grey coat hugged his lithe body and Margaret bit her lip, if only to stop herself from ogling him.

"Lord Greenwood," Margaret said, curtseying to him. "I'm delighted you were able to come this evening."

Oliver winked at her, but kept his voice neutral. "I would not miss it for the world." He turned to Daphne and Lord Winsome and smiled. "My congratulations on your engagement."

"Thank you, my lord," Daphne said, smiling at him. "Dare I ask if you intend to join our delighted state anytime soon?"

Oliver laughed at Daphne's question, his gaze meeting Margaret's. "Perhaps."

Margaret bit her lip and looked away, unable to keep a smile off her face.

When greeting duties were completed, she left Daphne in the capable hands of her mother and Lord Winsome and went to find Oliver. Discovering the ballroom empty of his presence, Margaret headed out to the balcony.

"Is it my beautiful wife come to fetch me?" Margaret turned and found herself in his arms and a laugh escaped her lips. "What took you so long?"

"Greeting duties," she said, sliding her arms around his waist and pulling him close.

He nodded his head sagely, his hand caressing her jaw. "You've brought about the match of the season. It's understandable everyone in London would want to greet you." Oliver leaned forward and kissed her lips and Margaret hummed in delight.

"When can we go home?" she asked.

Oliver laughed against her lips. "We should dance and toast the happy couple first, don't you think?"

Margaret frowned. "I'm sure Daphne would understand."

Shaking his head, Oliver kissed her lips once more. "Still…"

She sighed and stepped back, taking his hand. "Fine. One dance, a celebratory toast, and then we go home."

Oliver pulled her close. "Why the rush?"

"I want to spend the rest of the evening in bed with my husband," Margaret said with a wink.

On a balcony in Mayfair, an elegant ball took place, with elegant people and elegant music. The societal guests would never know that the growl they may or may not have heard came from the future Duke of Hedley as he picked up Lady Everly and gently deposited her in a secluded spot on the balcony. Nor would they know the muffled shriek of said lady soon turned to delighted sighs as the man in question kissed her senseless. But as Margaret relaxed against Oliver, she smiled to herself before sliding her fingers into his hair to kiss him again. The life of Margaret Reedy had just begun.

EPILOGUE

December 1821

THE INCESSANT POUNDING of hammers inside Bitch Manor had no doubt become the melody of the estate. In this case, they could only attribute the noise to the wholly necessary modifications required so that the Duke of Hedley could attend the holiday festivities that year. Along with the misfits of Baron Manor, Daphne and Winsome were along in tow, and Oliver had even managed to convince the Viscount of Averndale to join their celebration.

"I still can't believe you are building a ramp to the front door for my father," Oliver said, his voice a shout over the racket. Yet his words were still muffled, thanks to the tufts of cotton that had once again taken residence in her ears.

"What?" Margaret asked.

Oliver smirked at her before grabbing one clump and removing it, holding it up for her perusal. Pointing to the kitchen, Oliver motioned for Margaret to follow him, and with a sigh, she set down the notebook she was holding and followed him out the door and to the greenhouse where they were met with blessed silence. Gilbert, Salazar, Sisco, and Guinevere sat on a specially made shelf, their leafy greens giving the image of a forest along one paned glass wall. Baron had become their official home, the stable habitat of the greenhouse helping them to flourish again and again.

"Yes?" she asked, raising a brow at him.

"I said, I can't believe you are building a ramp for my father." Oliver wrapped his arms around her waist and pulled her into his chest, setting his chin on her head.

Margaret scoffed at his words and pushed against him. "Of course, we're building a ramp for him. How else would he be able to get inside the home of his own accord? Have Felix and Sam lift him in his bath chair? You and I both know he'd throw a fit over our audacity."

"And widening the doorways on the main floor so his chair easily fits through, and making the study into an easily accessible bedroom, is to merely tie over his outrage?"

Margaret pursed her lips and frowned at him. "No. It's to ensure that he can navigate the home comfortably and have his private rooms where he does not have to be attended to at all times."

Oliver smiled and cupped her cheek. "Do you have any notion as to how wonderful you are?"

Crossing her arms, Margaret scoffed. "Of course I do. You won't shut up about it."

With a chuckle, Oliver pulled her back into his arms, his familiar sandalwood scent wrapping itself around her like a warm hug. "And I'll continue to do so. I absolutely adore you, Margaret Reedy."

With a sigh, Margaret rested her head against his chest. "I love you too."

"The only thing I'm not overly fond of is that last

name. Any idea when you'll be persuaded to change it?"

Groaning, Margaret rocked her head back and forth against his chest. "We're already married in the way that has meaning to us. Why get the law involved as well?"

"Perhaps because I want to call you Margaret Ludlow? Maybe so you can officially become my future duchess? How about, so any children we end up deciding to have can have a simple future without all the unnecessary legalities that come with being born out of wedlock?"

"You have a point."

The past year of their courtship had been everything Margaret had dreamed of as a young girl. Oliver spoiled her with flowers of which she would never be able to recite the names, doted on Siris, who had finally settled into life as a city horse and spent nearly every moment with her. Their time together had slipped easily back into the comfortable routine it had been before, the only difference being location.

"However, your father is doing eons better. He's out of bed and now, with his chair, is capable of being active once more. He even mentioned attending parliament for the next session. There's no need to rush anything," she said, her words directed towards his feet.

Oliver cupped her chin and lifted her head so her eyes met his. "I'm more than happy to wait, Meg, as long as you're all right with me checking in on your thoughts from time to time?"

Margaret nodded and Oliver smiled, kissing her lips softly. "We should probably return to the crew."

"Yes, wouldn't want to miss out on all the hammering that is to be done," she said.

Oliver tickled her side and Margaret laughed, wiggling away from his perilous fingers. "We could always sneak up to the bedroom for a quick spot of tea," he said with a wink.

Margaret raised an eyebrow at him, but her lips pulled into a smile, effectively damaging her lethal stare. "Is tea supposed to be a code for something else? Another activity, perhaps." Margaret stepped behind a potting table and leaned forward. "A naked activity?"

Oliver growled as he stepped towards her, his hand reaching for her, but Margaret dodged him, placing a row of potted roses between them. Her laughter turned to a screech as Oliver gave chase, and Margaret skirted the edge of the potting table as she headed towards the door. Strong arms caught about her waist, picking her up and depositing her on the sturdy wood surface she had used as a shield a mere moment before.

"You had nothing but healthy appreciation for tea time this morning, Countess," he said, nibbling at the soft skin of her neck. "If I'm remembering correctly, you said something about partaking in tea time all day."

Margaret arched her neck, giving Oliver more room for teasing kisses. "Yes, and I believe you were the one that said we must work. Seems we are both going back on our original notions." A breathy sigh followed her response as his teeth nipped at her jaw, and Margaret turned her head, unable to wait any longer for his kiss.

Oliver's lips captured hers with a sweetness that matched not at all to the grip of his hands on her hips. His calloused fingers tugged at the fabric of her shirt with demand, while his kiss sang a sweet melody of love and devotion. The opposing nature of the two lit a fire in her, her hands coursing up his chest to bury themselves in his hair as she wiggled closer to him, eager for his body against hers.

A sharp rap against a glass pane of the greenhouse had Margaret pushing him away. It was not the first time they had been caught tangled up in one another, and certainly would not be the last, but Oliver still had a reputation to keep, even here in the wilds of Woodingdean.

"Sorry to interrupt, my lord," Marty said.

"Sure you are," Oliver said with a grumble that was rendered meaningless given the smile on his face.

"The crew said something about heading off for the night but weren't sure where the two of you disappeared to." Marty winked at Margaret, who could only shake her head at the woman's antics. "Will you be at the inn tonight?"

Margaret sighed and hopped off the table. "I'm afraid not. There are a few more pieces of furniture I need to adjust in the study before the duke arrives tomorrow."

Marty nodded. "Sounds absolutely boring. Seems as though I'll be forcing Averndale to keep me entertained. Well, have a pleasant evening then."

"Be kind to him, Marty," Margaret said.

The innkeeper smiled before blowing a kiss to Margaret and departing. Margaret shot a smile to Oliver, patting his forearm. "I'm sure she won't hurt him."

Oliver raised a brow at her words.

Two hours later, the once study now bedroom sat in more disarray than it had been before. Margaret and Oliver had moved the bed and side table several times, yet each configuration did not seem the right fit to ensure the duke had ample space to move in.

"You better cover your ears. I'm so frustrated I'm thinking of releasing a slew of curse words," Margaret said, hands on her hips.

"There's certainly no need for that," Oliver said, resting his hands on her shoulders and squeezing them. "Let's put it back to how it was before. We can have Papa navigate it tomorrow. Between Terrance and myself, we'll have it set up to the perfect arrangement in no time."

Margaret growled as she frowned at the pieces, but Oliver merely chuckled, kissed her cheek, and took her hand. "Come along, grumpy one. Help me move the bed back and then I'll feed you some dinner. Food should pacify your frustration. Hell, I'd say hunger is likely a part of it."

Margaret stuck her tongue out at him, but went to the other side of the bed and helped him move it back to its original spot. When the room was returned to how it had once been, Oliver took her hand and led her to the back of the manor for dinner. Vegetable soup, which he had left to simmer for most of the day, along with roast chicken, nourished their appetites, and a slice of blueberry pie made from the communal garden bushes for dessert, rounded out the meal nicely. In the past year, the garden had flourished, the blueberry bushes, along with the rescued perennials, had exploded over the landscape, as had the platitude of vegetables that, after they had flowered, provided provisions to the residence of the manor and the village.

When their dishes were cleared and the kitchen

cleaned, Margaret followed Oliver up to their bedroom. Brushing her hair, Margaret frowned as she pictured the study, her mind attempting different layouts, certain she had missed something. Calloused fingers smoothed over the space between her eyebrows before taking the brush from her hand and resuming her task. "Just close your eyes and focus on the motions," Oliver said.

Margaret followed his instruction, letting everything from her mind drift away except for the feel of the bristles against her scalp and the sounds of the brush stroking her hair. Its length was not nearly as long as it had once been, but it was getting there. While she missed the ease of her short hair, Margaret would be the first to admit that having Oliver brush her hair for her had become a guilty pleasure, and the longer the hair, the longer attention it received.

"Better?" he asked, setting the brush on the table before her.

"Mm." His arms wrapped around her shoulders and Margaret leaned back against his chest. "Thank you."

A soft kiss was pressed to her neck. "Thank you."

"Whatever for?"

Another kiss graced her skin, the scruff of his beard tickling her neck. "For making Baron a home my father can flourish in. For worrying about the proper layout of his room." Lips pressed against the shell of her ear. "For loving me."

Margaret arched her neck, giving his searching lips more room. "Thank you for loving me back."

Oliver's mouth pressed against the delicate skin of her neck, his kisses soothing while his hands lowered to her hips, his fingers gripping her shirt. His teeth scraped against her earlobe, and Margaret shivered, her breath escaping her lips in a soft gasp. Turning her head, she touched her mouth to his, and he groaned. It was that sound that set her aflame in his arms.

Spinning in his grasp, Margaret kissed him, hoping that the touch conveyed the sheer amount of love she felt for this man. Her hands skimmed up his clothed chest, and she buried her fingers in his hair as her teeth nipped at his upper lip, her tongue soothing the sting.

"Yes?" Oliver asked, pulling back from her embrace.

"Yes."

His strong hands gripped her arse and lifted her, and Margaret wasted little time wrapping her legs around his hips before letting her mouth fall back to his. With ease, Oliver stood and walked to the bedroom door, pinning her against it, his sex rocking against hers, and they both groaned at the touch. It still shocked and amazed her, the sheer longing that overtook her each time they came together like this as if it were the very first time.

"Too many clothes," he said against her mouth, and Margaret laughed at the outrage she heard in his words. "But I don't want to let you go."

Margaret chuckled, nipping his jawbone. "Sounds like a dilemma."

"Wench," he growled.

A giggle escaped Margaret's lips, and Oliver chuckled against her neck as he resumed his attack on her senses. "What if you put me down and we both undress really fast?" she asked, the words choppy.

Oliver groaned. "Deal." His fingers tightened on her

posterior. "Ready?"

Margaret nodded.

With a hurried grace, Oliver set her on her feet, and Margaret attacked her shirt buttons with vigor. Yanking the fabric over her head, she unbuttoned her trousers and shimmied until they collapsed in a pool around her feet. When she raised her head to check on Oliver's state, she became poleaxed. This man was a chiseled statue, designed by the most careful of hands, his muscles curving and dipping at the most interesting places. And he was all hers.

One side of his mouth curved up in a smile as his hand reached for her, pulling her closer as his lips met hers. Warm flesh met warm flesh and Margaret hummed at the feel of him against her. Her lips opened under his, her tongue twirling with his in a dance as old as time. Thick fingers skirted along her ribcage, under her breasts, his thumbs brushing her nipples until they stood at attention, begging for his touch.

"I want you against the door," he said, the words low. "I want to thrust my cock into you as you cling to me."

"God, yes." Her words were a rush from the image he painted so heady she wanted nothing more than to do it. To feel it. Placing her hands on his shoulders, Margaret jumped into his arms, and Oliver caught her, his hands squeezing the cheeks of her bottom as he backed her against the door, his hard sex rubbing against her quim. Margaret whimpered at the friction.

"Good?" he asked.

"So good." The words were a groan as she gyrated her hips, the feel of him exquisite. But it was not enough. Her core ached to be full of him, the nub of her sex throbbing for release and no matter how she moved, relief was nowhere to be found. Margaret whimpered as she moved against him, her teeth biting into her bottom lip.

Oliver's hand rose to cup her cheek, his thumb rubbing against her mouth, soothing the marks she had no doubt left. "None of that, love." His lips replaced his hand and the skilled digits fell to her quim, rubbing at the spot that eagerly craved attention. Margaret sighed, her head falling back against the door as he spun her in circles, both physically and literally.

"More," she said, the words a plea.

His fingers left her, but only for a moment as he aligned his sex to the opening of hers and Margaret melted, her core gripping him with a feral need. She squeezed his cock with the muscles of her quim and Oliver groaned. "I'm never going to last if you do that."

A smile pulled at her mouth as she cupped his jaw and kissed him. "I'm so close to exploding that I'm not sure I care."

Oliver's fingers returned with speed to the bud of her sex, rubbing and circling the needy flesh while Margaret clenched and released him, her peak so near she was certain she saw stars.

"Meg?" It was a question. A benediction. His hips swirled with her movements; the action instinctive as his pleasure tempted to peak. The thumb that had been conducting its own symphony kept up its paces even as its owner begged for her to reach her pinnacle. When her teeth sank into her shoulder, their sting the push she needed, her pleasure shoved her off the cliff, her cry filling the quiet room as she lost herself to the harmony Oliver had created.

With a shout, Oliver pulled himself from her, his seed spilling against her stomach as he shook against her. It was beautiful. He was beautiful. Resting her head on his shoulder, Margaret smiled against his warm skin, its sandalwood scent comforting her descent. When they were both cleaned up and tucked into the warm bed, Margaret kissed his cheek before snuggling against him and letting sleep claim her.

It was the slight chill of the room that awoke Margaret, the first few strands of light seeping through the curtain. Slipping out of the bed and Oliver's warm embrace, Margaret peeked out the window and gasped. Overnight, frost had covered the landscape, its icy appearance twinkling in the early morning light. A smile pulled at her lips as she looked back at the bed and the gorgeous sleeping man that resided in it.

"Oliver," she said beside his ear. "Oliver, wake up. I want to show you something."

"How is it possible you're awake before me?" he asked with a groan, wrapping his hands around her waist and pulling her into bed with him. His warm embrace tempted her, but only for a moment.

"No," she said, wiggling out of his arms. "Get up or I'm leaving without you."

Throwing on trousers and a long-sleeved shirt, Margaret pulled on thick wool socks before shoving her feet into her boots. With a glance at Oliver, she smiled as she watched him perform the same actions on the other side of the bed. "Grab your coat as well."

Pulling the quilt from the bed, Margaret grabbed his hand and rushed him downstairs and out the kitchen door.

"Bloody hell, it's cold," he said beside her, his hand wrapping around hers and pulling her close. "Are you sure this is what you want to be doing right now?"

Margaret smiled at him and with a nod, led him down the path toward Bellawink cottage. The snow crunched beneath their booted feet as they traversed the trail that they both could travel blindfolded. As of late, their visits to Bellawink were few and far between. Oliver had lent out the property to Sam and his family, as well as young Felix and Mr. Howell, the group an odd jumble of family in the cozy home.

"I know I've said it before, but it was a brilliant idea to lend out Bellawink to the Hemmings," she said.

Oliver shook his head. "It made more sense that they were closer to the property. Sam was walking from town each day, and the thought of his wife doing the same in her heavily pregnant condition just didn't sit right with me. Plus, I thought Mr. Howell and Felix could do for some familial comfort as well."

While his reasonings were sound enough, Margaret knew that proximity had little to do with his decision. No, it was his big heart and caring nature that had Oliver loaning Bellawink to the crew that helped them make Bitch Manor what it had become. Sam and his wife had taken over the care and maintenance of Baron when Margaret and Oliver were away in London, and the pair continued to welcome any and all lost souls that happened upon the property. The communal garden now supplied loads of fruits and herbs to not only Baron, but the village of Woodingdean, and Margaret could not be more delighted to learn that the property Walter had left for rubbish now ensured that not a single individual went hungry or homeless.

As they drew abreast of the meadow that separated the two homes, Margaret pulled to a stop. Shaking out the quilt, she wrapped it around Oliver's shoulders, albeit with some help from the man, then snuggled against him and wrapped the remaining fabric around herself. The quilt created a warm cocoon for the pair, and Margaret smiled as she leaned her head against his chest.

"Is this why we came out here?" he asked, wrapping his arms around her from behind.

"Would you like to be somewhere else?"

His chin rested on her head and he shook it. "No. Just intrigued by the trajectory of your thoughts."

Just then, a single strand of morning sunlight broached the hills that sat in the distance, its shimmery beam striking the frost-covered meadow, lighting the field up like a gemstone. "This is why we came out here," she said, her voice a whisper.

A hazy fog danced between the trees as the pink and purple streams of light illuminated the snow, making it a dazzling amethyst color. It was hauntingly beautiful and should a fairy or centaur choose to arrive at the moment, it would not have surprised Margaret in the least. Oliver's arms tightened around her, because of the cold or awe she was not sure, but a smile overtook her lips just the same. Yes, it had been the right choice, waking him up for this.

Turning in his arms, Margaret cupped his cheek and brought his gaze to her before navigating his lips to hers.

The kiss was soft. Comforting and sweet, just as the relationship between them was. "Marry me?" she asked the words a whisper.

"Yes," Oliver said, his lips forming a smile at the words. "When? Now?"

Margaret laughed and Oliver wasted no time pulling her in close and sealing her proposal with a kiss. She would marry this man as soon as the banns were read. Hell, if Gretna Green were closer, she would jump in a carriage and wed him straight away. It did not matter how or where. It did not matter when. She would marry Oliver every day for the rest of her life if it ensured that he remained in it.

The sun had crested the sky entirely by the time the pair returned home, nearly missing the duke's arrival. With pinkened cheeks and dampened boots, they cared not a bit, for they had each other, and that was all that mattered. The adventures of Margaret Reedy were finally coming to a close, and just in time, it would seem, for the future of Margaret Ludlow awaited.

Coming Soon!

Seasonal Habits of Husbands and Honeybees
Genus of Gentlemen Book II

Harrison Metcalf, the Earl of Everly, has only ever been in love with Margaret Reedy, his uncle's widow, but with her recent marriage to the Marquis of Greenwood, he is certain he will never love again. Alas, duty calls and he is still required to procure a wife and secure the line, but he could never knowingly marry someone who requires a love he could never provide.

Phoebe Kent never understood the point of balls and courtship. She would happily lose herself in beekeeping all day if it meant that she could avoid the uncomfortable noise and press of bodies that the season required. But with her parent's fear of spinsterhood looming on the horizon, she knows marrying is a must. If only she could find a partner as one did a business deal, as opposed to the nonsense of courting and love.

With a contact written and an agreement made, Phoebe and Harrison begin the deal that is their marriage, but a game of one-upmanship turns to flirting as they battle to outwit one another. A touch becomes a kiss, and a kiss becomes a night as they make contract modifications, twisting the two closer than they had planned. Can their new love survive when both are unsure if that is what they want?

ABOUT THE AUTHOR

Emmaline Warden Emmaline Warden lives in Colorado with her husband, four kids, and a menagerie of animals. Her love of romance began with an accidental copy of Susan Elizabeth Phillips and a trip to D.C. She's been reading and writing romance ever since.

emmalinewarden@gmail.com
Instagram: authoremmalinewarden
Twitter: @emmalinewarden
Facebook: emmalinewarden
Goodreads:
goodreads.com/author/show/18507128.Emmaline_Warden

Sign up for her newsletter and receive, **HEART OF STONE**, a historical paranormal short, as a special gift! www.emmalinewarden.com

Milton Keynes UK
Ingram Content Group UK Ltd.
UKHW031003250824
1368UKWH00003B/216